AN ISLAND HEATWAVE

LOVE ON THE ISLAND
BOOK 6

HELENA HALME

Helena HALME

Island Heatwave

An

LOVE ON THE ISLAND SERIES BOOK VI

CHAPTER ONE

The heatwave of the early summer has brought the first yachts into East Harbor. A light breeze sweeps through the masts, making the halyards rattle. The sun, already high up, is beaming from a clear blue sky. It's going to be another scorcher.

The brief movement of air does little to relieve the sweltering warmth, which has created a permanent layer of perspiration on Alicia's skin. She leans back in her seat, trying to catch a waft of cooler air.

She chose the table in the harborside café for its full shade. She takes a sip of her large glass of iced tea, which invigorates her a little, but not enough for her to carry on into town. Alicia is taking a break after a meeting with the organizers of a summer fair at the Fishing Village artisan center a few meters along the shore.

The new high-end potato chips that she and Liam have been producing since the spring crops were lifted are already on sale in two of the largest supermarkets on the islands, but sales have been disappointing. It was Liam's idea to start selling them at smaller shops, but Alicia is skeptical. The amount you can shift that way is minimal, but Liam says it's all about building the brand. He thinks they should give away packets for free, too, but so far Alicia has only agreed to providing bowls of loose chips for people to sample.

Alicia sighs and leans back in her seat. Her gaze turns toward the boats moving in and out of the long row of jetties in front of the cafe.

A huge yacht adorned with the name *Babushka* maneuvers into a parking spot at the end of the jetty closest to Alicia. As she watches the progress of the sleek white vessel, wondering how much such a monstrosity costs, she recalls that she didn't feel this exhausted the first time she was pregnant. She touches her tummy and feels a small movement within. The baby is also much more active than her darling Stefan, who had died aged seventeen, had been.

Her thoughts are interrupted by the sight of a man leaping onto the jetty from the large yacht.

The man is wearing a dark sailing jacket and trousers, and a navy baseball cap. A pair of mirrored sunglasses hide his eyes, but something about his bulky shape and movements, which are quicker and nimbler than his strong build would suggest, make Alicia certain that the man is who she thinks he is.

Surely it can't be?

Despite the heat, a sudden chill runs down her spine, and Alicia shivers. Unable to stop herself or look away, she watches in horror as the man stretches his hand out to help a long-legged blonde woman off the vessel. She's wearing tight white shorts and a blouse knotted around her midriff. Carrying a small bag in one hand and holding the woman, stork-like in her high-heeled wedges, with the other, the man walks along the jetty toward the cafe.

Alicia is relieved that she is wearing a sunhat, a bucket-shaped pink Marimekko thing she bought in the sales last summer. It hides her face, but she still feels vulnerable. Just as the man turns his gaze toward the cafe, Alicia grabs a newspaper off the table and buries her head behind it.

What is the Russian doing here? Surely Dudnikov must know that he has several police forces looking for him. That he will be charged with a multitude of offenses if he is caught. Among them will be the threats made against Alicia and her friends and family. He is also suspected of money-laundering, human trafficking, and loan sharking.

The horrible events of last Christmas come clearly into Alicia's mind. How the Russian had accosted her in the parking lot under Liam's apartment block in the center of Mariehamn. How he had grabbed her neck and threatened to harm everyone she loved if she didn't agree to launder cash through her new business. How he had kept calling her, issuing new threats, and how he had arranged the stabbing of her ex-lover Patrick, a Swedish journalist. He had even got one of his henchmen to hold her friend Brit's newborn baby hostage.

He had only given up when the police began closing

in on him. As had happened before, he had scuttled back to Russia, where Alicia had hoped he'd stay forever.

Luckily, Brit and her partner Jukka are away from the islands, taking their new baby to visit Jukka's grown-up daughter in Sweden. For a moment, Alicia wonders whether she should message her friend and tell her that Dudnikov is back in town, but she decides against it. The last thing Brit and Jukka need is a reminder of those awful events.

What is he doing here? What if he recognizes her?

After several minutes, when she thinks it's safe to do so, Alicia lowers the newspaper and glances around her. She looks inside the cafe, peers around the terrace where she's sitting, and along the jetty where the *Babushka* is docked.

There's no sign of Dudnikov or the woman.

Alicia turns around, carefully twisting her back, which has begun to bother her as her belly has grown. She spots the pair walking across the parking lot of the Arkipelag Hotel, up toward the center of the town. Next, she glances at the police station, situated just a block away from the hotel entrance through which Dudnikov is now brazenly leading his female companion.

What is going on?

Alicia gives another deep sigh.

It's critical that Alicia and Liam are successful in their new business venture. They have already sunk a lot of money into the equipment on the farm in Sjoland. And they've reduced the quantity of crops they are growing for the large American company. The margin on their own produce is much higher, so it makes sense in principle. But only if they can shift the packets of potato chips slowly filling their newly built storage unit.

Dudnikov turning up would be the final straw, Alicia thinks. She shakes her head. Her imagination must have been playing tricks on her. She gets up, holding onto her back, which is a little less sore now that she has rested. She decides that the short walk to Frida's apartment will do her good if she takes it slowly.

Frida, the girlfriend of her late son, Stefan, has recently returned from Romania, where she's been spending time with her new partner. Alicia hasn't seen the young woman for over six months, so she can't wait to catch up. She's also been missing little Anne Sofie, Frida's daughter. For a while, a couple of years ago, Alicia had been convinced the little girl was her grandchild.

Those times seem like light years away, Alicia thinks, and she touches her belly. Now she's to become a mother again herself, she's glad she isn't a grandmother as well. That would just be too weird!

CHAPTER TWO

F rida is trying to convince herself that life on the island with Andrei and her daughter is going to work out.

For the past six months she's been living in Romania, on Andrei's farm, which she now owns nearly half of. She had wanted to do some good with the money her mom left her, so she had decided to help Andrei with his family homestead. But Andrei, a proud man, did not find taking money from Frida easy. They came to an agreement, where she was given part-ownership of the place. Some major modernizations of the house and the barns were needed so that Andrei's brother, Mihai, would be able to run things while Andrei was away.

It took months to convince Andrei that his little brother could manage on his own. The worries he had about Mihai and his abilities had become ridiculous, and eventually Frida had confronted Andrei.

'You don't want to leave Romania and this farm,'

Frida said one night when they'd been arguing for over an hour. They were sitting up in bed, in a newly renovated room with an ensuite bathroom. They talked in hushed tones so that the rest of the household, including Frida's daughter, Anne Sofie, Mihai, and Andrei's sister Maria, couldn't hear them.

Frida felt at her wits' end. When they had decided to come to Romania together, the plan had always been to return to the islands after four weeks. Andrei would leave the farm in his brother's care. With the improvements Frida had promised to fund, looking after the dairy cows would be so much easier. They'd agreed that Andrei could also travel back at short notice to help if ever there was a crisis.

But weeks became months and when nearly half a year had passed, Frida couldn't stand it any longer.

Andrei, putting his arms around Frida and looking into her eyes, replied, 'I do. But I don't think I can leave yet.'

Frida had shaken his arms away.

'He is ready. The new barn has been built and the kitchen is renovated. Mihai can operate the new milking machine well. What is there to worry about? Anne Sofie needs to be at home. She's missed months of pre-school. And she misses Alicia and her mom. They're like family to us.'

'I know,' Andrei had sighed.

They'd made up in the way they always did, by making love. But when, afterward, Frida had tried to get to sleep, she couldn't shake off the idea that Andrei was stalling. That night, feeling lonelier than she had in years, she had made a decision. She would wait another two weeks and then return to her lovely apartment in Mariehamn on her own, if Andrei still didn't want to leave the farm behind.

She loved Andrei more than she had ever loved anyone – apart from Anne Sofie of course. But during the past few months in Romania, she'd come to understand that she couldn't leave her home to be with him. She didn't love the country the way Andre did, the way she loved the Åland Islands. Romania felt strange to her. The language was incomprehensible and the people so different from those on the islands.

Perhaps it was because she didn't speak the language, but there was none of the friendly banter in the shops that there was at home. On the islands, even if there was nothing to say, she'd get a silent nod from the island people she knew.

Here everyone just stared at her.

Although Andrei denied it, she knew that the villagers considered Frida to be a spoiled, rich Scandinavian woman who had never had to work in her life and who couldn't understand the struggles their country had endured.

They were right, of course. Not about being rich, because having a lot of money was new to Frida. But even if she learned about Romania's history, she could never fully understand its past suffering.

What it amounted to was that she'd been desperately homesick.

She'd missed the sea breeze of the islands, the sound

of the ships' masts softly jingling against the rigging in the wind. She'd missed watching the cruise liners from her kitchen window as they motored in and out of West Harbor. And she'd missed the long summer nights when the sun set for just an hour, making the night never fully dark.

She'd longed for the quiet of the islands after the tourists had left at the end of the summer, and even missed the bitterly cold days of winter when she had to dress Anne Sofie in so many layers that the little girl could hardly move.

Frida couldn't stay in Romania for much longer. She had to get back to the islands soon. But if Andrei couldn't leave his farm, their relationship had no future.

That night, Frida had given into the feeling of total hopelessness and silently cried herself to sleep.

Now back on the islands, she is almost as miserable as she was in Romania. She's standing at her kitchen window, looking out to sea. But when she thinks about seeing Alicia, a smile spreads over her face.

If she must be contented with a life on her own as a single mom, so be it. She's done it before. She met Andrei less than a year ago. She will get used to being by herself again. She has no money worries, which she's grateful for.

And she has Alicia and her family.

The new baby is bound to cheer everyone up. Frida will help as much as she can, to pay back some of the kindness that Alicia and her mom Hilda have shown her over the years. She will love Alicia and Liam's baby as much as they love Anne Sofie.

She turns around and glances at her daughter, who's sitting in her highchair eating a snack of carrot sticks prepared for her earlier. The baby will be a new little friend for her daughter too.

I will manage.

Alicia leaves the cafe and hurries along Nygatan toward the police headquarters. It's only about 500 meters from the Club Marin Cafe where she'd been sitting, but it's hot and she's carrying more weight than she's used to. The road veers slightly uphill and the effort in the heat is making her back twinge again. Beads of sweat are forming on her forehead and along her spine under her billowing cotton dress.

'You must learn to take it easy. You are a pregnant woman in your forties, not twenties, as you were when you were expecting Stefan.'

She can hear husband Liam's words and she wonders what on earth she thinks she's doing. Why didn't she just phone Ebba from the cafe?

After everything that Dudnikov has put them through, she wants to be there when the man is arrested. She wants to see the look on his face when he is hand-cuffed, and he's led away by the island police. To be put away for a very long time, she hopes.

It's only when she opens the heavy glass doors of the station that she remembers her friend, the police chief,

Ebba Torstensson, is not there. She's away, visiting Stockholm, together with her wife, Jabulani.

'Oh no,' Alicia says under her breath.

A young police officer in his shirt sleeves comes out of the station and sees Alicia standing there, panting after the walk up the hill. 'Can I help you, Mrs O'Connell?'

Alicia considers her options for a moment. She tries to think of the officer's name. He had helped Ebba last Christmas when Dudnikov was trying to get Alicia to launder money for him. Johan something?

Alicia doesn't want the police to mess this up. She knows Dudnikov is a slippery character and the fact that he's here, boldly walking into the Arkipelag Hotel in broad daylight must mean that he knows that the charges against him won't stick, or that he can escape without being caught. Whoever handles this needs to be a very experienced officer who knows everything about the Russian.

'Johan, isn't it?'

The young man nods and stretches out his hand to help Alicia up the steps.

'Are you OK?'

Alicia straightens herself up and doesn't take the man's hand.

'I'm still able to walk!'

'Sorry…' the policeman's face turns a dark red color and Alicia regrets her harsh tone. She is so fed up with people treating her like some geriatric, although the term 'Geriatric Mother' is how they describe her at the maternity hospital.

'It's fine. I just remembered Ebba is on holiday. I was going to say hello. Nothing is wrong, don't worry.'

Alicia turns around, as swiftly as she can manage, leaving Johan Ledin (she just remembers his last name when it's too late) staring at her back.

CHAPTER THREE

Seeing the jetties full of boats of various sizes and types rocking in the water makes Patrick's heart ache. He gazes out to sea and stops to watch a sailing yacht, a 40-footer, he estimates. A new one too, and a bit larger than his own boat had been.

Watching the skipper, a man in his fifties, with a weather-worn bronzed face, gray hair escaping from his cap, his thoughts go back to his many summers on these quirky islands. How Patrick misses sailing in the archipelago on beautiful sunny days, islands small and large dotted around him. He'd be with his two daughters or, as time went on, on his own. Out there, with only the wind and waves for company, he could think.

Had he appreciated his good fortune in having a yacht of his own? Now that he's lost everything, he wonders how much he'd taken it all for granted.

During the last six months he has done a lot of thinking. There was no one to share his thoughts. No one he wanted to trust with his innermost feelings. All the fear, frustration and bewilderment his head was filled with. He now knows that he needed the solitude to get to know himself again after everything that had happened. Traveling up to northern Sweden, to where he had been born and raised, had seemed the best option when no one wanted him around down South.

Except perhaps the Russian.

Patrick's mouth pulls into a grimace. But Dudnikov just wanted to break his bones, so that didn't really count. He truly hoped the criminal was now behind bars, or at least hiding out in deepest, darkest Russia.

There was someone else he would have wanted to talk to while he was in his self-appointed exile.

Alicia.

But that was not possible. Besides, not seeing her made it easier in the end. Being away from her, the islands, from the influential Eriksson family that he had been part of, but still keeping in touch with his two daughters, Sara and Frederika, had cleared his head.

He's made his decision and he will not veer from it.

He smiles to the skipper, who's now tied his boat up and has stepped onto the jetty. The man touches his cap and nods. He must have seen Patrick watching his skillful docking. Two sailors recognizing each other.

Patrick feels an uplift in his heart as he continues along the boardwalk and turns toward the center of Mariehamn. He is meeting his ex-wife. Of course, after the short ferry crossing from Stockholm, he could have gone straight to the restaurant, a fancy tapas place that Mia had suggested, but he had wanted to calm his mind before what he feared would be a fractious meeting.

All dealings with his ex-wife were difficult, but he knows this one would be especially so.

She will not like what he has decided.

How can the heat be so oppressing on an island in the middle of the Baltic? The temperature is nearing 30°C when Mia steps out into the mid-morning heat from her parents' air-conditioned summer villa. There is barely any wind and, as the heat hits her face, she's reminded of a girls' weekend in Spain a few years back. She smiles to herself when she thinks of the guy she met there. She'd had a brief but passionate affair with a local business-man. She cannot for the life of her remember his name, but she recalls his body and what he could do with it.

Just the thought of the Spaniard's taut, tan limbs makes her own skin tingle as she steps into her Mercedes and turns on the engine, the AC on full blast. Before she puts the car into drive, she checks her face in the mirror. Her signature red lipstick seems a bit too much in this heat, but she needs it today. She smiles at her own image, pleased with her immaculate make-up. The short walk in the heat between the villa and the car hasn't smudged anything.

Mia moves toward the gates, which open automati-cally, and she turns into the road toward Mariehamn.

She hopes Patrick is already at Boquerian, the latest place in town, which serves passable food with a Spanish vibe. That must be why she's had the Spaniard on her mind today, she thinks, smiling to herself. She briefly wonders if she kept his address but shakes off such thoughts. She must concentrate on Patrick and her family now.

No more fun for Mia.

She deliberately drives slowly, ensuring that she is at least ten minutes late. This will infuriate Patrick, no doubt, but she doesn't care. Let him wait! She's angry with him for upping sticks and leaving her with their two daughters like that.

Mia steps off the main shopping street, Torggatan, into a small courtyard now filled with tables. Beyond them is a glass-covered space with beautiful Moorish tiles on the floor and the back walls. A tall wooden bar, with stools, stands in the center and there are black leather sofas and tables along one side. On one of the sofas, at a spot she specifically booked, Mia sees a familiar shape perusing the menu.

She sighs and steps inside the busy restaurant.

'So, how have you been?'

Mia stares at Patrick. She tries not to be affected by his handsome face with the piercingly blue eyes, and tall frame, which has somehow become more athletic. He's clearly lost some weight. Has he been working out?

She brushes these thoughts away and reminds herself that she is angry at her ex-husband.

'Is that all you have to say after all these months? When you disappeared and left me holding the babies. Your babies!'

Mia spits out the words.

But Patrick doesn't react. Instead, he smiles and leans back in his seat.

He's on the leather sofa facing the restaurant while Mia is forced to perch on a rather uncomfortable wooden chair. In the past, Patrick would have offered her his place, knowing that she hates having her back to the action. But when Mia appeared and he looked up and noticed her, all he did was stand briefly and then sink back into the comfortable sofa.

She was – is – too proud to ask for him to swap. She glances behind her to see if they could change to another table, but the place is heaving.

'These babies you talk of, they are Sara, aged fourteen, and Frederika, thirteen?'

A smile hovers around Patrick's lips as he says this.

Mia doesn't have time to reply before he leans forward and asks, 'How are they? I spoke to Sara yesterday, but Fred is still at camp, isn't she?'

Mia sighs.

'Just because they're no longer small, doesn't mean that they are easier to look after.'

This seems to get through to Patrick. He leans over and places his hand over Mia's.

'You're right. I'm sorry.'

His sincerity throws Mia off course for a moment. To buy time, she pulls her hand away and picks up the menu. She lowers her eyes toward the folded sheet and opens it up slowly, even though she knows exactly what she will have.

She needs to maintain her defenses and not be affected by those eyes. Have they become sharper in the last six months, or is it just that absence has made him even more handsome?

Something catches in her throat and Mia has to take a couple of deep breaths to calm herself down. She steals a glance at Patrick, who is also studying the food on offer.

Pull yourself together!

Images of the happy times they had when they were first married flash in front of her. How different Patrick had been from the guys she had dated previously. He was clever, witty, and always so attentive toward her. At the time, she could tell he didn't care what her family thought of him. Or, rather, he didn't care about the Eriksson's money and status.

Naturally, this drove her Mom and Pappa crazy.

They were both skeptical about his prospects, and his chosen career of journalism, although he had done well at *Journalen*. He was the youngest deputy editor at the newspaper. Mia knew her father had received good reports about him from the editor, who just happened to be his friend. What Patrick hadn't known then was that Kurt Eriksson knew everyone who was anyone both on the islands and in Stockholm.

Suddenly, Mia recalls one hot summer's afternoon, very much a day like today. They'd just returned from their honeymoon and decided to spend the weekend on the islands. Patrick had rented a yacht for a couple of days and had convinced Mia to go sailing with him. She'd felt sick almost as soon as she'd stepped onboard, so they'd only sailed to the nearest guest harbor, a couple of hours away. They'd stayed there for the entire weekend – most of it in the double bunk.

Mia's cheeks feel hot when she remembers how they'd explored each other's body. She has never since let a man get so close to her core. She gave herself completely to Patrick that weekend. They shared their innermost secrets with each other. Patrick told her how much he wanted to become a respected writer and journalist, and Mia admitted to the body insecurities that had always haunted her.

'That's silly,' Patrick had said. 'You are the most beautiful woman I have ever seen.'

Those words have since been engraved on her soul.

Mia lifts the menu up to hide her face. She takes a few breaths, counting four out, four hold, and four in as taught by her life coach. She tries to do this as quietly as she can.

But Patrick must have noticed, because he pulls the menu down and asks, 'Are you OK, Mia?'

He seems genuinely concerned and Mia doesn't know what to do. Her heart is beating so hard that she thinks she might faint. Perhaps she's having a heart attack? She keeps staring at those bright blue eyes and that furrowed brow.

'Just concentrate on your breathing,' Patrick says, but Mia can't get enough air into her lungs to reply.

Instead, she nods.

CHAPTER FOUR

P atrick can see that there's something wrong with Mia. Is she having a panic attack?

At that moment, a waiter, in a long apron, comes over to their table and says cheerfully, '*Hejsan*!'

'Can you give us a minute,' Patrick says.

'OK,' he replies, glancing from Patrick to Mia and back again.

He seems to be rooted to the spot.

'A minute?' Patrick repeats and at last the man gets the message and walks back toward the open kitchen, glancing over his shoulder a few times as he does so.

Patrick looks hard at Mia, who is as white as a sheet. She has a panicky look in her eyes, which are scanning the room. Patrick takes her hands and crouches down by her side.

'Let's go out to get some air. It's so stuffy here.'

'Yes,' Mia croaks.

Patrick pulls her up gently, putting Mia's arm into the crook of his. He picks up her large handbag – Louis

Vuitton, he notices absentmindedly – and leads her slowly out of the restaurant. He waves toward the waiter and mouths, 'Sorry'.

They make their way onto Torggatan, which is baking in the midday heat. Patrick glances around and sees that there is a vacant bench in the shade of a tree.

'Let's go and sit over there,' Patrick says, looking down at Mia. She's still panting, but the breaths seem to be less frequent now.

She nods and they walk slowly away from the restaurant.

'Just take it easy,' Patrick says, lowering Mia onto the bench.

He sits down next to her.

Patrick glances across to Mia and sees that her usually immaculate red lips are slightly smeared. Perhaps she ran the back of her hand over her mouth? That is so unlike her that Patrick is even more concerned.

She has her arms wrapped around herself as if she is trying to hold herself upright with them. She's wearing a sleeveless white cotton dress, with an embossed logo. Is the dress Louis Vuitton too? It has an upturned collar, buttons down the front, and a belt with a large golden buckle. As usual, she looks stylish, and out of place in Mariehamn, which is only a small town despite being the islands' capital.

Patrick couldn't help but admire her when she'd stepped inside the restaurant. He noticed a string of other men – and women – give her admiring glances. Her canvas wedges, strings neatly wrapped around her thin ankles, made him remember their lovemaking when first married. Glancing at those same long legs now, he thinks how vulnerable the straps make her look. He is surprised to find that he feels a huge amount of tenderness toward his ex-wife.

He is pretty certain that Mia is having a panic attack. He's read about them but has never seen anyone have one. The last person he thought would suffer from any kind of anxiety is his ex-wife. Strong, willful, and selfish, she didn't seem to have a nervous molecule in her body.

Perhaps he has misunderstood her all this time?

He leans over and gazes into her face. Her head is hanging down and she's still taking slow, deliberate breaths in and out.

'How you doing?'

Her eyes meet his and she says, in a quiet, breathless voice, 'Better, thank you.'

Patrick takes a tissue out of his pocket.

'May I?'

'What?'

'Your lipstick …'

Mia is now facing him, and her hands have fallen onto her lap.

Patrick takes hold of her chin with his left hand, and as gently as he can, wipes the excess lipstick from around her lips with his right.

'I'm not sure I'm doing a very good job, but …' he says and looks into her eyes.

They stare at each other for what seems like minutes.

Patrick notices how Mia's eyes are darker, and there

are tears pooling in them, yet she doesn't look as if she's about to cry. There's something else in those eyes and Patrick is again transported back to the early, happy days of their marriage.

No, don't be fooled. This is Mia, remember! The treacherous, selfish woman you never want to be tricked by ever again.

But Patrick isn't listening to his own warnings.

He moves his eyes to her lips. He sees that they have parted, revealing the white tips of her teeth. The lack of lipstick makes them seem somehow fuller.

Before the thought has even entered his mind, he has placed his lips over Mia's.

CHAPTER FIVE

Having decided not to mention her possible sighting of Dudnikov to the young police-man, Alicia walks toward Frida's house. The sun is blazing down from a cloudless sky and it's so hot that she has to find a bench in the shade to rest her swollen feet for a moment. She feels foolish and old. How can it possibly have been the Russian she saw earlier? He would not be so stupid as to come over to the islands, where he knows there's a warrant for his arrest. Not only that, but the man she saw had docked his beautiful yacht boldly in the harbor, then walked with his girlfriend along the main street into the largest hotel in Mariehamn.

Surely even Dudnikov wouldn't be that arrogant?

She needs to forget about the man. She watches a mom with a young baby having a coffee on the terrace of one of the new coffee bars that have opened on Torggatan and touches her own belly. The 'flutterings', as her old midwife used to call them in London, years ago when she was pregnant with Stefan, have become more frequent and occasionally she can feel a real kick now. Poor Stefan. Once again, she wonders if she is ready to have another baby.

'It's too late now,' a voice in her head says and she smiles at her own thoughts.

How many times has Liam told her the same?

'This little one isn't going to replace Stefan. And she or he is going to know that there was an older brother, so you mustn't feel guilty,' Liam had added.

The woman in the cafe pulls down the strap of her striped, yellow cotton dress, and briefly revealing a swollen breast, starts to nurse the baby. Before placing a cotton cloth over her breast and the baby, she gazes down as the little mouth works hungrily on the nipple.

Alicia is filled with such a sense of well-being and happiness that she feels as if her heart is going to burst. When has she been this contented? Not since she was last expecting.

She's one of those lucky people who thrive in pregnancy. Even the heatwave that has hit the islands doesn't make her feel particularly uncomfortable, just a little tired and hotter than normal. But in every other way she feels calm, at peace with herself and the world. It's as if she was in a happiness bubble filled with all the things that make her smile.

Like the mother and baby in front of her, or the mound of fresh strawberries being sold by a girl with long blond curls wearing a red scarf an apron decorated with berries. There's a small line, and customer after customer gives the girl a wide smile when they receive their box of berries.

Alicia resolves to buy some strawberries herself. They will be a perfect welcome present for Frida. It seems strange that her friend has come back from Romania without Andrei. Last time Alicia FaceTimed Frida and little Anne Sofie, Frida had said that they were all moving back to the islands together. She hopes all is well between the couple. Perhaps Andrei had to stay behind because of some last-minute issues with his farm?

After Alicia has bought her own tub of berries, she continues along Torggatan toward Frida's apartment, which is situated along one of the side-streets. Once a large family home, the wooden turn-of-the century house has been divided into three good-sized apartments. Frida occupies the ground floor, which has direct access to a beautiful private courtyard with a small garden, a sand box, and swings for the children. After her mom died, and Frida unexpectedly inherited a fortune, she'd bought the place outright. Alicia couldn't be happier for her. Frida had lost so much. Her mom, Stefan, as well as their friend Daniel, who turned out to be Anne Sofie's father.

Deep in her thoughts, and suddenly worried that things hadn't worked out between Frida and Andrei, Alicia doesn't see Patrick and Mia until she's virtually standing by the bench.

·   ·   ·

Patrick's eyes are wide and his lips parted as he takes in Alicia's form.

'Don't you make a pretty couple,' Alicia says.

When she first saw the embracing pair on the bench, she didn't recognize who it was. As soon as she did, her first instinct was to flee. But Mia's eyes were on her with a flash of glee as soon as she saw who it was.

Ignoring Patrick, who is openly staring at her belly, Alicia turns toward Mia.

'Nice to see you two have reconciled.'

As she watches Mia's reaction to her words, Alicia sees that the mirth that she thought she saw in the woman's eyes is actually tears. Usually immaculately turned out, Mia's face is pale and her lips without their customary red lipstick. They look as if she's roughly wiped them.

Of course, they've been kissing. But why the tearful look in Patrick's ex-wife's eyes?

Mia turns her pale lips into a smile, but it doesn't look convincing.

Since no one speaks. Alicia adds, 'Well, it was nice to see you.'

She turns away and continues to walk toward Frida's apartment. She only has a block to go, and she doesn't feel so tired anymore.

'Alicia!'

She hears Patrick's voice behind her, and then a hand grabbing her arm. Alicia very nearly drops the bag containing the strawberries.

'Watch it! What are you doing?'

Alicia pulls herself away from the man.

Patrick brings his hands up, palms facing her.

'Sorry, I didn't mean to … I just didn't want to let you go without an explanation.'

Alicia stares at Patrick.

What is the matter with him? The affair they had is long since over and done with.

Alicia wants to forget about that mad summer two years ago when she first came back to the islands, still raw with grief for her son. She'd first met Patrick on the ferry and they'd had an instant connection. A connection that was just physical, although she hadn't recognized that then or months later.

She'd even been foolish enough to move in with him in Stockholm, which was where she'd discovered his capacity for lying and deceit. And his inability to detach himself from his unfaithful ex-wife and the wealthy Eriksson clan.

As if she needed a reminder of how far apart they now were, the scene she'd just witnessed could not have made it clearer.

Alicia shakes her head as she gazes at Patrick, who is standing gaping at her.

'What do you want?'

Alicia realizes she's still angry at Patrick for all that she's given up for him in the past. Her relationship with Liam. The last few months with her stepdad, who had died while she was living with Patrick in Stockholm.

Not to mention all the trouble he's caused her.

Last Christmas, when Patrick had been stabbed, very likely by one of Dudnikov's henchmen, and ended up in hospital, she'd rushed to his side.

But so had Mia.

When the hospital called, Alicia had taken the next ferry over to Stockholm without thinking twice, not least because Dudnikov was threatening her at the time and she'd been foolish enough to think that she alone could stop him from hurting everybody she loved. She hadn't even told Liam about the trip, which she regrets bitterly now. She should have trusted her husband (who so nearly became her ex-husband) and asked him to come with her. Instead, her actions had fed Liam's suspicions about how much Patrick still meant to her, threatening their own reconciliation.

'I just wanted to explain. We're not, you know...' here Patrick pauses, running his fingers through his hair. Alicia notices that he has some very light gray hairs at the temples, where the usually straw blond of his hair has gone darker.

'No need,' Alicia says and glances toward the bench where Mia is sitting with a small mirror in her hand, applying lipstick.

A leopard doesn't change her spots.

'I want to talk to you. Please.'

Patrick's blue eyes are peering at Alicia and she can see something in them that she hasn't often seen before: sincerity.

She sighs.

'OK, but not now. I'll call you.'

'Thanks, but could we make it soon. Like tonight?'

Again, Alicia hesitates.

'Tomorrow? I'll meet you at the Svarta Katten.' She

glances at her diary on her phone and adds, 'Half past three?'

'Thank you.'

Patrick steps forward as if to give her a hug, but Alicia moves backward. His eyes widen, and then his lips shift into a grin.

The old Patrick returns.

Alicia turns on her heels, giving a quick glance toward Mia, who is watching them intently.

As she walks slowly up the hill toward Frida's apartment, she wonders why she agreed to meet up with Patrick. She is so over the love triangle between her, Patrick, and Mia! And what is she going to tell Liam? That she bumped into her ex-lover and decided to have a coffee because he pleaded with her? Perhaps she should just not go?

But the islands are such a small place, she'll see him at some point, and what if he turns up in Sjoland? What will she say to Liam then, if it comes out that she'd agreed to meet Patrick.

For goodness' sake, you're five months pregnant! It's hardly going to a be lovers' tryst.

CHAPTER SIX

Frida's apartment stands on a high hill overlooking the water to the west of Mariehamn. When Alicia knocks on the door the first thing she hears is meowing.

'Alicia, you look very well!' Frida says while her cat, Minki, stretches in front of Alicia, at the same time producing short, high-pitched sounds.

'I've missed you too, Minki,' Alicia says and extends her hand toward her. The cat gives it a quick lick and disappears inside the apartment.

'How are you?'

Alicia gazes at Frida and is struck by how grown-up the young woman now appears. Her hair, all the colors of the rainbow in the past, is now its natural strawberry blonde, cut into a bob. She has bangs, which suit her and soften her face. Her eyes are blue and her cheeks rosy pink. Frida is wearing a pair of tight-fitting white jeans and a lacy blue top with billowing sleeves. Her toes are

painted a pale peach color inside a pair of tan Birken-
stock sandals.

But when Alicia gives Frida a hug, she senses something isn't right.

Just as Alicia's about to ask Frida what's wrong,
Anne Sofie, who is sitting on the sofa, notices her and
squeals in delight.

'*Famo* Alicia!'

The little girl runs straight into her arms, nearly
knocking over the box of strawberries that Alicia has
taken out of the carrier bag to give to Frida. The child is
the spitting image of her mother. Alicia battles tears of
joy at seeing and hearing her. Anne Sofie calls her
Famo, short for *Farmor*, or grandmother.

Passing the berries to Frida, Alicia stoops to sweep
Anne Sofie into her arms, then immediately realizes that
the girl is too heavy for her.

'Goodness you've grown, my little darling!' she
says, crouching in front of Anne Sofie and pulling her
into her arms instead.

She plants several kisses on her forehead. The fair
hair that used to be just short wisps framing her face
now nearly touches her shoulders.

'Mamma says I grow too fast,' the girl replies as
Alicia releases her from her grip. Her large round eyes,
which are fixed on Alicia's, are the bluest of blue and
her complexion is fair, though her cheeks are bright red.

'She's teething again. For the last time now, I think,'
Frida says and ruffles the little girl's hair. A smile appears
briefly on her face, disappearing as soon as it arrived.

'Coffee?' Frida asks, turning her gaze to Alicia.

Anne Sofie stares at Alicia's tummy. '*Famo* is fat!'

Alicia smiles widely at the girl, but doesn't know what to say.

Frida puts her arm around Anne Sofie's shoulders. 'That's not very nice! Besides, Alicia hasn't got fat, she's expecting a baby.'

At her mom's words, Anne Sofie's mouth opens, and her eyes become round and wide.

'Baby! Does it hurt?'

Frida shakes her head at her daughter and, smiling, turns toward Alicia.

'Come in and sit down before we get deeper into this conversation. I feel there are going to be a thousand questions fired at you and your belly soon.'

Alicia enters the large kitchen and living room of Frida's mid-town apartment.

'Did you say yes to coffee?' Frida asks.

'No, sorry, could I have tea instead?

'Of course.'

Frida starts to busy herself with the drinks.

'I've also got some cinnamon buns from Hilda.'

Alicia digs in her shoulder bag and brings out a parcel smelling deliciously of butter and spices. When her mom had heard that Alicia was going to see Frida, she'd insisted Alicia take a few of the freshly baked sweet buns.

Alicia had rolled her eyes but accepted the gift and was now glad she had. Her mom's baking never failed to cheer people up. And judging by Frida's face, which looked puffy, as if she'd been recently crying, she could do with some cheer.

'What's up?' Alicia asks when they are facing each other across Frida's kitchen table. Frida has put on a Disney movie for Anne Sofie in the living room, and the girl is transfixed by the cartoons. It suddenly occurs to her that Frida hasn't once mentioned her Romanian lover.

'Is Andrei OK?'

Frida's face crumbles and tears fill her eyes.

Alicia puts her hands over Frida's which are clasped together on the table in front of her.

'Has something happened?'

Frida shakes her head.

'That's the problem. He is fine. In Romania.'

Frida's face hardens and she gets up to refill their cups with more coffee and tea.

'But I thought he was going to hand over the farm to Mihai – that's his younger brother's name, isn't it?'

Frida nods.

'Mihai is lovely, as is his sister Maria.'

She sighs and continues, 'We were only supposed to stay for a couple of weeks.'

Frida tells Alicia how a few weeks in Romania had turned into six months. Week after week, Andrei had promised they'd return to the islands. Yet, time after time, he'd eventually argued that his brother wasn't ready to take on the farm.

'I didn't know what to do. In the end, I just left. What if Andrei is never ready to leave his family or the farm. What am I going to do then?'

Alicia tries to console Frida as well as she can. At the same time, she fears the young woman's instincts are right. She thinks back to how she had missed her own home on the islands while living in London. How she never properly settled in England, always feeling like a stranger. However much she loved Liam, their son Stefan, and the beautiful house in North London, she had always longed to be in Åland instead.

As she watches Frida dab at her eyes, smearing her make-up, Alicia reminds herself that it doesn't have to be that way. People can move, and many do, happily living in another country.

Look at Liam.

He isn't regretting his decision to join Alicia on the islands.

Alicia gets up and puts an arm over Frida's shoulders to give them a squeeze.

'You have to give him time.'

Frida turns her head toward Alicia and tries to pull her mouth into a weak smile. She nods, but Alicia can see that she's not convinced.

She reaches her hand out and touches Frida's fingers.

There's a brief silence, suddenly broken by the sounds of singing flooding in from the lounge. Anne Sofie is belting out the words to *Frozen*.

Both women smile.

'Can you not talk to Andrei about all this?' Alicia asks.

'The thing is, it's not just the farm,' Frida says.

Looking at Frida's tear-filled eyes, Alicia already

knows what the girl is going to say next. But she waits while Frida takes time to articulate her concerns.

'He doesn't like my money.'

'Oh, Frida.'

'Or rather, where it has come from.'

Alicia knows that Frida herself isn't fully at ease with being wealthy. When her mother was alive, the two of them had a modest existence. It was only when her mom died that Frida found out she'd been sitting on a fortune. She had savings amassed via an unknown benefactor – believed by Frida's lawyer to be her father, whom she has never known.

What's more, Frida believed that father to be none other than Alexander Dudnikov, the very same villain who has been terrifying Alicia and her family for years.

What would Frida say if Alicia told her that she'd seen him in town only an hour or so earlier?

Was it really him?

At that moment, Anne Sofie walks into the kitchen. She climbs into Frida's lap.

'Don't cry, *Mamma*.'

Alicia sees that Frida is trying to smile through her tears.

'I'm OK,' she says as she hugs her daughter close to her.

'What if we play hide and seek?' Alicia suggests and the little girl's face lights up.

'Yes! Yes!' she says, jumping up and down. 'Me hide first! You count.' Anne Sofie points her little finger at Alicia, who dutifully puts her hands over her eyes and begins counting slowly. 'One, two, three …'

When the girl has disappeared from the kitchen, Alicia takes Frida's hand and squeezes it.

'But no one is certain that Dudnikov really is your dad, are they? Even Ebba doesn't know for sure.'

'Famo Alicia, Famo Alicia, I hiding!'

The little girl's shouts are quite clearly coming from her bedroom and Alicia gets up to pretend to look for her in each of the other rooms, before finding her hiding in her bed. There are shrieks of delight when Alicia lifts the sheet.

When they've done a few rounds of the game, Alicia sits back down at the kitchen table and sighs. 'You've tired me out, little one!'

'Again, again,' Anne Sofie says and pulls at Alicia's hand.

But before she can reply, Frida lifts her daughter and swings her around the kitchen to Anne-Sofie's obvious delight. Over the giggles of the little girl, Frida says, 'What about a little bit of lunch? Would you like some meatballs?'

Frida straps the girl into her highchair and puts a bowl in front of her. Once Anne Sofie has settled between the two women and is concentrating on eating her food, Alicia gazes at Frida.

'Has Andrei given a thought to what he's going to do here? I'm sure if he got a job, he'd feel that he didn't need to live off you.'

Frida's face grows serious.

'I'm not sure. All he knows is farming, really. He hates the idea of me, you know, paying for everything.

But as I said to him, I have money, so why should he worry about it?'

'Everything will turn out OK, you'll see,' Alicia says and places her hand on Frida's arm.

Frida's eyes meet Alicia's.

'I know he doesn't like where the money has come from.'

Alicia thinks for a moment.

'Why don't you take matters into your own hands and do a bit more investigating? You were good at research when you worked at the newspaper. Why not put those skills to good use and find out once and for all who your dad is?'

Walking back to her car, Alicia thinks about what Frida has just told her about Andrei.

She liked the guy from the beginning, as soon as she met him last summer. Alicia still feels terrible about his brother Daniel, who died in a fishing accident while working for Uffe, her late stepfather, on the farm in Sjoland.

Her stepfather had had no idea that his farm manager and accountant had been cheating him and employing illegal labor on the farm. Andrei believed that his brother's death had something to do with this, and that it was connected with Dudnikov. However, Alicia's friend, the police chief on the islands, assured everyone that poor Daniel had perished at sea due to his own inexperience. Alicia understood that Andrei had finally accepted this.

But what if he hadn't?

Frida also told Alicia that she had invested heavily in Andrei's farm in Romania.

'Andrei is, after all, little Anne Sofie's uncle, so I'm only investing in a family venture,' she'd told Alicia. 'I now own half of the farm, so Anne Sofie will always have a connection to the country her father was from.'

Alicia had nodded. Frida is a wealthy young woman. And it was a noble thing to have done, but Alicia now wonders if it was a good investment. And now that Andrei has the farm on a better footing, won't it be more difficult to leave it? Perhaps he doesn't care for Frida and little Anne Sofie enough to abandon the life he has in Romania? Alicia knows only too well how strong the pull of your home country can be.

CHAPTER SEVEN

Struggling to decide what to pack, Hilda is standing in front of her wardrobe, gazing at the summer dresses that she's kept at the back of the walk-in space. None of them inspire her. A red shift dress, which she loves because it is sexy and close fitting, will be uncomfortable during the long ferry and bus journey to Stockholm. A loose-fitting cream maxi dress would be perfect, but it makes her look pregnant.

The thought of expecting a child makes Hilda smile and forget about what she should wear. She can't believe how lucky she is that her daughter is going to give her another grandchild. After the heart-breaking loss of Stefan at the tender age of seventeen, Alicia and Liam are expecting again.

Stefan perished in a motorcycle accident on a slippery London street in late November over two years ago now. None of them have truly overcome that tragedy, but Hilda hopes that the new baby will bring Alicia and Liam the happiness that they deserve.

That they managed to reunite after more than a year apart, during which both had found comfort in someone else's arms, is a miracle. And to have another child when they are both in their forties is just wonderful.

Hilda's heart aches when she thinks how Uffe, her late husband, would have relished a new baby. He was so good to Alicia, whom he had adopted when she was just a year old. He was such an exemplary step-dad that Alicia had never asked much about her own father, Leo.

Of course, Hilda had told her he was dead, but the truth came out when Leo reconnected with his daughter last year. The lie is almost forgotten now. Alicia has forgiven Hilda and Leo is back in their lives.

Hilda turns back to her wardrobe. Glancing at her wristwatch, she sees she has only half an hour before she must leave. She grabs hold of a light blue linen trouser suit and a white short-sleeved cotton T-shirt. That will have to do. The trousers will be wrinkled after the ferry and car journey, but at least the jacket will hide most of the damage.

She packs another two tops and chucks in the red shift dress, as well as the billowing maxi one. One of those will be good for the evening's dinner date. As she carries her small wheelie bag down the stairs of the house, she wonders if she's doing the right thing.

She has been here before.

In the kitchen, she peers out of the window and sees that Alicia's car isn't parked outside. Where is she? Again, Hilda glances at her watch. She left nearly two hours ago! She tries not to panic but feels herself go rigid with fear.

Has something bad happened to Alicia?

Hilda finds her cell in her handbag and dials her daughter's number.

'Hi, Mom, I'm just pulling in. Are you ready?'

Alicia has promised to drive her to the ferry port. This time, Hilda has been honest about meeting up with Leo. Last winter, just before Christmas, she'd gone to see Leo in Helsinki, in the expectation of spending a couple of days with him, but she had kept the rendezvous secret from Alicia. That trip had ended in disaster.

Six months have passed, and she has finally agreed to meet up again. After losing Uffe, she feels so lonely. She knows her late husband would have wanted her to find someone else, and who better than her ex?

Even though Alicia hasn't said so, Hilda is aware that she would love her parents to get on well, even if they don't get romantically involved again. Her daughter just wants Hilda to be happy.

Alicia knows her too well. Hilda needs people around her. It's not enough that Alicia and Liam are living across the yard from her. Even with a new grand-child, she needs a life of her own. She's just over sixty – she could live another twenty, thirty years – time that she certainly does not wish to spend on her own.

She'll feel sidelined enough with the impending move into Alicia's cottage. Although the house-swap was her idea, she dreads living in what used to be Uffe's office and an old milking parlor. Of course, it makes sense that Alicia and Liam would live in the large house, especially as Alicia runs the farm and they have their new gourmet potato chip company on the premises.

But.

Hilda is used to her large kitchen, and she loves throwing parties in the spacious dining room and lounge, which can accommodate at least fifty people. Alicia's small space can barely take ten, if that. And in the house she shared with Uffe for forty years, and where he was born, she feels close to her late husband.

Alicia must know – or guess – at all this because she's so keen for Hilda to reconnect with Leo.

This time Hilda has insisted they go to a neutral place. She herself found the hotel, Reisen, a small place next to the Royal Palace in Stockholm. She saw an article about in a Swedish women's magazine, and it seemed perfect.

She's booked a room overlooking the water and Leo has arranged a restaurant somewhere in the trendy South part of the city, which he said is just a short taxi ride from the hotel.

Without discussing the matter, they have reserved two bedrooms. After what happened last time, Hilda doesn't want to take the risk of everything going wrong again. She thinks it must have been the pressure of being intimate after so many years – decades! – that made the newly sober Leo turn to alcohol again. If it happens this time, Hilda can just flee to her own room. And if it does happen again, she will not have anything more to do with Leo.

She's told him, as well as Alicia, that this is definitely his last chance.

CHAPTER EIGHT

The view of the Finnish capital from the deck of the cruise liner is as beautiful as ever. Sipping his cold alcohol-free beer on one of the wooden picnic tables on the aft deck, Leo watches the sun light up Helsinki Cathedral, which dominates the city skyline, but without fully appreciating the view. He hardly takes in the way the early evening rays pick out the gold crosses on the seven circular domes.

His thoughts are on all the unhappy times he's made this journey. Although, this time, he's going all the way to Stockholm and not stopping at the Åland Islands. He plans an early night in the large cabin he's booked for the crossing. He has treated himself to a berth fit for an admiral. It has large windows, a balcony, and a vast bed with a separate sitting area. The breakfast is served in a private lounge on one of the top decks.

Sleeping in swanky suites and eating apart from those with cheaper cabins is not really Leo's scene but he wants to make this trip feel special. He wants to banish all those other times when he'd lost control of himself.

The idea for this self-indulgence came when he'd discussed the trip with his sponsor.

'Is there any way you can make it different this time?' the sponsor had asked.

Leo had told him that they were not going to meet on the ferry, as they had last time. Hilda was going to make her own way to Stockholm. And choosing the Swedish capital as their meeting point was another change. They'd only visited the city together once, during a mad dash to confront that Swedish reporter about a defamatory article he'd written about Hilda's late husband's farm. But Leo and Hilda had never been to Stockholm on vacation. Not during their short marriage some forty years ago, or since.

Of course, Leo could have flown, but he feels the need to banish the demons on the ferry. He knows he needs to take the same ship to the islands to meet his daughter Alicia at some point in the future, so he must get used to the surroundings without falling into the trap of picking up the bottle.

Especially now he is going to become a grandfather for the first time. In fact, this will be the second time, but he never got to meet his grandson, Stefan. He'd already died by the time Leo decided to search for Hilda and Alicia. He'd lost contact with his former wife and daughter after an awful row in which he'd hit Hilda across the face. That was decades ago, but even now, after all this time, he can't forgive his actions. Nor can he explain them.

That night has marred his life ever since.

After his shameful act, his wife left him, taking their new baby girl, Alicia. For weeks, Leo tried to contact Hilda, and when she wouldn't talk to him, take his calls, or see him, he had turned to drink.

At their daughter's request, Hilda's parents hadn't revealed that Hilda was staying with them in northern Helsinki, only a tram ride away from Leo and Hilda's small flat.

The guilt and the separation from the love of his life and his new baby had driven Leo crazy and his drinking became even worse. He now knows that Hilda and Alicia were still in town when he had the first of many benders, some of which lasted for weeks.

Later, after he'd run out of money and had to stop, emerging into the world bleary-eyed, he'd tried to get in touch with Hilda again. This time her parents told him she'd left Helsinki. They would not say where she had gone. Leo made phone calls, looked up names in phone-books, pleaded time and time again with her parents, but to no avail.

To his shame, he eventually gave up.

Drinking had made him forget, until, decades later, he'd had a heart attack and the doctor had given him just months to live if he didn't change his lifestyle.

It was then that he realized he needed to see Hilda and his daughter. He couldn't die without making peace with them. As luck would have it, he found them living in the Åland Islands.

Since that first meeting two years ago, he's been sober for 14 months, 21 days and – Leo checks his watch – 16 hours. Except for the two occasions he'd fallen foul of the drink, both witnessed by Hilda.

CHAPTER NINE

The heat seems more intense in the city than it had on the farm in Sjoland. Hilda realizes that she's brought all the wrong clothes, as she unpacks her small suitcase in the plush hotel room near the Royal Palace. Luckily, the room overlooks the water, and there's a slight breeze coming in through the open window.

Hilda takes off her blue linen trousers and white shirt, which she'd worn on the ferry with a blue blazer adorned with gold buttons. She hangs the jacket in the wardrobe, knowing she will not be wearing it again in the coming days. She glances out of the window and sees that the small thermometer stuck to the frame shows 28°C.

It's just gone six o'clock, so there's not much hope of the temperatures getting much lower in the next few hours. Hilda sighs and wonders if she has time to nip into NK, the large department store in the center of town.

She surveys the wardrobe where she's hung her clothes and sees the short-sleeved, cream maxi dress that she feels fat in. It's not what she wants to wear this evening, but it'll have to do. All the other clothes she's brought will be too uncomfortable. Hilda resolves to go shopping the next day, whether Leo wants to come along or not. This is as much her holiday as it is his. Besides, they don't have a schedule as such.

Hilda wants to keep things casual.

They're going out to dinner tonight, to a place Leo had been recommended. Situated in Söder, the south side of the city, it apparently serves traditional Swedish home cooking –*husmanskost* – with a great selection of alcohol-free beers on tap. Afterward, Hilda plans a walk along the waterfront close to their hotel.

If Leo wishes to join her, it's up to him.

They are shown to a table in the corner of the room in Restaurant Pelikan. It's a sparsely decorated space with dark wooden tables and chairs. Each table has a single tall candle, and there are large palms dotted around the room. It's a buzzy place, with almost all the tables occupied, and the clientele is obviously well-heeled. Everyone is dressed for the occasion and Hilda feels a little out of sync in her chosen outfit. Oh, well, she knows the maxi is fashionable at least, even if it isn't expensive.

Looking around the room, she feels as if she's been transported back in time, especially when she spots a huge 1930s style artwork adorning the back of the bar.

Hilda is about to point this out to Leo, who's facing away from the backlit bottles and glasses, but changes her mind at the last minute. Wouldn't showing him a shelf full of liquor be like taking a child to a candy store and then telling them they can't have any?

She looks at him briefly. He's reading the menu, a large cardboard thing, half obscuring his face. His reading glasses are perched on his nose, which makes Hilda smile. She herself hasn't yet needed glasses, but they suit Leo. The rimless frames make him appear more distinguished.

Hilda wonders whether he's still vegan. When he first visited Hilda and Alicia on the farm in Sjoland, his peculiar diet came as a complete surprise to her. All the dishes she'd prepared were unsuitable for Leo, and she had felt mortified. She was a feeder, but how could you feed someone who didn't eat anything?

Hilda says a silent prayer that she doesn't ever have to cater to his new-fangled diet again. Alicia has told her time and again that Leo is doing it for his health, but Hilda doesn't believe that a healthy lifestyle has to exclude good home-cooked food.

Good local fare, which she's been preparing for decades. Eggs from the lady two houses along from the farmhouse in Sjoland, elk from the hunt in the fall, and beef from local cattle farms. Besides, she's read that vegans eat a lot of processed food, which she knows is bad for you. Not to mention all the salt and sugar that they add to make the stuff tasty.

Well, she won't interfere in his choices, but if he

mentions his 'healthy diet' again, Hilda might just give him a few choice words.

'What are you going to have?' Leo now asks, lowering the menu.

'I think I'm going for the meatballs. It's what this place is famous for.'

Hilda inspects Leo's face for any reaction, but to her surprise he says, 'Me too.'

He smiles in such a sweet way that Hilda's heart melts a little. Perhaps her old Leo is back. The Leo that she'd fallen in love with all those years ago.

Earlier, when they'd met in the hotel lobby, at seven o'clock as agreed, Leo had looked tired. He had new lines across his brow and his hair was mussed up. She'd asked him if the ferry journey had been too long, but he shook his head and gave her a tight hug instead.

No kiss, not even on the cheek.

Well, Hilda had thought. There was a small sting of disappointment that he didn't want to make a more intimate gesture, but she took it as a good sign. He wants to take things slowly too.

In the taxi, he told her that he had to take a cab from the ferry port to get to the hotel in time, which explained his slightly disheveled appearance.

'You should have sent me a message. I'm sure we could have put the reservation back half an hour!' Hilda exclaimed.

But Leo had looked at her with those pale eyes of his. Placing his hand on her knee and giving it a light squeeze, he'd smiled.

'I would run to the end of the earth to be with you.'

His words had filled Hilda's heart to the brim. They'd literally taken her breath away and she hadn't been able to reply. She'd just smiled back at him, and they'd stayed like that, gazing at each other as if they were teenagers again until the taxi stopped outside the restaurant and they had to get out. That broke the spell, and inside the Pelikan, Hilda again began to wonder if she was doing the right thing.

Her head is swimming with conflicting emotions.

She's dizzy with affection – love? – for Leo. But is she just in love with the memory of their past?

She remembers how she felt when they first met. It was love at first sight. He was a lead singer in a band, and she was an adoring fan. When he'd looked at her from the stage, and then after the gig talked to her, and told her he wanted to see her again, she'd been delirious with happiness.

Their short marriage had been a good one, until Alicia was born, and they'd run out of money.

And he had hit her.

Is forty years enough to forgive and forget?

It obviously is, since this is the third time Hilda is meeting Leo on a date.

But how can she forget the past? She's still angry at him for everything he's put her through. Not just at how their marriage ended, but how he has behaved since coming back into her and Alicia's life.

'How is Alicia?'

Hilda is stirred from her thoughts by Leo's question.

She realizes that they've sat in silence after the waitress, a young woman wearing an old-fashioned outfit complete with a white hat, had taken their order. Hilda must admit that she wishes she had a large glass of white wine in front of her, but she has decided not to drink a drop this weekend. She doesn't want a repetition of the trip they took to Helsinki.

'Good. She's at the blooming stage and there have been no complications so far,' she replies.

Leo is nodding and fiddling with the napkin. They are rescued from the next prolonged awkward silence by the arrival of their drinks. Hilda has opted for a mocktail of bilberries and elderflower, while Leo has his customary zero-alcohol beer.

'Cheers!' Hilda says and lifts her tall glass adorned with whole berries.

Leo takes a gulp from his drink. 'You can have wine, you know. I won't be tempted. Not this time.'

Their eyes lock.

It's Hilda who looks away first, even though it should be Leo who is embarrassed.

After the debacle of their last date, when Leo had got drunk on the ferry and then pushed Hilda violently in the back of the cab while trying to get into an argument with the driver, Hilda had refused to have anything to do with him. They hadn't spoken for a few weeks after that, but then they'd begun exchanging messages again, then longer emails, and after that, phone calls.

'I'm sorry,' Leo says.

Hilda puts up a hand with her palm out as if she is trying to stop traffic.

'Don't.'

Leo leans in across the table and takes hold of Hilda's hand. Their palms together, elbows on the table, they gaze at each other as if they are about to arm wrestle in the middle of a smart Stockholm restaurant filled with well-heeled city folk.

Leo pulls his other arm out and covers Hilda's hand with both of his.

'I know I've said all this over the phone, but now that we are face to face, I want to say it again. I am so sorry. I don't know why I started drinking again. It was the joy of being with you, but I was also scared. Afraid that you'd not like me anymore. That we – us –wouldn't work.'

Hilda pulls her hand away because she's seen from the corner of her eye that people in nearby tables are giving them sly looks.

'I wish I could understand,' she says.

Leo sighs and leans back in the chair.

'I know it's difficult. But if you can forgive me, I can show you that I can do this. That I am not afraid anymore.'

Hilda nods. She doesn't say anything, but the look Leo is now giving her does something to her body. She can feel her heart expanding and something else, a tingling inside that she hasn't felt for a very long time. She reaches out her hand and places it on top of Leo's palms, which are open on the table.

'I forgive you. I already did.'

CHAPTER TEN

They are half-way through their meatballs, which, it turns out, had also come in a vegetarian version.

Not vegan, thank goodness.

Hilda had sighed, but she hadn't let Leo's refusal to eat meat spoil the mood. Especially as Leo had ordered her a large glass of Malbec to go with Hilda's choice.

Hilda is now sipping her drink, and instead of looking longingly at her glass, as he had done on that fateful trip to Helsinki last year, Leo is smiling at her and asking if the vintage is as good as the long description on the menu had indicated.

Before Hilda has time to answer, she hears a woman's voice shouting his name.

'Leo! We must stop meeting like this!'

The woman is dressed in a neat sleeveless black dress with matching kitten heels. She's petite, and when Leo gets up to greet her, he towers over the woman's slight frame. They hug.

It's as if they've known each other for years.

Hilda looks down at her oversized dress, the large amount of fabric that has gathered on her lap making her look like she's hiding a huge tummy. She tries surreptitiously to smooth it down with her left hand while she shakes the woman's proffered hand with her right. She's refusing to get up, although Leo is treating the woman as if she was royalty.

'Hi, I'm Hilda. Nice to meet you,' she says, staying seated, while glancing sideways at Leo.

How does he know this woman?

'Olivia.'

The woman gives Hilda a friendly but slightly cursory smile and then quickly turns toward Leo again.

'Well, it looks like you're having fun.'

Somehow, there is a certain amount of reproach in Olivia's tone of voice.

'Yes,' Leo says simply.

Leo's face reveals how uncomfortable he is. It's as if he wishes the earth would open and swallow him right up.

When it's clear that Leo isn't going to elaborate, Olivia turns toward Hilda again and says, in a conversational tone, 'It's funny that I should see Leo again so soon. We took the ferry together and he told me he was meeting a business associate. You must be that "associate".'

What is this?

Hilda's eyes find Leo's and she can see that he really doesn't want to talk to Olivia.

She nods and says that, yes, she is indeed in business with Leo.

'That is interesting. Because, you know, as I was admiring the wonderful cabin that Leo had got us on the ferry, he never once mentioned that this associate was a woman. Did you Leo? Or that the meeting would take place in a restaurant. Or in the evening.'

Olivia is regarding Leo as if she's caught him doing something he shouldn't.

Then it hits Hilda what the woman said.

'You shared a cabin?'

'Yeah. We go way back.'

'Right.'

Hilda tries to catch Leo's eye again, but he's now looking sideways at the other diners, then at his hands. Anywhere else but at either Hilda or Olivia.

There is a long, awkward, silence.

Hilda doesn't know what to think. Is this Leo's woman friend? Someone he's comfortable enough to share a cabin with. Is he sleeping with her?

Is Leo two-timing her, Hilda? Surely, he wouldn't dare do that after everything.

It's true that Hilda and Leo aren't in a relationship, but surely this reconciliation is aimed at a possible future together? Or has Hilda completely misunderstood the situation?

Eventually, Leo takes Olivia's hand.

'It's good to see you again so soon.'

The woman is not keen to leave, but now she has no choice.

'Nice to meet you, Hilda,' she says and walks out of the restaurant.

When they are alone again, Hilda doesn't know what to say. She has also lost her appetite, so she just finishes her wine in one large gulp, while trying not to look at Leo.

'Do you want another one?'

'Yes, please,' Hilda says, adding, 'It's OK, I can get it myself. I need the bathroom anyway.'

Hilda stands up and, straightening her back, concentrates on walking away from their table with a confident gait, although her whole body is shaking. Once inside a cubicle in the bathroom, which turns out to be in the basement at the far end of the bar, Hilda sits on top of the toilet lid and tries to take deep breaths.

There's no fool like an old fool.

What did she think would happen? Leo has never been reliable. First the drinking and the lack of money when they were new parents. He never took responsibility for his family. Going out at all hours when Hilda and baby Alicia needed him at home. Then when she had the audacity to ask his parents for money, he had hit her.

Last summer they had tried to reconcile, but that, too, had ended with Leo disappointing her once again. Turning to violence, as usual.

Hilda knows he is an alcoholic, and perhaps she wasn't supportive enough. Still, is this what she wants for herself? A man who is so volatile? She is not that desperate! She's seen how other men look at her. Even here in the Pelikan, several older men gave her a second glance as she passed their tables. Even when she is wearing a dress that makes her appear at least two sizes bigger. Why should she settle for someone she gave up on long ago?

And now this! He's quite clearly intimate with another woman while trying to patch things up with her!

No, no, no!

Hilda is now so angry that she wants to go back to the table and tell Leo some home truths. But why should she bother?

How she misses Uffe now. If he hadn't died so suddenly the winter before last, Hilda wouldn't have to be here in Stockholm having dinner with someone who clearly doesn't respect her. She flares her nostrils to stop the tears that are threatening to ruin her makeup.

Leo is not worth even one single tear.

She thinks back to the route she took to the bathroom. She can quite easily get out of the restaurant without Leo noticing. He has his back to the bar. She gathers herself and opens the door to the line of copper sinks facing a large antique mirror. She corrects her make-up, applies more lipstick, aptly named 'Bittersweet', and snaps her handbag shut.

If you think you can make a fool of Hilda Ulsson, you have another thing coming!

CHAPTER ELEVEN

Leo feels like a lemon sitting and waiting in the buzzy restaurant for Hilda to come back from the bathroom. She was visibly shocked by what Olivia said about being in his cabin and now he curses his decisions to invite the woman in.

He hardly knows her.

She's always been kind to him at the meetings, that's true, but she's not his sponsor, nor is he interested in her in that way. He thought he had that clear during the meetings they've shared, but he now wonders if he's been sending confusing signals.

He turns around to see where Hilda is, but instead of his ex-wife, he sees the bar full of drinks that he knows he cannot have.

Would one beer make such a difference? Yes, it would.

As much as he tries not to think about it, the events of last winter, when he got so drunk on the ferry with Hilda that he pushed her hard in the taxi, enter his mind.

He made a complete fool of himself and hurt Hilda – again.

He can hardly remember what happened, but he knows that the driver was somehow bothering them – or Leo had got it into his head that he was – and he had kicked off. He was so drunk that he didn't know his own strength. Bad things always happen when he is drunk.

He's got a fresh chance with Hilda now and he is not going to throw that away.

After half an hour, Leo's biggest fears are realized.

Hilda is not coming back.

He sends her a message, tries to call her, but she doesn't answer.

Leo calls the waitress over and pays the bill. Instead of grabbing a cab back to the hotel, he decides to clear his head by walking along Götagatan toward the subway station at Skanstull. Surely Hilda would have gone back to the hotel? He must get hold of her and explain that nothing at all happened with Olivia on the ferry. She must believe him when he tells her that being sober on a booze cruise when everyone else is beyond inebriated is one of the most difficult situations for an alcoholic.

But how can he explain what a strong tie you can form with the people in an AA group? Seeing one of them outside the sessions, in a situation where there is temptation everywhere, felt almost like a gift.

Both Olivia and Leo are only months into their sobriety, and both have had setbacks in the past. Talking about it felt good, especially in the privacy of his luxurious cabin.

Leo had also felt a little sorry for Olivia. She has lost her money gambling while drunk, and her accommodation for the overnight crossing was in the depths of the ship's hull. Leo had a bed and a sofa bed in his suite, so it had seemed natural to offer Olivia a place to stay.

Walking along the street, with a pub or a bar on almost every corner, Leo tries to remember whether there had been any moments during the whole evening when he had felt uncomfortable, but he can't think of any. Even when they were getting ready for bed, Olivia had told Leo to go to the bathroom first, because she would likely take longer.

'You think this face and body happens without considerable effort?' She had joked.

Leo had laughed politely and complemented her by saying, 'I think you're a natural beauty.'

Leo stops walking. He halts so quickly that a group of young men, full of beer, behind him curse at him.

'Sorry, sorry,' Leo says.

As he watches the youngsters enter an Irish bar a few doors down, Leo has a sudden memory of Olivia's expression at that moment. Her face had softened and her eyes had widened. With a slight flush to her cheeks, she'd replied, 'Oh, Leo, you say the nicest things.'

Had she thought he was coming onto her?

In the restaurant, Olivia had behaved as if Leo was two-timing her when that couldn't be further from the truth.

No wonder Hilda got the wrong idea.

. . .

The door to the Irish Bar is wide open and Leo can hear loud music and laughter coming from inside. He thinks of the wonderful taste of beer, real beer, not the watery alcohol-free stuff he now drinks. The feeling of that first, and even second, beer is so unique and wonderful. Why should he deny himself? Just two beers would be enough to get the buzz.

After that, he can carry on to Hilda's hotel and tell her that she is the first and the last woman he is ever going to love.

After a small hesitation, Leo takes a few steps toward the open door and walks inside.

CHAPTER TWELVE

Frida sits alone in her lovely, light-filled kitchen. She's just bathed and read Anne Sofie her bedtime story. She was so tired from playing hide and seek with *Famo* Alicia that she didn't protest when Frida put her down to sleep.

When Frida peeked inside the pink-walled room a few minutes later, she saw the little blonde head on the pillow, her eyes tightly closed. With her little mouth slightly open and her small hands curled up together underneath her chin, she looked so angelic that the sight brought tears to Frida's eyes.

Frida tiptoed out of the room and made herself another coffee.

The conversation with Alicia is playing on her mind now as she watches the ships from Finland and Sweden sail into the West Harbor. The small red shapes move slowly one after another, getting larger as they approach the narrow straight into the harbor.

How Frida has missed this kitchen with its view of

the Baltic Sea! Romania was wonderful, and she loved getting to know Andrei's family, but she'd felt homesick after only a couple of weeks.

The farm where Andrei had grown up in the southern part of the country is isolated, far from the sea. Once Andrei took her and Anne Sofie to the River Out to see a vast reservoir, but it wasn't the same as smelling the saltiness of the Baltic. Frida had kissed Andrei on the mouth while they were standing by the banks of the river, gazing at the water running toward the flat, wide basin in the distance.

'Swim, swim!' Anne Sofie had shouted, pointing at the water and trying to wriggle her hand out of Frida's hold.

Andrei had picked up the little girl and told her, in his faltering Swedish, that the water was too cold.

'And look how fast it flows!' Frida had added. 'Even *Mamma* wouldn't want to try to swim against that.'

Anne Sofie had then gazed at the water and turned her serious face toward Frida. She'd nodded, with her blue eyes wide. She was only two but seemed a lot older.

After the excursion, Frida had come to realize how much she needed to be close to the sea. She'd grown up in Mariehamn, and hadn't truly appreciated the beauty of the archipelago surrounding the small town until she had lived away. She needs to be by water, she now realizes, as she watches the cumbersome maneuvering of the first of the Marie Line ships as it reverses into the harbor.

Frida places her cup on the counter and sighs.

Andrei.

How she misses him! She wants to smell his scent, to

feel the roughness of his unshaven chin, see the serious, intense look in his eyes last thing at night when they lie opposite each other in the back room of the old wooden farm building in Sibiu.

She knows it's not just the farm and his sense of responsibility for his siblings that are keeping him away from Åland. No, she knows he is unhappy about her wealth. Or perhaps not the money itself but where it came from.

Frida had tried to explain to Andrei that she isn't certain Dudnikov is her father. Or that her mom's money had come from the Russian criminal. The lawyer, Karls-son, never actually disclosed the identity of her father, or who was behind the vast sums that had been deposited into her mom's account every month for years – including the whole of Frida's life.

The old man simply hadn't denied it when she'd suggested that Dudnikov was behind the money. All she had to go on were the rumors about her mom having had a Russian lover.

What if Alicia is right and she can prove that the Russian wasn't her father? What if she could find out for certain who he was?

If she could prove that Dudnikov had nothing to do with her or Anne Sofie, Andrei might be more willing to settle on the islands.

Frida gets her laptop and begins searching. Soon she finds what she needs and clicks 'Buy now'. In a couple of weeks' time she will know something about her DNA.

That's a start.

· · ·

After Frida has closed her laptop, there's a knock on her door. As usual, her cat is there first. Frida picks up the creature.

'Has anyone ever told you that you're a cat, not a guard dog?'

Frida buries her face in the cat's fur. Immediately, Minki begins to purr loudly.

Outside the door stands a tall, blond man. He's wearing cut-offs and a faded T-shirt.

'Hello?'

'Hi, I'm so sorry. My name is Ollie Streng. I've just moved in next door. I forgot to buy coffee and I can't start the day tomorrow without any. You couldn't lend me a cupful? All the stores are closed by now…'

'Oh, of course.'

Frida bends down to drop the cat on the floor and gestures for the man to come in.

Minki jumps onto the hall table and assumes what Frida calls her statue pose. Her eyes are not leaving her new neighbor's face.

Ollie looks a little disturbed and gives a nervous laugh.

'Don't worry about her. She doesn't like strangers.'

Apart from Andrei, whom she loved from the first moment.

'I'm not good with cats. They seem to hate me for some reason,' Ollie says, tailing Frida into the kitchen. Minki follows them, running fast past Ollie and jumping onto the kitchen window ledge.

'Really, she's fine,' Frida says with her back to the

man. She brings out the coffee jar, and begins filling a small container.

'That's too much – honestly, I just need a few spoonfuls.'

Frida closes the container and hands it over to her new neighbor.

They stand awkwardly for a moment.

To break the silence, Frida asks where Ollie has moved from.

'Oh, Sweden. My mom is from Åland and I've always wanted to live here, so when a job came up, I jumped at the chance.'

The man shifts his weight from one foot to the other and Frida suddenly realizes she's not asked him to sit down.

'How rude of me, please take a seat. Would you like a beer?'

'That'd be great.'

Ollie pulls out one of the kitchen chairs, while nervously glancing at Minki, who's still staring at him.

'She really doesn't like me, does she?'

Frida glances at the cat. She is behaving rather strangely, she thinks, but says, 'She's always like that with people she doesn't know.'

She grins at Ollie, who returns her smile. The gesture opens up his face and makes him look even more handsome.

Frida gets two tins of Sandels lager out of the fridge and asks if Ollie would like a glass.

'No, this is great. To tell you the truth it's been a bit of a day. The removals van was late – they missed the ferry connection and barely made the last Ålandsfärjan. Now it seems half my stuff is stuck in Customs. Including my coffee.'

Ollie is just about to take a sip of his beer when the cat, meowing loudly, lands on the kitchen table, only to spring back up and rush straight at Ollie.

Beer spills on his clothing and he stands up, shouting. 'Bloody hell!'

Frida is horrified. She gets a cloth and starts wiping Ollie's shirt.

'I'm so sorry.'

Her new neighbor composes himself.

'Don't worry. I'm fine.'

He attempts a smile and picks up the coffee.

'I'd better leave you. Thank you for this.'

CHAPTER THIRTEEN

Back at the hotel, just before turning to take the elevator to her room, Hilda hears voices and laughter coming from somewhere. She cranes her neck and sees the sign to Bar Reiss. She looks at the large clock in the lobby and notices that it's barely gone eight o'clock.

She turns away from the elevators. What she needs now is a drink. It's too hot to go to bed yet. The temperatures haven't fallen, and the AC in the hotel isn't up to much. Hilda knows she will have a sleepless night ahead of her so she might as well have a few drinks to help her relax. Besides, the bar is the last place Leo would come looking for her, she's certain of it.

Seating herself on one of the barstools, which, unusually, have proper backs and are surprisingly comfortable, she orders a glass of wine.

'Hilda?'

The deep voice behind her sounds familiar, but it isn't until she turns around that she realizes who it is.

'Well, I never! Nils von Brask!'

The man in front of her is grinning widely. His dark green eyes have the same mischievous smile they had when the two of them met on the stricken ship last Christmas Eve. Nils ended up spending Christmas with Hilda and her family. Neither of them had ever had an evening like it, she is certain of that.

The police chief on the islands, Ebba Torstensson, who went to school with Alicia, had suspected Nils of being in cahoots with the Russian criminal Alexander Dudnikov.

As if!

Hilda still feels embarrassed that Ebba had treated her guest as though he was a common criminal, and taken him across the yard to Alicia's cottage for questioning.

Getting down from her stool, she remembers how tall Nils von Brask is. He is head and shoulders above her.

They hug a little awkwardly.

Nils' body is taut, in a way that no man of his age should be. As he is about to release her, Nils bends down and gives Hilda a kiss on her cheek.

'Can I sit here?' he asks when Hilda has recovered a little.

Hilda nods. She'd been very tempted to turn her head so that Nils would kiss her on the mouth, but she'd managed to resist that temptation.

Be sensible!

She is most likely still in shock over another bitter disappointment handed down to her by Leo.

There's no denying that Nils von Brask is a handsome man. Tall and slim with a characterful face, he is dressed in a deep-blue button-down and dark trousers. On his feet, he's wearing fashionable tan sneakers. Hilda notices that his belt is the exact same color. On his wrist, he is wearing an expensive-looking Rolex.

'I'd forgotten about the once over you give people so unashamedly,' he grins.

He's teasing me again. Just as Uffe used to do.

Hilda can feel her cheeks burn and she hopes to God she hasn't blushed like a teenager. She sits a little straighter on her barstool, and says, in what she hopes is a playful tone, 'I appreciate your impeccable style, that's all. I ran a fashion boutique for years.'

'That explains it,' Nils says drily, but his eyes betray the playfulness that the comment was meant to convey.

They sit there for a moment, just smiling at each other.

'So, what are you doing in Stockholm? Are you staying here?' Nils asks while seeking the barman with his eyes and nodding to him.

The man rushes over and Nils queries what Hilda is drinking, but at that moment another barman brings her the wine.

'Please put that on my tab,' Nils says confidently to the barman.

Hilda wants to protest but decides against it. Let the man do his thing, she thinks, and sips her wine.

Nils orders a glass of whisky. Hilda is reminded of the night they met, when he had a long conversation with the barman about the choice of whisky. This time, he seems to know exactly what to order.

'Still drinking whisky, then?'

Nils returns her smile. 'You didn't reply to my question.'

'Ah, that's a long story. I was supposed to spend the evening with a friend, staying here for the night, but it turns out it's going to be a lonely one.'

Nils brings his glass toward hers and touches the rim.

'Well, that is good news!'

'Is it now?'

Hilda cannot help but flirt with this guy. After the disastrous Christmas, which she managed to save by offering her guests copious amounts of good food and drink, they've only exchanged a few emails. In truth, Hilda was so mortified by the way Alicia and the police chief had treated him, that she couldn't bring herself to keep in touch.

'I must thank you for last Christmas,' Nils says as if he's read her mind.

'Oh, please. I must apologize to you for everything.'

'No, no. It wasn't your fault that I found myself in the middle of all that. On the contrary, you saved my Christmas. Besides, being interrogated by the island police was an experience.'

'Please, let's not talk about that awful night.'

'OK, but tell me, have they caught the criminal I was supposed to be working for?'

'Don't think so.'

Hilda is quiet for a moment. The fact that Alexander Dudnikov is a free man is a constant cloud over their heads. She knows that Alicia is afraid he might pop up at any moment, as is she.

Hilda regards Nils. She wonders if she could tell him how the man terrorized her when she had her fashion boutique in Mariehamn. She feels so utterly guilty about that too. Although it was Uffe who first introduced Dudnikov to her, she had fallen for his lies. She'd got herself so indebted to him that she had lost the boutique. In the end, Uffe had to sell some of his land to pay the Russian off.

'That's a shame. But listen, I'm at a bit of a loose end too, so why don't we spend the evening together. I have an invitation to the opening of a new jazz bar in Östermalm. It's not far from here. You enjoy live music, don't you?'

Before Hilda can reply to Nils' invitation, her phone pings.

Where are you? Please Hilda, I can explain.

She reads the message but doesn't reply.

'Something important?' Nils asks, his face full of concern.

Hilda shakes her head and finishes her wine. It's a rather excellent Italian Gavi di Gavi.

'No, no one important,' she says.

'So, what do you say? Are you going to keep me company?'

Hilda smiles.

'Why not?'

'Well, this deserves a toast. Another one?' Nils says, grinning.

Once again, he turns toward the barman, who immediately comes over.

'Mr von Brask, what can I get you?'

So, he's known here, Hilda thinks. She wonders if she's crazy for accepting his offer to go to this new jazz bar. It does sound like something Hilda would enjoy. And when does she ever just think about herself?

It's not as if Nils is a stranger. She knows him, and even the island police have vetted him, haven't they? She thinks about Alicia, who is always telling her to be careful, and she decides to let her daughter know about the change of plan later.

While Nils is giving the barman the order, Hilda's phone buzzes again. This time Leo is trying to call her. Hilda presses refuse call and turns to smile at Nils.

Her relationship with Leo is ancient history. It didn't work the first time, and Hilda feels stupid for trying to rekindle something. She will only get hurt. After losing Uffe so suddenly, she was momentarily blinded by the attentions of an old flame. But going back is never a good idea.

The only good outcome out of all this is that Leo has reconciled with Alicia.

She can meet her father on her own in Helsinki, or wherever she prefers. If he comes to the islands, Hilda can always escape to Stockholm, because one thing is certain: she doesn't want to see her ex-husband ever again.

CHAPTER FOURTEEN

Leo wakes up with the sun streaming in through the curtains. He looks around and sees that he is in a small bedroom, on top of the covers in a narrow bed. Pale curtains flutter against the open window.

Where is he?

He tries to get up, but his head throbs so much that he puts it back down again and closes his eyes.

What happened?

And then he remembers.

The Irish bar, the Guinness, the vodka shots, the young lads he'd seen go in before him. How he'd told them about Hilda, and Olivia, and how they'd laughed. Sniggered at the old man with women troubles.

Leo takes hold of his head and is suddenly nauseous. He sees that a red bucket has been placed on the floor next to the bed and he throws up in it. Afterward, he lies back again and tries to remember what else happened.

Did he get into a fight? His head throbs, but that's probably just the hangover.

What he needs is a beer.

He tries to get up again, slowly, and knocks over a side table and a glass of water.

'*Perkele,*' he swears to himself.

As he tries to get up, the door opens and who should stand there but Olivia.

'Good morning,' she says.

She walks over to the bed and picks up the glass from the floor.

'How did I get here?'

'You don't remember?'

Olivia sounds cold, even angry.

Leo gets it.

He's let everyone down again, including the woman who has an unreciprocated crush on him.

He rests his hands on his head. If he could, he would cry. How did he mess up again?

'I've called your sponsor.'

Leo nods but doesn't look at Olivia. He can't face anyone today. He wants to be home, wants to crawl into bed, drink a bottle of beer and sleep.

'You haven't any beer, have you? I can't go cold turkey yet.'

Olivia stares hard at him, but then nods and leaves the room. After a few minutes she's back with a can of Carlsberg. Leo takes the beer and opens it with shaking hands. He downs half in one long gulp.

Wiping his mouth against the back of his hand, he

says, 'Tomorrow'. His eyes are on Olivia and he can see that she understands.

She pulls a shirt from a small wardrobe opposite the bed, then a pair of underpants from a drawer, and hands the two garments to Leo.

'There's stuff in the bathroom for you to use. Including a toothbrush. Get washed and changed and come into the kitchen to meet my brother.'

About half an hour later, Leo feels a lot better. Following the sound of two people talking, he enters a tiny kitchen.

Olivia and an older man with gray hair and a neat salt and pepper beard sit at a small table set against a window. There are just three chairs around it. Both Olivia and the man turn to look at Leo as he appears in the doorway.

'I'm sorry about last night. I don't really remember much but thank you for giving me a bed.'

'Don't worry. I'm used to it,' the man says tightly, glancing briefly at Olivia.

Olivia gives a short laugh.

'Ricky has dragged me away from a bar many a time before now.'

'All the same, I'm grateful.'

Leo has been in these situations before, but usually with people who have been drinking with him. Many a time in Helsinki, he's woken up on a stranger's sofa, or even on a bare floor. During those times, the drinking has continued, until he has found himself at home, or on occasion in a police cell, with nothing to drink and a hangover so bad that he hasn't been able to move for days.

Now he stands here with two people who are stone cold sober, who have seen him delirious the night before. Who no doubt saved him. Or did they?

With the buzz of the first beer in his veins, he's wondering why Olivia didn't just let him carry on drinking? He could have had one last bender. How he longs for oblivion now. He wants to forget about last night, about Hilda and the look she gave him after Olivia had left their table.

And why had he allowed her to share his cabin on the ferry. Why hadn't he just bid her goodnight and let her go to the cabin she had booked. If he hadn't been on the ferry, she would have had to do that anyway.

Now his good act had messed up his chances with Hilda for good.

What is the point in trying to be good?

A thought jolts his brain into gear.

Alicia.

Suddenly he remembers his daughter and the grandchild she is carrying. He cannot let them down.

Stay sober for them.

'Coffee?'

Leo is shaken out of his own thoughts by Olivia's brother.

Ricky gets up and turns toward the kitchen counter where a coffee machine stands. He is stockily built, unlike Olivia, who has a very petite frame. Both have dark hair and piercingly green eyes, though.

'Thank you,' Leo mutters.

He sits himself diagonally opposite Olivia at the tiny table. The large window, which seems completely out of proportion with what Leo has seen of the apartment so far, looks over the street below. When he looks down, he can see the sign for the subway. Leo doesn't know Stockholm that well, but it looks as if Olivia's brother lives somewhere on the south side.

He hasn't come that far from the Irish pub then. He hopes not, at least.

He moves his eyes toward Olivia. She's smiling at him now.

'Don't worry about grumpy head over there. He's never been very good with drunks, although, as he says, he's had plenty of practice with me.'

At these words, Ricky turns around. He's pouring coffee into a cup.

The siblings start faux fighting, with words going back and forth.

This leaves time for Leo to wonder what really happened last night and whether he can ask Olivia about it. Although Ricky now seems more relaxed, Leo is ashamed enough to hold back.

'Do you remember much from last night?' Olivia's brother asks as he places the coffee in front of Leo.

'No, not after the second beer.'

Ricky glances at Olivia, who briefly shakes her head at him.

'Please, I know it's bad, but I do want to know,' Leo says.

Olivia places her hand over his on the table. 'Just

have your coffee first, and then perhaps you could face a bit of breakfast?'

She glances at her phone and adds, 'or lunch.'

This makes Leo panic.

'What time is it?'

'Nearly noon,' Olivia says, adding, 'Why?'

Leo takes a few sips of the coffee, but it's too hot and it burns his mouth. He gets up and pats Olivia's shoulders.

'Thank you again, but I must go,'

He's nearly out of the door when he hears Olivia shout after him, 'Where to?'

Leo is right; he is still in Söder. He runs to the subway. He ignores his head, which has started throbbing again, and gets to the platform just as the train going back to Centralen arrives. The time is now nearly ten past twelve. He has twenty minutes before the bus leaves the central station.

As soon as the doors open, he runs along the platform, up the escalators and across the central train station to reach the buses that take day trippers to the harbor north of Stockholm where the ferry leaves for Mariehamn. He knows Hilda is going to be on the one leaving at 12.30. Unless she's changed her plans, that is.

CHAPTER FIFTEEN

Leo gets to the bus just as it is about to leave. He digs in his pocket for his wallet and pays for a ticket. Panting, as the bus begins to move away, he stands in the aisle scanning the passengers. Finally, he sees Hilda sitting in the middle of the coach, gazing through the window to the other side of the platform. She's deep in thought and hasn't seen him.

For a moment, Leo wonders if he should just tell the driver he's made a mistake and step off the bus.

Hilda will never forgive him.

How many chances can he expect to be given? Besides, he knows that his sobriety needs much more work. Whenever he's fallen off the wagon, he's been with Hilda. His feelings toward her are obviously still too complicated and raw for him to be with her.

But he must talk to her and explain about Olivia.

As he makes his way slowly toward the middle of the bus, he remembers the beer he had this morning, and all the alcohol he had last night. His breath must be reeking. He digs in his pockets again. As luck would have it, he finds a tube of mints in his back pocket. He slips one inside his mouth and stops next to Hilda.

'What are you doing here?'

Hilda cannot believe her eyes. The bus has just left the central station and Leo is standing in the aisle

'Can I sit down?'

The coach is on a traffic circle and Leo is having trouble keeping himself upright. When he nearly falls backward, Hilda takes pity on him.

She nods and turns her face toward the window again.

'You are not coming on the ferry.'

The bus drives around the large waterfall at Sergels Torget. Before Leo interrupted her train of thought, Hilda had been recalling the times she has taken this bus after attending fashion shows in the city.

'Of course not. I just wanted to explain,' Leo says.

Hilda turns her head and glares at Leo. He has a nerve. She can't control her anger anymore.

'Explain!' she cries out, raising her voice.

A Swedish couple sitting behind them stop talking and Hilda can feel their eyes burning into the back of her head. From the corner of her eye, she can also see another passenger, a young woman, looking at them.

Lowering her hand and her tone, she continues, 'You come here, unannounced, and corner me in this bus. You reek of alcohol, and no doubt you've spent the night with that woman, that hussy, that you had already entertained on the ferry. Well, you are welcome to her. I do not wish to have anything more to do with you.'

She moves away from Leo and looks out over Stockholm. They are now driving through the business district, where the tall windows of high-rise buildings glint in the midday sun. She tries to steady her breath and temper. She mustn't shout at Leo, however infuriating he is. She will not embarrass herself on this bus, which is probably full of islanders. She is well-known because of the boutique, as well as Uffe's farm and Alicia's connections with the Eriksson family.

Leo seems unperturbed.

'Olivia is on the same AA program as me. I felt sorry for her…'

'I do not want to hear this!'

Hilda is hissing now, covertly keeping an eye on the other passengers. Many are wearing earphones, but they are mainly young. Hilda is more concerned with the older folk, who may have heard of her or visited her shop.

Leo continues his tale.

'I let her sleep on the sofa bed in my cabin. I got a comfortable one because I thought I needed a nice space. I promise you, nothing happened. And last night, well, I started drinking when you didn't come back to the table, and Olivia and her brother gave me a place to crash.'

Hilda takes a few deep intakes of breath. She tries to keep her voice level.

'And what about your perfectly serviceable hotel

room? I know you weren't there because I checked with the hotel staff. I was worried about you!'

Hilda is taken aback by her own sudden feelings of relief. She had been concerned about Leo after she found out that he hadn't come back at all.

At first, she'd been afraid that she'd bump into him at breakfast. But when he was nowhere to be seen, she had enquired at the hotel reception, telling them Leo was her brother.

She hadn't had any more messages or calls from him after she and Nils had left the hotel for the jazz bar. It turned out that Nils was an investor in the place, and they got the best table, right next to the stage.

It had been a magical night, but Hilda had been careful not to flirt with Nils. She asked to leave before the last set, and when they were outside, waiting for Hilda's cab, she had turned her head away when he tried to kiss her.

Hilda had tried to smile. 'I'm sorry, it's been a difficult night. Until I met you, that is.'

Being a gentleman, Nils had just touched her arm and replied, 'In that case, I bid you goodnight. I'm sorry I can't escort you all the way to the hotel, but I have to stay here until the bitter end. You understand, don't you?'

Hilda had been relieved. As the night had worn on, she had become more and more concerned about Leo. She was angry with him, but she also realized that he was weak. What if he turned to drink after she left him? She knew he couldn't stop once he started. He was no longer a young man and Stockholm was a dangerous city for anyone as vulnerable as he was.

Nils had hugged Hilda and added, 'Can I call or message you? I would like to see you again.'

Hilda agreed, although she wasn't certain she wanted to see Nils again. At least not romantically.

He was a good-looking man, but she wasn't ready for a new relationship. What the evening with Leo had shown her was that she had most probably rushed things. She hadn't sought to replace Uffe – that she would never be able to do – but she'd been too quick to find someone else to share her life with.

Leo was there, she knew him, had been married to him, so she'd thought she could just pick up with him again, as if the last forty years hadn't happened.

She'd read somewhere that grief makes you do strange things. And that you should take time before making changes in your life after you've lost a loved one. How true that is! Hilda wished that she'd taken that advice sooner. She would have avoided all the painful encounters with Leo.

'Look, can we start again?'

Leo places his hand on Hilda's arm, but she removes it from the armrest and crosses her hands on her lap instead.

'Please.'

'Stop it!'

Hilda's words are so loud that the woman behind them leans forward and touches Hilda's shoulder.

'Is this man bothering you? Would you like us to tell the driver?'

Leo's face drops.

Hilda turns toward the woman and smiles as naturally as she can muster.

'No, I'm sorry if we're disturbing you. It's just a small disagreement, that's all. We'll keep our voices down, won't we?'

Hilda looks at Leo, and he nods. He appears a little abashed by the situation he has created.

'You're not disturbing us at all, but I'm glad you're OK.'

The woman's eyes go from Hilda to Leo and back again. She's obviously concerned that there's some kind of abusive situation going on.

If only she knew their history.

At last, the woman gives up and leans back in her seat.

Hilda could cry. Why did she think she could rekindle some teenage love affair? Even if the disheveled man sitting next to her was her husband and the father of her only daughter, they are ancient history. She is so tired after that humid night in which she woke up several times wondering what had become of Leo.

'We are different people now.'

Hilda is painfully aware of the couple behind them. She knows they can hear every word they utter.

Leo's face brightens. 'That's my point! I am different, I promise you. I know I messed up last night, but when you left me like that, I was, I was …'

Now it's Hilda's turn to put a hand on Leo's arm to stop him from talking.

'Look, I know last night was a disaster. Another disaster,' she says, emphasizing the last two words.

'Yes, but …'

Leo places his hand on top of Hilda's, but this makes Hilda pull hers away.

'Please, Leo, can you just listen to what I am telling you?'

Again, Hilda cannot help but raise her voice.

'Sorry,' she says turning toward the woman behind her. She raises a hand, with her palm up.

'Please don't be.' The woman smiles, as does the man next to her.

Hilda turns around and tries to calm herself. She is mortified for creating such a lot of commotion on the bus.

'OK,' Leo replies after a moment.

His shoulders have slumped, and he is staring at the back of the velour seat in front of him. The interior of the bus is a garish lilac and red, and the AC is nonexistent. Hilda feels the back of her thighs sticking to her linen dress. She brushes her hair off her forehead.

'It's so hot here!'

'Yeah, but that's not what you wanted to tell me, is it?'

Leo's eyes have a little sparkle to them now and Hilda can't help but smile.

'No.'

They are both silent for a moment. The bus has left the city and is making its way along the freeway with increasing speed. Hilda wishes she could open a window, just to get a little fresh air, but there are no openings anywhere. The temperature is near 30°C and the bus, just like her hotel room last night, isn't designed for this kind of heat. Summers in the north aren't usually this hot.

'I've recently lost my husband, the love of my life …'

Hilda sees Leo wince at the words, but she continues.

'Uffe was a wonderful man. He became Alicia's dad and, without question, took us both in when I so desperately needed a safe haven. When he died so very suddenly, I think I went a bit crazy. I didn't realize that I needed time to grieve rather than jump straight into another relationship.'

Leo's eyes are wide, and Hilda thinks she can see tears pooling there. She places a hand on his arm again.

'I loved you too. Once. But it was over forty years ago now. And you have your own issues to resolve.'

Leo nods. He's not looking at her and Hilda guesses it's because he doesn't want to show her that he is about to cry. Hilda herself feels a lump in her throat.

'It's not as if we won't see each other again, is it? We have a daughter together and a new baby, a grandchild, to look forward to. That's something, isn't it?'

During the rest of the journey to the Kapellskär harbor, Hilda and Leo talk about Alicia and the pregnancy. They don't mention the previous night or make plans to see each other again. When the bus turns into the harbor area and Hilda sees the Marie Line ferry is already loading cars onto its lower decks, she turns to Leo and says, 'Will you be OK? Is there a bus back?'

He shrugs his shoulders and says, 'If not, I'll get a cab. Don't worry about me.'

Outside, after the other passengers for the bus have walked over to the ferry terminal, Hilda and Leo stand facing each other. Hilda is holding onto her small roller suitcase.

'Well, this is me.'

'Right.'

Leo doesn't know what to say or do. Will Hilda push him away if he tries to hug her? Or kiss her on the cheek? Should they shake hands? No, that's too formal.

Leo decides to take a step closer to her, and when she doesn't react, he lifts his arms up.

'Can I give you a hug?'

He can't decipher her expression, but she nods and Leo pulls Hilda toward him.

For some reason, they start to rock from side to side, and then both begin giggling like teenagers.

'Look at us! We're too old for this.'

Hilda grins and her positive frame of mind gives Leo hope. But he knows he shouldn't expect a reconciliation. Hilda doesn't want any kind of relationship with him. Apart from a friendship, perhaps.

If he's lucky.

'You'd better go before the ferry leaves without you,' he says.

They gaze at each other.

Leo can't believe that, once again, he is letting this woman, the love of his life, go.

He watches Hilda walk into the terminal building, until she disappears around a corner.

I still have Alicia and the new baby. I have to be strong for them.

CHAPTER SIXTEEN

P atrick is sitting at the far end of the cafe, in one of the last rooms that make up the Svarta Katten. The place used to be a private house, and it's Alicia's favorite place because it's so homely. Each room is furnished as a fancy salon, with a few tables and old-fashioned sofas and dining chairs to sit on.

Perhaps he wants to be discreet about our meeting, Alicia thinks. Suits me.

It's quiet here today. Most people would want to sit by the sea, because of the heat, Alicia guesses. She notices with pleasure that there is a large fan set to maximum speed next to the table where Patrick is sitting.

Just walking the short distance from the car park, trying to keep in the shade of the trees, has caused beads of sweat to form on her forehead and on the top of her lip.

She's conscious of how she must look, then stops

herself.

It doesn't matter.

Patrick gets up as soon as he spots Alicia across the room and watches her walk to the table. They are the only people occupying this last room.

They stand for a moment facing each other. Alicia is trying not to be affected by Patrick's strong physique and those blue eyes peering at her.

As when she saw him with Mia, he runs his fingers through his blond hair. His arms flex under his customary white T-shirt (does he ever wear anything else?). He's obviously been working out during the months he's been away from the islands.

He points toward the chintz-covered sofa where he was sitting. 'Do you want to sit here?'

'Thank you.'

Alicia doesn't like to have her back to a door, which she'd have had to do if she'd sat in the chair opposite him – a winged seat covered in moss-green velvet. It annoys her that Patrick knows this fact about her, but she tries not to think about it.

'Coffee?'

'No, thank you, but if they have mint tea, that would be nice.'

'OK,' Patrick says, making his way out of the room to the sales counter at the entrance to the cafe.

His disappearance gives Alicia a little time to recover. She finds a paper tissue and wipes her face. The fan is doing its job and she feels a lot cooler already.

When will his body stop having this effect one her?

As long as you don't do anything about it, it'll be fine.

She knows his attentiveness is because he wants to get something out of her. But what can it be? He can see she's expecting, and he must guess who the father-to-be is. He must realize this means she is fully committed to her marriage to Liam.

Patrick appears in the doorway, followed by a young girl holding a tray. She puts down a pot of tea and two cups and saucers decorated with sprigs of pink flowers. There are also two Pepita cakes, prettily covered in a pink glaze.

When they've thanked the girl for pouring the tea, and she has disappeared out of the room, Alicia glances at Patrick, who has settled on the green chair opposite.

'How did you get her to serve us? They never do that for me. I can barely get them to speak when I get a drink from the counter!'

The place was known for its surly staff – youngsters who preferred gazing at their cellphones to serving customers.

Patrick gives Alicia one of his lopsided smiles.

'Why, I charmed her, of course!'

Alicia shakes her head and takes a sip of her fragrant drink. Since she became pregnant, she's become obsessed with lemony and minty flavors. She's completely gone off coffee, which for her is very unusual.

'Congratulations are in order, I believe?'

Patrick points at Alicia's belly.

She puts a protective arm around her bump and gives him a brief smile.

'Thank you.'

'You OK? Not too hot?' Patrick chin nods toward the fan, which is whirring around, fluttering their napkins as the air reaches the table.

Alicia touches her face. She thinks she must have looked as hot as she felt when she arrived, but she tries to remember that how she looks to Patrick doesn't matter. Still, she feels self-conscious and shifts a little on the seat, pulling her back straight.

'What do you want, Patrick?'

A young couple, holding hands, enter the room and sit at a table along one of the side walls. Alicia is conscious that anything they say will now be overheard.

Patrick – and Alicia to a certain extent by association with the Eriksson family – is a bit of a celebrity on the islands. She saw the girl glance briefly at their table and immediately understood that she knew who they were.

The main newspaper on the islands, *Ålandsbladet*, owned by Patrick's father-in-law, Kurt Eriksson, didn't run any stories that could be construed as gossip. Which meant her brief affair with Patrick two years ago had been kept out of the limelight. Both of them worked on and off for the paper, so it would have been difficult to know who could have written such a story anyway.

Those rules didn't, however, apply to online posts about the Erikssons and their checkered family life. Alicia has come across many island gossip sites where

Alicia and her 'torrid affair' with the 'Swedish heart throb' and the ex-husband of Mia Eriksson is mentioned.

Alicia didn't care about what people thought, but she doesn't want Liam to come across stories about her and Patrick. Not now when everything is going so well between them.

Since Patrick still hasn't told her why he wants to see her, Alicia decides it's time to go.

'It was nice seeing you and welcome back,' Alicia says, getting up.

The young people at the other table visibly prick their ears.

'Wait,' Patrick says, also rising from his chair.

'Let me walk you to your car. You shouldn't be out in this weather at all in your condition, now should you?'

Alicia flashes Patrick an angry look, but he seems oblivious. She's just about had enough of men thinking she's a weakling just because she's pregnant.

Patrick raises his eyebrows at her.

'I know Liam will be happy for me to have taken care of you,' he adds sweetly.

Alicia sighs and nods.

When Patrick puts his hand under Alicia's elbow, she brushes it off and steps around him to walk out of the cafe. As they pass the other couple, he smiles and nods at them.

Outside in the small car park, Alicia hisses at Patrick.

'What was that all about?'

Patrick shrugs his shoulders.

'I was just giving them something to write about on their blog.'

'What? You know them? And they write a blog?'

Patrick nods. He presses his lips together.

'I came across them last year. We did some work together online, but we've never met in real life. Nice couple.'

Alicia opens up her car and a waft of hot air hits her face.

'Oh my God, when will this heatwave end?'

She puts her keys in the ignition and racks up the AC. She goes around and opens the passenger door, hoping for a draft that will make her drive back to Sjoland a little more pleasant. The sun is glaring down on them from a cloudless sky.

Patrick stands watching Alicia. He's got his hands in the pockets of his cotton pants, a stance that makes the muscles in his arms stand out.

'What is it you want, Patrick?'

Alicia is standing gazing at him over the top of her old Volvo.

'You know I went up North when they released me from hospital after Christmas.'

'Yeah,' Alicia says, nodding. She puts her bag on the passenger seat, grabs a fan that her mom got for her in Spain a couple of years ago, and flicks it open. 'You've got exactly one minute.'

'I did a lot of thinking.'

Alicia fans her face harder while staring at Patrick.

'And I came to the conclusion that I still love you.'

Alicia's hand stops. She stares at the man in front of

her. The handsome, sexy, funny, and wholly, totally, unreliable man.

The scenes from two years ago flash in front of her eyes.

Their first kiss at the Erikssons' Midsummer party, when they somehow ended up alone by the shore and made out while the party went on a few meters behind the dunes. Their passionate lovemaking on board Patrick's yacht. The tense weeks when she didn't know whether he was just toying with her.

And the few weeks when they lived together in Stockholm, in what she thought was his apartment. It had never occurred to her to ask how he'd managed to get such a good divorce deal from Mia, allowing him to have a large condo in a prime spot of Stockholm, overlooking the Riddarfjärden water. Of course, it later transpired that the apartment belonged to the Eriksson clan and that Patrick was only renting it on the goodwill of his ex-wife. That was the first of many lies and betrayals.

No more.

Alicia flings the fan inside the car and bangs the passenger side door shut.

'Goodbye Patrick,' she says and walks as quickly as she can around the Volvo to seat herself at the wheel.

'Go to your wife and be happy with Mia. Although I can't say I like the woman, I think you two deserve each other.'

With that, Alicia starts the car and drives away.

.   .   .

Patrick stands on the sidewalk, watching Alicia make her way along the road to the sea and then turn onto the main thoroughfare past the East Harbor.

Has he finally lost her? Just when he knows exactly what he wants, Alicia seems to have moved on. Pregnant with her ex's baby, she has chosen her old (boring) life against what he could offer her. He'd planned to move back to Mariehamn to be with her. He'd even toyed with the idea of buying her a ring – he would have even married her if she'd insisted on it.

Patrick bites his lower lip and thinks hard.

I've left it too late.

But he knows Alicia still has feelings for him. Just the way she looked at him. He felt the same strong connection he'd sensed between them the first time they set eyes on each other two years ago. Surely, she'd felt it too?

Why can't she see that they are meant to be together?

Patrick gazes out to the boats gently rocking along the jetties in the East Harbor. There aren't that many yachts there yet – it's early in the season, but he can see a couple of beauties.

How he wishes he still had his old yacht. He'd take it out now, even though there's hardly any wind and sailing would be difficult. Instead, he'd motor toward the Sjoland canal and from there to the open waters of Lumparn. Patrick longs to feel the wind in his hair and the total sense of freedom he gets from being at sea.

A thought comes to him. If Mia is so keen on having him back, perhaps she could convince old Eriksson to buy him another boat. He's been dreaming of a catamaran for a while now. A few years ago, before Mia began having affairs, he'd seen a beautiful 45-footer at a boat show in Stockholm. It would be more comfortable for the girls. He'd dreamt of taking it over to Stockholm, and even sailing as far as the island of Gotland. With a catamaran being so much more stable, longer distances become easier.

But then Mia asked for a divorce.

Now she's changed her mind and wants him back, but Patrick is still in love with Alicia.

He needs to think and clear his head, so he decides to make his way down to the harbor and take a walk along the wooden jetty. Perhaps he'll see someone he knows who will offer to take him out for the afternoon.

As he makes his way along the boardwalk, Patrick sees a yacht named *Babushka* with a Russian flag moored to the end of the jetty closest to the harbor master's office. She dwarfs all the other boats in the harbor. Although she's a motorboat, something that Patrick would never consider owning, he thinks she is beautiful with her sleek sides, blackened portholes, and teak decking.

Patrick can't resist having a closer look, but just as he is a about to step onto the jetty, he sees a man sitting on the forward deck. He's wearing dark sunglasses and smoking a cigar. He's holding a newspaper, which half hides his face, but Patrick would recognize the Russian a mile away.

Although he's only met Alexander Dudnikov once, he's spent hours, days, looking at images of the Russian villain on his computer screen.

He has the same heavy-set build, high forehead and hairy arms. The short sleeves of the white polo shirt fit tightly over his muscular biceps.

What is Dudnikov doing here? Does he not know that he is a wanted man all over Scandinavia?

Patrick does a ninety-degree turn and walks slowly away from the jetty toward the center of town. He wants to run, but he keeps himself in check. He doesn't want the Russian to be alarmed in any way until he has had time to talk to the police chief.

No, he's going to call Alicia instead.

Or will she think that this is a desperate attempt at reconciliation? She may not even believe that he has seen the Russian villain.

Suddenly Patrick stops and turns back toward the harbor. He shades his eyes against the sun, which is glaring down from a cloudless sky. The deck of the yacht is now empty. Whoever was sitting there has disappeared.

Was it really Dudnikov that he saw? Surely he wouldn't be so stupid as to visit the islands when he knows he is a wanted man? And to sit on his super yacht, which is hardly inconspicuous, in the middle of the day, reading a newspaper in full view of everyone?

Patrick isn't exactly on good terms with Ebba, the police chief on the islands. She is a good friend of Alicia's, and he's always had the sense that the police chief doesn't like him. He's a journalist, after all. His job is to report news, not keep the police informed. In the past, Ebba has accused him of withholding information, or writing about something that the police wanted to keep secret.

What if the man in the beautiful super yacht isn't Dudnikov after all? Reporting the sighting will make a complete fool of Patrick in front of the police chief and the whole island police force.

No, that won't do.

If he's to move back to the islands and make a life for himself here, he needs to try to build a good relationship with Ebba Torstensson. He'll need it when he takes up a post in the local newspaper. Mia has hinted on several occasions that the post of Chief Editor is soon to become vacant when old Nuotianen retires.

Patrick knows that swinging the editorship at *Ålandsbladet* in front of his eyes is just another way in which Mia is trying to entice him back to her. Which is why he has feigned a lack of interest in the post, but if he is honest with himself, it is exactly what he wants.

The girls are now of an age when they need him less, and he would relish the chance to make his mark on the local paper.

Or on any publication!

Patrick would have to have total editorial freedom from the owner, his father-in-law, and that won't be easy. But that would be his condition for taking the job – and Mia back – so Kurt would just have to agree.

Plus he'd have to shell out for a beautiful boat too.

Patrick takes another glance at the Russian yacht in the distance.

I'm going to let sleeping dogs lie.

CHAPTER SEVENTEEN

After she lost her husband of nearly 40 years, Hilda began spending more time than she liked to admit on Facebook. Now that she is trying to forget another disastrous attempt at a reconciliation with her ex-husband, surfing the site for her favorite pages is a welcome distraction.

There are many groups that she now follows and sometimes checks several times an hour. There are groups for women who've been suddenly widowed, like her, groups on fashion, or on being a woman of a certain age. Then there are the celebrity gossip pages. One of these is linked to a blog. It's run by two young people from Mariehamn who write on the goings on in Åland, in particular stories that are never reported in the local newspaper. She knows Alicia despises such sites, but Hilda can't help reading each post as soon as its written.

Many of the stories on the blog called *The Island Papers* are about the Eriksson family, especially Mia

Eriksson. Each time Hilda reads about the latest Swedish playboy Mia's been seen with, she feels a little guilty, because of her own connection with the family.

That said, she's never liked Mia, not even when Alicia was at school with her. The girl would never give her daughter the time of day. Once or twice, Alicia came home in tears because of something nasty the girl had said to her. Mia Eriksson had everything, yet she felt the need to bully her daughter! And her behavior since then has been far from exemplary.

Patrick, Mia's ex-husband, who had a brief affair with Alicia, is still governed by her whims. Alicia had told her how Mia had asked Patrick for a divorce in order to marry a Swedish aristocrat she had fallen for. But as soon as the divorce had been finalized, the Swedish cad had left Mia, no doubt because he didn't fancy becoming the new daddy to Mia's two pre-teen daughters. It's the children Hilda feels sorry for.

While their mother moves from man to man, they just want their dad back. Or that's what *The Island Papers* claim. Hilda sometimes feels the urge to contact the young people behind the blog to tell them what she knows about Patrick. How he slept with Mia in Stockholm while Alicia was in Mariehamn looking after her mother, who'd just lost her husband. Alicia had to witness the two canoodling at her own stepfather's funeral.

Hilda is certain Mia would never have wanted Patrick back had he not moved Alicia into his apartment in Stockholm. That girl has always had something against Alicia, or perhaps it's jealousy?

As Hilda clicks onto the new blog post, she thinks Mia Eriksson deserves everything coming to her. But the image that comes up first on the page stops Hilda in her tracks.

How can you unsee something you've stared at for what seems like hours on the computer screen? How Hilda wishes she'd never read the latest blog posts by the snooping pair on *The Island Papers*! She stands up and goes over to the kitchen, which overlooks Alicia's cottage. She can spot Liam sitting at the desk in the office. It used to belong to Uffe, and he'd often go there to hide from her and the many tasks she'd set for him. Since Hilda modernized the space for Alicia, and installed roman blinds, which are invariably pulled up, she can see whoever is sitting at the desk.

Where is Alicia? Hilda cranes her neck to try to see if her daughter is sitting at her usual spot at the other end of the desk, but she can't see her. She needs to warn Alicia before Liam comes across the article, although she's certain Liam doesn't read the kind of rubbish she's fond of. Still, these things go around social media so quickly now. You never know, some so called 'well-wisher' might bring his attention to the story. It concerns his wife after all.

Hilda shakes her head when she thinks of the title of the story.

Secret Lovers' Rendezvous?

What is Alicia thinking! After everything Patrick has done, why would she want to meet up with him? Hilda thought that the man had moved away, back to northern Sweden where he'd been raised. Good riddance, Hilda had thought at the time. But now the troublemaker is back on the islands.

The article is short, mostly filled with several pictures of Alicia and Patrick. In one, he's holding Alicia's hand on the table, and they seem to be arguing. The trouble is, you can't see Alicia's expression because she has her back to the camera.

This is true about most of the shots. Apart from the last one, where Alicia and Patrick are leaving the cafe, which Hilda recognizes as Svarta Katten in town. In this one, Alicia and Patrick are walking side by side, and Patrick has his hand in the small of Alicia's back.

The last sentence of the article takes Hilda's breath away.

This secret little meeting between the ex-lovers makes us wonder, whose baby is Alicia Ulsson carrying?

Hilda hears the door go, and she quickly shuts the lid on her laptop.

'Hello, Mom.'

Alicia comes into the kitchen and looks directly at Hilda.

'What's wrong?'

Hilda gets up smartly, trying to avoid her daughter's gaze.

'Coffee?' She says, making her way toward the machine sitting in the serving hatch between the kitchen and the dining room.

When she doesn't hear a reply, she turns around and sees Alicia still looking at her. Her hands are now on her hips.

'C'mon what's happened? You know I'm not drinking coffee, haven't done since this little one came along.'

She pats her extended tummy.

How stupid of her!

Pull yourself together.

'Sorry, a senior moment. Mint tea. Or do you want lemon and ginger today?'

Again, her daughter refuses to reply. Instead, she walks behind Hilda and puts her arms around her mom.

'I'm OK for a moment. I've just had a mint tea in town. Guess who with!'

Hilda doesn't have time to reply before Alicia tells her all about her meeting with Patrick. She tries to look surprised, and thinks she has succeeded in fooling Alicia, until, unwisely, she exclaims, 'What an earth made you decide to be seen with him in public! In Svarta Katten of all places!'

Alicia's face quickly tells Hilda that she's made a grave mistake.

'How did you know that's where we went?'

'Oh, darling!'

Hilda embraces Alicia, but her daughter's body is stiff.

She pulls herself away, and with a serious expression in her eyes, says, 'What are you trying to tell me?'

Hilda sighs and reaches for her laptop. She opens it

up and points at the article on *The Island Papers* website.

'Oh my God!'

Alicia sits down heavily in front of the computer. Her left hand has flown to her mouth, while her right uses the mousepad to scroll through the article. How did they write it so quickly? It can't be more than an hour since she left Patrick. She sees there are several spelling mistakes in the story, but it doesn't matter. What matters is what it says. And the images are damning enough without any words.

'That bloody man!'

A tear rolls down her face as she turns to look at Hilda.

'I'm so sorry, darling.'

Hilda puts a hand on her daughter's shoulder.

'It's not at all what it looks like. It's all lies!'

At that moment, Liam appears at the door.

'What's all lies?' he asks.

Without thinking, Alicia closes the laptop and turns around to face her husband.

'Oh, some silly article mom is reading on one of her celebrity gossip sites.'

Relieved that Liam hasn't seen the images, Hilda takes the lead from Alicia and tries to distract him.

'Liam, would you like some coffee? I've made a fresh batch of cinnamon rolls.'

Alicia watches Hilda take hold of Liam's arm and

steer him into the kitchen. She knows he can't resist a still warm pastry, especially one of Hilda's famous sweet buns. She wipes her cheek and hopes Liam didn't see how upset she was from the expression on her face.

Being alone for a few moments lets Alicia think about what she has read and the pictures she's seen.

She's fairly certain Patrick had known that the two bloggers were going to be at the Svarta Katten. But she cannot understand what he is playing at. Did he invite the two bloggers to the cafe so that they would witness their 'rendezvous'? Why would he do that to her?

Unless he wants to sabotage her relationship with Liam. But surely, even if that happened, he must know Alicia wouldn't run back to him? Besides, Liam and Alicia's relationship is stronger than that.

Or is it?

Why didn't she come clean just now instead of lying about what she'd been looking at? What if he finds out about the article himself and comes to the wrong conclusions? The same ones the bloggers were peddling.

She knows he abhors social media and hasn't even got a Facebook account, but anyone could tell him about it. Alicia quickly thinks about the people he knows on the islands who would be reading the blog but she can't think of anyone. She can't imagine Ebba, or her wife, Jabulani, would lower themselves to the level of a gossip rag. And if her friend Brit read the article, she'd never tell Liam without first discussing it with Alicia. She hopes Brit's partner, Jukka, would do the same. Besides, they are all away on holiday.

At the same time, Alicia knows that any acquaintance of Liam's could drop the bombshell. People on the islands like to talk, which feeds gossip sites just like the one Hilda follows.

CHAPTER EIGHTEEN

L ater that evening when they are lying in bed and Liam is reading *The Times* on his iPad, Alicia glances at his profile. She recalls when she first fell in love with him at Uppsala University, where she was studying English. Liam had been attending a medical conference. Four years Alicia's senior, he had seemed so grown-up and sophisticated. What's more he was living in London, a place Alicia had long wanted to visit.

How flattered she'd been when Liam had showed such interest in her, listening carefully to each word she uttered and quite obviously admiring her every molecule. He didn't seem to be able to get enough of her during that snowy day (and night) they'd spent together.

The two years that followed, when they were both still studying, Alicia for her bachelor's degree and Liam training to be a surgeon, had been difficult. There was really no internet to speak of, or at least not like now, with instant messaging and internet calls.

Sometimes Alicia wonders how they'd managed to keep their relationship going when they only saw each other a few times a year, but they did. She had been so in love then, and had absolutely no doubts about moving to England to be with her husband.

She was so naive, but there must have been something in that love, because look at them now. After everything that they have endured, loss of a child, infidelity on both sides, separation, moving countries, they're still going strong.

One large reason why they are now together is honesty.

It hadn't always been the case. They'd forgotten to be straight with each other even before Stefan perished. Then afterward, when Alicia had found out about the Polish nurse, she hadn't said or done anything. She'd let Liam think she didn't know that the late nights at the hospital were often nothing to do with his job. Perhaps she hadn't cared?

Liam had done the most awful thing and had been unfaithful, but Alicia hadn't confronted him. She can now admit that it had suited her that Liam was at fault for the marriage breaking up. But the reality was that they had both been at fault.

Besides, Alicia had gone further. With the pain of Stefan's death blinding her, she had moved permanently back home to the islands. And she hadn't even asked Liam to come with her. She didn't even tell him of her decision until she had built what she thought was a new life with Patrick.

How foolish she had been!

She doesn't regret coming back to Åland, but she regrets jumping into a new relationship so fast. Patrick was never reliable, nor was he free of his own complicated relationship.

But he allowed Alicia to feel something, even if it was just a fleeting passion.

When she looks back at that summer two years ago, she thinks of herself as completely deranged.

Is that what love is?

Because she recognizes that madness from when she first fell for Liam.

Is she just a serial romantic?

'What's the matter?'

Liam has put down his iPad and is holding Alicia's hand.

'Why?'

Liam moves his hand over her extended belly, and smiles. 'You just gave a really deep sigh. Is the baby kicking already?'

Alicia places her hand over Liam's and smiles at him.

'No, I was just thinking.'

'Penny for them?'

Alicia considers Liam's features once more. If possible, he is more handsome now than he was as a younger man. A few strands of gray have appeared at his temples, and he has a couple of deep lines across his forehead and on either side of his mouth. But his lips are full, his eyes bright, and his jaw is as strong as ever. He's kept his solid frame, with muscular arms and chest, which she always found so attractive.

Alicia bites her lip, but decides that she will be honest, just as they have decided they will be with each other when they rekindled their relationship last winter.

'I met up with Patrick today.'

Liam removes his hand from Alicia's belly and turns his face away.

'He's back.'

This comes out as a statement rather than a question.

'Don't be mad, please. He was with Mia, but he said he had something to tell me.'

Now Liam faces Alicia again, but this time his expression has changed from the happy open one he had only a moment ago. His eyes are dark and his lips are pressed together.

'And you asked how high as soon as he told you to jump?'

'Please, Liam, don't be like this. As I said, he was with Mia, I think they are back together now.'

Liam pushes the duvet off him and gets out of bed. He is not wearing anything – the heat of the day is still lingering in the old milking parlor that Hilda had converted into accommodation for Alicia after Uffe died. Alicia cannot help but admire his body. The strong athletic thighs and neat buttocks. Liam pulls on his loose pajama bottoms.

'Where are you going?'

'I need a drink of water,' Liam says before disappearing out of the door. Alicia can hear him run the tap. But he is away for much longer than drinking a glass of water would normally take, so Alicia gets up too.

She wraps herself in a dressing gown, which

stretches over her middle and pads barefoot to the small kitchen, built between the office and the living quarters. Soon they will swap with Hilda and move into the big house across the yard.

Alicia finds Liam holding onto the small countertop with both hands and leaning onto them. She goes behind her husband and tries to hug him, but her large tummy gets in the way. Instead, she rubs his bare back and says, 'Darling, I'm sorry. There's something else. The reason why I went to see Patrick. Nothing to do with us. I love you and don't want to even see Patrick, but I needed to hear what he had to say. Please turn around and come back to bed so that I can tell you what happened.'

'Are you certain it was Dudnikov you saw?'

Liam is now sitting up in bed, his eyes wide. He cannot believe Alicia. Why would she put herself in danger again with the Russian?

'I think I am. I know it sounds incredible, but I know what he looks like.'

'But you didn't tell Ebba?'

Alicia looks down at her hands.

'Well, I wasn't certain, and there was no one at the police station that I recognized. And I didn't want to spoil Ebba's holiday. You know how tetchy Jabulani gets about Ebba's work. They've been looking forward to going away for such a long time…'

'Alicia!'

Liam's frustration is about to boil over.

'I'll call her first thing in the morning.'

'And we'll both go to the station tomorrow.'

'OK.'

Sometimes Alicia is the most stubborn person Liam has ever known.

'And Patrick didn't know about Dudnikov?'

Now Alicia is biting her lip.

'I didn't ask him.'

'What? You said…'

'I didn't want to tell him. I thought when he said he wanted to talk to me and that he had something to tell me, it would be about the Russian.'

Liam knows what's coming. That bloody Swede is not going to give up, is he? Even when Alicia is about to have the child – his, Liam's child – the man still tries to pursue Alicia. Will he ever move on?

He doesn't want to ask, but he can't stop himself.

'What did he want?'

'Oh, that's not important.'

'Alicia?'

Alicia leans back in bed, lowering herself underneath the duvet so that half of her face is covered by the sheet.

'Just nonsense.'

'He wants to get back together with you?'

'Uh, uh.'

Liam removes the sheet from Alicia and gives her a kiss, a long lingering kiss.

'The man is a fool, you know that, right?'

Alicia nods and leans back for a second kiss. Liam feels his desire rising. After the first weeks of pregnancy when she had often felt unwell, Alicia has been up for sex more than he can ever remember her being. Her newly rounded body is turning Liam on more than he would ever have expected. He doesn't want to analyze it too much; just enjoy their beautiful and newly invigorated intimacy.

He has done what he thought he'd never be able to do. Win Alicia back and a have a second chance at fatherhood. Now as a bonus, their sex life is at a new height.

How can anything, least of all an out-of-work Swedish journalist, or a wanted Russian criminal, spoil their happiness.

CHAPTER NINETEEN

The next morning, Liam manages to convince Alicia to send a message to Ebba before breakfast. To their surprise, the police chief is already at work, and calls Alicia back straight away. They have a long conversation about Alicia's possible sighting of the wanted man.

'What did she say?' Liam asks after Alicia has ended the call and is sitting down at a table in the corner of the large room. While Alicia was talking to Ebba, Liam has set out a pot of yogurt, washed some berries and prepared two bowls of organic granola for breakfast. He's sipping a cup of coffee, but he sets it down so that he can pour hot water over some lemon and ginger for Alicia.

'Thanks darling,' Alicia says. 'She was fed up with me for not letting her know sooner.'

Liam nods. He doesn't want to point out that he was right, Alicia will know it anyway. Dudnikov's presence on the islands is bad news for everyone.

'Did she have anything to say about why he might think it's safe to be here?'

Alicia shakes her head.

'No, she is as puzzled as I am. Let's hope it isn't him, or that Ebba and the police catch him before he leaves again. I'm so tired of having him hanging over me.'

Liam goes over and puts his hands on Alicia's shoulders.

'Don't worry, I'm here now and I will take care of you.' Liam lowers his hands around Alicia's belly. 'Of both of you.'

Alicia turns around and takes Liam's face between her hands and smiles.

'Yeah, but you do know I can take care of myself.'

Liam nods. He's overstepped the mark again. At the same time, he knows Alicia is vulnerable. He smiles at her.

But his wife is also strong and brave. And proud. She'll never admit to not being able to cope. These are some of the many reasons he loves her.

'I know, I know. You're a grown woman.'

They agree to have dinner that night in one of the new restaurants in town.

'Soon we won't be able to go without a baby-sitter,' Liam says when he suggests the night out. 'Besides, the sales figures are finally looking good, aren't they?'

Alicia kisses Liam on the lips and pulls away, smiling.

'You are a very special man; did you know that?'

Liam knows she needs to take her mind of Dudnikov.

Looking at him as he fusses with the breakfast, Alicia wonders how she thought she could ever be with anyone other than Liam. She knows the reason they lost their way was Liam's infidelity, but she also knows that she didn't care when she found out about it. They had already lost each other by that point. When they then lost Stefan, the marriage was all but over. They both needed to fight to keep their relationship afloat, but neither of them had the energy to do that.

What a wonderful second chance they now have! Not only to rebuild their relationship and marriage but to rebuild their family too.

'What?' Liam says, looking directly at Alicia.

'I'm just wondering how I deserve a second chance like this.'

Pulling her toward him, he hugs her as much as the bump allows.

He places his palms on either side of Alicia's face and looks deeply into her eyes. 'It's me who should be grateful.'

'Oh, Liam,' Alicia says, and she takes hold of Liam's palm and kisses it. 'I love you.'

'I love you too, sweetheart. Now, let's have something to eat, and tonight we will forget all about the past, including the Russian, and look forward to the future.'

Liam places his other hand on Alicia's belly, and as if to order, the baby moves into his palm.

They both laugh, and Liam kneels down to give the bump a kiss.

. . .

Ebba contacts Alicia twice that day, both times after doing a thorough sweep, first over Mariehamn and then over some of the more luxurious hotels around the archipelago. The police have come out empty-handed on both occasions.

'He's not here, and we haven't found any record or sightings of a yacht called *Babushka* either,' the police chief tells her just as Alicia is getting ready to go out. She's wearing a loose Marimekko kaftan, one that she bought from her mom's boutique before it closed down. It perfectly covers her growing belly, and it's cool while still being quite dressy.

'That's good news,' Alicia replies.

Before she has time to say goodbye, Ebba adds, 'But next time you think you've seen him, call me straight away. Whether I'm on duty or not. Understood?'

Alicia is aware of the thinly veiled criticism in Ebba's words.

'OK, you win. I made a mistake, but it seems such a strange thing for him to do. I just wasn't sure of myself.'

Alicia can hear Ebba sigh at the other end of the telephone.

'Still, you need to call me.'

After the conversation Alicia smiles to herself. To anyone who doesn't know the police chief, Ebba can come across as quite short, even rude. But Alicia has got used to her old schoolfriend. Though they were never friends when they were in the same class on the islands.

Who would have thought that Alicia would now be so close to the odd, gangly girl from school?

They hadn't seen each other for decades when Alicia bumped into Ebba on a skerry two years ago. She and Patrick had been out on his sailing boat when they'd stumbled upon poor Daniel's dead body out in the archipelago. Alicia had just started working for the local paper, where Patrick had also been employed on a temporary basis while on holiday from Stockholm.

At the time, Ebba had considered Alicia and Patrick as a bit of a nuisance. She probably disapproved of Alicia because she was a married woman on a romantic jaunt with a married man on his expensive yacht. What's more, Patrick was the son-in-law of the most influential business magnate on the islands.

Alicia had been blind to all of that, of course. And she hadn't known anything about Patrick's relationships, just that his marriage was breaking up, just like her own.

CHAPTER TWENTY

When Frida sees the email from the research company with the results of her DNA analysis, she takes a few breaths before she opens it up. What if it says that she has nothing but Russian blood? When her mom was alive, she knew there were rumors that she had a Russian lover. But her mom had shrugged her shoulders when Frida, then just turned thirteen, had asked her about it.

'Jealous people make things up,' she'd said and then changed the subject.

Frida had wondered what these people had to be jealous about. They lived in a not particularly well-to-do suburb of Mariehamn in what she then believed was a rented apartment. Of course, after her mom died, she'd found out that it was her own property.

For as long as Frida could remember, her mom had worked as a waitress at Arkipelag, the largest hotel in town, owned by Kurt Eriksson, the local businessman.

They never had much money, although they never went without either.

With shaking hands, Frida clicks on the email and opens the attachment.

She stares at the screen for a long time, without fully understanding what it's telling her. There is a pie chart, which is almost totally one color. Only three other segments are a different shade. The title of the chart tells her in large letters that 93% of her DNA originates from one country: Finland. Some 5% is from Sweden, and other Scandinavian countries, while the rest, 2%, is from Italy.

Italy?

What is most interesting is that there is not a trace of Russian DNA in her body.

Frida can't believe what she is seeing. She checks that the information is correct and that the name and birth date are right. She even checks the number she'd noted down when she sent the sample off, and, yes, it matches the one on the screen.

That's when she jumps up and pumps her fist up and down. 'Yes, yes, yes!'

Quietening down, she stares at her laptop for a few more minutes and then picks up her phone and calls Alicia.

'That's incredible news! How wonderful. Have you told Andrei yet?'

Frida takes a few deep breaths and confesses, 'No, I don't know what to say. I mean, is this really proof? What if Dudnikov is Finnish after all? How do we know he doesn't have Finnish parents?'

Alicia is quiet at the other end of the phone.

'Well, yes, I guess that is possible, but I would very much doubt it. Let me call Ebba and see if she has any information on his parentage. But really, I think you can eliminate him as a possibility?'

'Do you really think so?'

'I really do. But to put your mind at rest, let me talk to the police chief.'

When Frida's phone rings a few moments later, she's delighted to hear Andrei's voice.

'Hello, you!'

Frida's heart is filled with hope. She's been waiting to hear from Andrei for two days. She hasn't wanted to call him after he didn't reply to three of her messages in a row. She hoped he was dealing with whatever it was that was keeping him back in Romania. Perhaps he was delaying calling her until he knew exactly when he would come over to the islands?

'Hi, how are you?'

Andrei's voice is dry, there seems to be no warmth to it.

'I'm good,' Frida says, trying to keep smiling.

'And Anne Sofie?'

'She's happy. I got her a place at pre-school. She's starting tomorrow.'

'Good.'

For a moment they are both quiet. Frida is listening to Andrei's breathing. She doesn't know what to say.

'Do you want to FaceTime?'

'Hmm, better not. Not sure how strong the signal is. I'm out on the field with the cows.'

'OK,' Frida replies, not knowing what else to say.

She considers for a moment whether to tell Andrei the good news about her DNA analysis, but it doesn't seem like a suitable time.

'What have you been up to?' Frida asks, trying to fill the silence between them.

'Well, you know.' Andrei takes in a long breath and adds, 'Farming.'

'Uh, uh.'

As their conversation peters out, Frida decides to end the phone call, mustering all the strength she has not to shout, cry or start accusing Andrei of being deliberately obtuse, or distant.

'I'd better let you get on, then.'

'OK.'

Is he not even going to say he loves me?

Frida waits, but all Andrei says is, 'Bye then,' and with that he's gone.

Before Frida has time to dissolve into tears of both frustration and despair over Andrei's strange behavior, her phone rings again.

It's Alicia.

'You're in the clear, girl!'

Frida is speechless. Now the tears she'd been trying to hold start running down her face.

'Are you crying?'

Frida is unable to speak. She begins sobbing like a fool.

Ever since she found out about the money in the

wake of her mom's death, she's been feeling guilty about it. She's given a lot to a charity that aims to stop human trafficking, and invested in Andrei's farm in Romania, but she didn't give all of it away.

She's used much of it to make her and little Anne Sofie's life more comfortable. To know that the criminal Dudnikov isn't behind all the cash has lifted a massive weight off her shoulders. A burden she hadn't even realized was such a terrible load until now.

And it isn't just the money. Frida can't bear the thought that her mom had been with such a despicable person. And that half of Frida's own genes were given to her by a criminal. Not to mention Anne Sofie, who would have a quarter of the man's blood running in her little veins. While Frida is trying to control her emotions, Alicia speaks again.

'Please, don't be upset.'

'I'm not…'

'I know, I know. But listen, now you must find out who your father is. Don't they do DNA matching at the research lab?'

CHAPTER TWENTY-ONE

'I'm sorry, I have to go again,' Alicia says and gets up to visit the restroom for the third time during their dinner at the new restaurant.

It's a trendy place with an indoor courtyard right next to Sittkoffs mall. When they entered, Alicia immediately felt too old and too pregnant, but Liam seemed very pleased with the place.

'Feels almost as if we are in London,' he'd said, so Alicia hadn't had the heart to tell him how uncomfortable she felt. It was buzzy, that is true, and the food being delivered to the other tables by white-aproned serving staff looked delicious.

Alicia's nerves had settled when their server, an older woman with a wide smile, had enquired about her due date and they'd had a brief chat about babies. She had also recommended a great alcohol-free beer and dishes that Alicia could eat.

The food was mostly vegetables, but they were fresh

and prepared to perfection. She had also ordered a local dish, smoked perch, which had passed the test.

As Alicia gets out of the cubicle and is washing her hands in the brass sink, she glances at her face in the mirror. Next to her stands a slim blonde woman, who is applying bright red lipstick. Alicia is just about to make a joke about the low lighting in the restrooms, which makes applying makeup almost impossible, when her eyes lock with those of the woman.

'I know you,' Alicia blurts out before she can stop herself.

The woman quickly looks away from Alicia and drops her lipstick into her large designer handbag. She leaves without a glance at her image in the mirror, or at Alicia, who's left gaping after her.

She moves her head to face the mirror again and at that moment realizes exactly where she's seen the blonde before.

When Alicia enters the busy dining room, she scans it to find the woman and another, even more familiar face. And there he is, just getting up from a table in the corner of the room. Their eyes meet, and for a moment Alicia is rooted to the spot.

This time she's not seeing a ghost.

There stands Dudnikov, tall and muscular as ever. His face is unreadable, but then his lips turn into a smile. He nods toward Alicia, and then leads the blonde woman away. When the woman, who seems to be agitated, glances back at what the Russian was looking at, her face drops.

Dudnikov throws some notes on the table, where the

meal is only half-consumed, and the couple hurry out of the restaurant.

Quickly, Alicia fumbles with her handbag and finds her cell. She dials the familiar number and tells Liam that they need to leave NOW.

'What? Are you OK? Is the baby coming, It's far too early…'

'No, Liam, quickly, I'll explain in the car!'

CHAPTER TWENTY-TWO

'You didn't have to come with me.'

'Really?'

Liam is mad, but Alicia knows she's doing the right thing. It's dusk now and she's following a car up a narrow road toward the northernmost tip of the islands.

'You insisted,' she says while trying to make sure she doesn't lose sight of the headlights in front of her. Luckily the road is deserted.

'Yes, because you are five months pregnant.'

Liam's voice is low.

'That doesn't mean that I am an invalid!'

How many times does she have to tell him that she is perfectly capable of looking after herself? Hasn't she shown that in the past few years?

'And, I was going to say, putting not only your life but the life of our unborn baby in danger!'

Alicia takes a couple of deep breaths while she tries to calm herself. She doesn't want to argue with Liam. If the truth be told, she's glad he is with her, but she needs him to understand that this is her one and only chance of getting Dudnikov behind bars.

'Ebba and the rest of the police are right behind us.'

Alicia glances at Liam's profile and hopes that her statement is true. She'd only managed to leave a message with the police chief. She didn't call the police station, because she wasn't sure they'd take her claim to be following the Russian criminal, wanted in two countries for human trafficking and money laundering charges, seriously.

'This is stupid,' Liam says as they watch the car in front turn off the long straight road and onto a small track.

'Please, park the car here, Alicia. I mean it.'

Alicia can hear from the tone of Liam's voice that he is serious, so, reluctantly, she stops the car at the side of the road and turns toward him.

'We are waiting here until the police arrive. That road looks like a dead end, so they are literally cornered.'

Alicia looks down at her lap. She's studying a map on her cell. Liam is right, the road leads down to the sea and ends there.

'But what if they have a motorboat waiting for them?'

Liam turns to face her and places his hands under her elbows.

'Please Alicia, you saw there were several people in that car. What can we do? How could we possibly stop a gang of criminals from leaving or doing whatever they are here to do, even if we wanted to?'

Before Alicia can answer, there is a hammering on the rear window. Large knuckles then hit the windscreen. A grinning face comes into view.

'What the hell!' Liam yells.

'Did we lock the doors?' Alicia asks in a panic, but her question is immediately answered when the passenger side door is yanked open and Liam is uncere-moniously dragged out of the car by one arm. Immedi-ately, he begins to fight back, but a shove from a man, at least twice as wide as her husband, is followed by a blow that knocks him straight out.

Shrieking, Alicia clambers out of the car and runs toward him. Kneeling down beside Liam, she can see there's blood running from the side of his mouth. She rubs his cheek, trying to revive him when she hears a familiar voice speaking in broken English behind her.

'Good evening, Alicia.'

Before she can protest, she is dragged off Liam by the tall, heavily built man and roughly manhandled down the track and into the back seat of the car they've just been following. A smaller Russian thug sits next to her. He glances at Alicia, but quickly looks away as if the sight of her makes him uncomfortable. Then Liam's limp body is pushed in and the door banged shut. They're stuffed into the back seat like sardines. Alicia cranes her neck past the Russian in the middle toward Liam to see if he's regained consciousness, but his head is hanging over his chest.

Dudnikov takes a place in the passenger seat and

says something in Russian to the larger of the two men, who starts the car. They drive along a dark bumpy lane for a short distance. Alicia leans forward and tries to get another glimpse of Liam, but the man next to her pushes her back.

There's a taste of bile in Alicia's mouth, but before she can react, they stop. This time, Dudnikov gets out of the car first and takes hold of Alicia's arm.

'You stupid woman. A mama out here playing games with big boys!' the Russian says, and he pushes her toward a small building. He leads her through the porch. There is a light inside, but the steps are dark and uneven, and Alicia stumbles.

'C'mon!' Dudnikov says, almost carrying Alicia inside.

There is a tattered sofa in the middle of a one-roomed cabin. Large windows face the sea in the twilight. A small side window is open. For a mad moment, she wonders if she could wriggle free and run to it, but then realizes her belly would never fit through it. Perhaps if she wasn't pregnant, but now it would be hopeless.

'Please sit,' Dudnikov says, grinning.

The large man who hit Liam has him on his shoulders like a human pelt. He drops him down next to her. Alicia puts an arm under her husband's armpits, trying to keep him upright. His head is still lolling over his chest, so instead of trying to hold him in a sitting position, she guides him sideways so that his head rests on her shoulder. She sees his eyes are closed, but to her great relief she can hear that his breathing sounds normal.

What have I done now?

Alicia's heart is racing. She looks around the cabin, which seems clean and well-tended, even though there's very little furniture and the small kitchenette in the corner nearest to the sofa has a pile of dirty dishes in the sink.

She decides she needs to buy time. As soon as Ebba picks up her message – and she hopes to God the police chief has already done that – help will be on its way. She shared her location with Ebba and so far, Dudnikov and his two heavies haven't thought to ask for her cell. She's grateful for her quick thinking, which allowed her to hide it in her bra while her husband was dragged to the ground. Even if they find it, Alicia is certain her signal would be traced to this godforsaken cottage in the woods.

All she needs to do is delay Dudnikov's departure and hope that she doesn't provoke him into hurting them anymore. She glances at Liam, who looks as if he is sleeping peacefully, leaning on her.

'What are you doing here?' She asks Dudnikov, who's got himself a bottle of vodka and a single glass from a cupboard above the sink.

The Russian takes his time to sit down on the chair opposite the sofa. The two other men are standing by the door in the back of the small space, their feet wide and their hands crossed over their chests.

'I ask you same question!' Dudnikov says, his voice loud now.

Alicia's mind races again as she tries to find a feasible answer to the question.

'I wanted to talk to you,' she says. She's surprised by her own boldness, but she knows she needs to buy time. Ebba, she prays and hopes, will be here in a matter of minutes.

There is a smile hovering on Dudnikov's lips.

Since their last meeting, over six months ago, Alexander Dudnikov has lost some of his heft. He seems leaner, and perhaps a little more wrinkled. His hair is slicked back, but Alicia can see gray hairs at his temples and that his hairline has receded since the last time he accosted and threatened her.

'Miss me?'

Alicia ignores Dudnikov's leer.

'Do you know that there is an arrest warrant on your head?'

At this Dudnikov laughs out loud, echoed by the guffaws of the two henchmen.

'I so scared!'

'You should be!'

Dudnikov stops laughing abruptly and leans back in his chair. 'You have not been silly and phoned useless island police, have you?'

Alicia doesn't say anything, but Dudnikov must see from her face that this is exactly what she has done.

He speaks in Russian to the two men, and one of them – the slightly smaller one – comes over and pulls her up. He starts patting her down.

Alicia keeps her eyes peeled on the man, who is obviously embarrassed about having to do this to a woman in her condition.

'I hope you are proud of yourself. Molesting a pregnant woman like this,' Alicia says. She stares at Dudnikov and then at the man who is now feeling up her hips and either side of her legs. The Russian blushes and Alicia is filled with hope. At least one of them has some morals.

Dudnikov shrugs his shoulders and takes a large glug of vodka.

'A good point. Who is father? Or perhaps you not know?'

Again, there is laughter, but this time Dudnikov is alone in his hilarity. When Alicia glances at the bulky henchman who hit Liam and is still standing by the door, she can see that he also looks sheepish.

This is something I can use.

Alicia is surprised at how brave she is. She feels as if she's a lioness, defending her unborn cub, as well as everyone else. She glances briefly at Liam, who is still unconscious. She hopes he isn't seriously injured.

Suddenly, the Russian man comes across Alicia's cell. He rests his hand on top of her chest, but he doesn't know how to retrieve the phone. His eyes are wide, staring at Alicia's. It's clear he doesn't feel comfortable putting his hand down her front.

Dudnikov barks an order in Russian and the man glances over his shoulder. He removes his hand from Alicia's breast, turns around, and shrugging his shoulders, says something to Dudnikov.

Alicia crosses her arms, tucking her right hand underneath her armpit, over the place where her cell is. Trying to keep her voice from trembling, she gives out a low moan as she sits back down on the sofa.

Dudnikov glares at her.

'I left it in the car,' Alicia says, her voice now trembling. She hopes the Russians will think it's because she's in pain. 'Could I have some water? Something's not right with the baby.'

Dudnikov continues to look at her angrily, then directs his gaze at the man who'd been patting her down. Dudnikov waves his arm, and again speaks in Russian. Alicia understands that he is sending the other, heavier, guy to search the car for her phone.

The other man goes over to the kitchen and brings Alicia a tumbler of water.

'OK?' He says, looking at her with concern.

Before Alicia has time to reply, Dudnikov is behind the man, whispering something angrily in his ear. The man gives Alicia a concerned look and moves back toward the door.

CHAPTER TWENTY-THREE

'So many babies… I hear the Romanian rat also has a *svoloch*.'

Alicia cocks her head at Dudnikov's words.

'What are you talking about?'

'You know, a child you have with whore. No father.'

Dudnikov's malice makes Alicia catch her breath. How can he talk about Frida and the beautiful little Anne Sofie like that? She can't reply and just shakes her head. At least the disgusting criminal is talking. This is buying her time.

'What she name?' Dudnikov asks.

'You mean Anne Sofie?' Alicia replies.

In spite of trying to keep her voice level, she can hear a tremble in it.

'I do no care what she called… I know where she lives. And her mom.'

Dudnikov moves closer to Alicia. She nearly gags when his horrible grin comes close to her face. She uses all her willpower to keep from turning away from the man's foul alcohol-filled breath. Alicia is trying not to be riled by the Russian, and keeps her mouth shut.

Where is Ebba and the island police?

'I hear she has money. I have very good investment proposal. Perhaps I will pay her visit.'

'You wouldn't dare!'

The words come out of Alicia's mouth before she's had time to think.

'How you going stop me? Look at you! Alone in middle of forest. And your no hope husband. I feel sorry for him. He going to raise a cuckoo? Perhaps you open your legs for the Swedish reporter again?'

Alicia wants to get up and slap him across the face, but she stops herself just in time. She mustn't rile Dudnikov up. She knows he is dangerous, especially if he feels threatened. Besides, she isn't able to get up quickly enough. She'd have to perform an embarrassing shuffle to the end of the seat and then push out with her hands. One of the Russians would force her back down in no time.

All her limbs suddenly feel limp. She lowers her head and fights the tears that are welling up inside her eyelids.

This is hopeless. Isn't Ebba coming after all? Perhaps she didn't get the message.

The door opens and the heavier Russian walks inside. He shakes his head at Dudnikov.

'You lied,' the Russian says to Alicia.

Alicia doesn't have time to reply, because at that

moment, Liam wakes up with a cough. He has blood under his nose and trickling down his chin from the side of his mouth. Alicia goes to touch his face, but Dudnikov tuts loudly, which makes Alicia pull back her hand.

'Ooh, the hero waking!'

Alicia longs to ask Liam how he is and to wipe away the blood. But she knows that showing concern for Liam would only give the Russians more reason to hurt him again. And Liam might start fighting back, which could end up very badly for him.

Dudnikov glances back at the pair of heavy men. They exchange a few words in Russian, laughing with each other.

We are the butt of their jokes now.

Anger rises inside her, but then she feels the baby move and it quickly dies down.

Liam, sitting upright as much as he can, is looking at her.

'Are you OK?' Alicia mouths silently to him, and he nods, but so imperceptibly that she would have missed it if she had blinked. At least they're on the same page.

Keeping the Russians calm and talking.

Turning toward Dudnikov and lifting her chin up in defiance, she asks, 'We've thought all along you were Frida's father. Who is it, if not you?'

Dudnikov places the glass of vodka, which he's been taking large glugs from, on the low table between them.

This makes Liam lick his lips audibly.

'Can he have some water?'

Alicia can't help herself. She has to look after Liam.

Dudnikov shrugs his shoulders and gives one of the men a nod.

The smaller of the two, the one who let Alicia keep her phone and who hadn't touched Liam, goes to the little kitchen and gets a glass of water. He stands above him as Liam, with shaking hands, brings it to his lips. It spills over the front of his shirt, which Alicia sees is stained with blood and torn badly. He empties the cup and, nodding to the Russian, gives it back to him.

Alicia reaches her hand out and touches Liam's arm, but this makes Dudnikov get up. 'No touching!'

Alicia wonders what he's afraid of? Perhaps that Alicia will pass a note to her husband right under the Russian's nose?

Hardly.

She pulls her hand back and, gives Liam a quick smile, a gesture she hopes is reassuring. She turns back to Dudnikov.

'We thought you were Frida's father but you're not are you?'

The Russian gives a belly laugh. He turns around to say something to the two others and they all snigger for a long time.

'You crazy! I not touch ugly island women!'

Alicia takes a deep breath in and out, trying to calm herself again.

'So, if not you, do you know who Frida's father is?'

The Russian narrows his eyes and leans in toward Alicia. She fights the nausea she feels and tries to keep her expression neutral.

'You want know?'

'Yes.'

Dudnikov again turns to his mates and says something in Russian. The two guys guffaw in response.

While Dudnikov is entertaining his troops, Alicia has time to think. She's only talking to the Russian about Frida to buy time, but she hopes Dudnikov hasn't realized this. She knows he likes to think he is informed about everything that goes on in Åland via his criminal contacts here, but she doubts even he knows the mystery behind Frida's wealthy parentage.

Alicia thinks fast. If she had to choose an ally, she might try to appeal to the Russian who left her cell alone and gave Liam water. But she hasn't heard him speak anything but Russian, so it may be futile. She glances at him covertly. His eyes betray emotion, Alicia thinks, turning quickly back toward Dudnikov.

'C'mon tell me, I'm dying to know.'

'Dying, eh?'

Alicia curses her choice of words. She can feel Liam shift position next to her, but she's too afraid to look his way.

'It's an expression,' she says as calmly as she can.

Dudnikov has an even wider smirk on his face when he replies, 'You will not believe me.'

'Try me,' she replies.

He lights another cigarette and smiles at Alicia.

'Curiosity kill the cat.'

Dudnikov leans back in his chair and pours himself more vodka from the half-empty bottle on the table. He has a smug expression on his face.

'That also an expression.'

CHAPTER TWENTY-FOUR

Dudnikov's infuriating boasting about island people has given Alicia more energy. She suspects that he doesn't really know who Frida's real dad is. However, it's good to hear it from the horse's mouth that it's not him, at least.

They must get out of here. If only Ebba would come soon! She has no idea how long they've been cooped up in this small cabin.

'What are you hoping to gain by keeping us here?'

Liam is sitting up straight. He doesn't look at Alicia, but he has his eyes peeled on Dudnikov.

'I did not want you here. You follow me.'

The Russian villain has the same self-satisfied smile on his face that Alicia has come to loathe. It was what he looked like when he threatened her in the underground parking lot, and before that, when he nearly drove her off the road on Föglö two winters ago.

His expression changes and he leans forward in his chair.

'Enough chit chat.' He flashes a grin at Liam. 'See, I learn all your expressions.'

Dudnikov turns toward Alicia.

'We need discuss business.'

Alicia shudders. She is beginning to lose faith in the island police ever finding them.

'Since you come to me, I think you change your mind, yes?'

She stares at the Russian. Perhaps if she agrees to whatever illegal scheme he has in mind, he will let them go, and Ebba can get him another time.

'What do you want?'

At Alicia's words, Liam turns to face her.

'No, you can't do this. It's my business too. We are fifty-fifty partners.'

Dudnikov ignores him and continues.

'Deal not so good anymore. Now I take 80 percent, you have 20.'

He turns the palms of his hands up and shrugs. 'Sorry. It business. You have no – how do you say it – power of bargain. I have you by the *yaytsa*.'

Dudnikov gets up and puts one hand over his crotch. The word he uses, and his crude gestures make the men behind him howl with laughter again.

At that moment, a loud pinging noise stops the men's hilarity short. It's coming from under Alicia's armpit. She freezes and tries to retrieve the cell. But Dudnikov is quick and he tries to grab the device from her bra. His left hand is holding her waist and his right is inside Alicia's dress, but she manages to snatch the cell out of his reach.

'Here!'

Liam has his hand outstretched too. As if by a miracle, Alicia throws the cell and Liam catches it. He moves quickly toward the open window and throws the phone out.

All the men, including Dudnikov, run at Liam and wrestle him to the ground.

Alicia screams.

The Russians are all piling on top of Liam, and suddenly Alicia realizes she could get out if she moved quickly now. But could she run?

She gets up as swiftly as she can and stumbles to the door. But before she can pull the handle, a hand comes over hers.

It's the smaller of the two thugs, but instead of stopping her, he opens the door for her and gives her back a nudge, putting his finger to his lips. Alicia glances quickly at the floor where Liam is putting up a good fight against Dudnikov and the other man.

When did he learn to fight like that?

But as the door shuts behind her, Alicia hesitates. Can she leave Liam? What if they do something even more awful to him? What if they kill him?

She must get help. She has no phone, but she has the car. As she runs into the darkened road, she listens for the men's footsteps but there are none. She doesn't dare look round. The track isn't long, as far as she remembers. Her legs are heavy, and she feels impossibly slow, but to her surprise she is at the main road much quicker than she thought.

Seeing her old Volvo where she left it, she almost

cries out in relief. The door is open, and she quickly gets in. Locking the doors, she dares to gaze back along the tracks.

There is no one following her.

Glancing down at the dashboard she sees the keys are still there where she left them. Her hands trembling, she's just about to start the car when she sees lights emerging behind her.

Several police cars come to an abrupt halt next to her, and the first person she sees, is Ebba. She winds down the window.

'Quickly, a cabin down that path. There's Dudnikov and two others. Liam is there.'

Ebba places a hand on Alicia's arm. 'You OK?'

'Yes, yes, GO!'

Ebba tells Alicia to wait in the locked car. She won't hear of her doing anything else, and Alicia agrees.

But after a few minutes, she can't bear it any longer and gets out of the car and walks back and forth on the edge of the deserted road. She listens intently for any sounds – gun shots or shouts, but there's nothing. The thick forest on either side of the track must be the perfect sound barrier. The temptation to drive down the track to see what is happening is overwhelming, but in her condition, she'd probably be more of a hindrance than a help.

She must remain sensible.

But her concern for Liam is overwhelming, and after what seems like half an hour, she gets into the car and starts it. At that moment, a police car appears. As it pulls out onto the main road in front of Alicia's Volvo, she sees that it contains Ebba, another police officer, and, to her immense relief, Liam.

Alicia springs out of her car and rushes over to Ebba's open window. The sight of Liam makes Alicia gasp. His face is black and blue and one of his eyes is swollen and closed.

'He's safe,' Ebba says, putting her hand on Alicia's. 'We'll take you both to the hospital.'

She stretches behind her and opens the door.

'Did you get them?' Alicia says, once inside the police car, next to Liam and holding his hand.

Ebba nods.

'All but one.'

'No, not Dudnikov?'

Alicia can't bear it if the Russian criminal is still at large. Will this nightmare never end?

Ebba cracks a smile. She's leaning over from the passenger seat toward the two of them in the back.

'No, we've got him.' She nods at a blue and white police car that is speeding away from them.

Her eyes seek Alicia's again.

'But there was only one other man with him. You said there were three?'

Alicia nods.

'I'll tell you everything later, but the third one probably ran away when he let me out.'

She smiles at Liam and goes to hug him. When he winces, she quickly lets go.

A policeman sitting in the driver's seat looks at her through the rearview mirror.

'We think he has some broken ribs, so best not to squeeze him too hard.'

'My poor hero,' Alicia says and takes hold of Liam's hand.

He tries to smile but grunts as soon as he moves his lips. But his eyes are on Alicia, and she can see how relieved he is to be safe with her.

'I love you,' Liam whispers through his almost-closed mouth.

Struggling with tears, Alicia replies, 'Me too.'

CHAPTER TWENTY-FIVE

F rida puts the phone down and sits on the sofa. She can't believe what the police chief just told her.

Alexander Dudnikov has been caught!

Can she really believe that this man, this villain who's responsible for the misery and possibly the deaths of so many people is no longer a threat to anyone?

In spite of the heat that lingers in the apartment even after the sun has set, a shiver runs down her spine. She can't help it, but she still thinks of this horrible person as her absent father. Even after the results of the DNA test, it's difficult to brush off the months of guilt she'd felt about her parentage. Not to mention the shame she's felt all this time for using her mom's inheritance, which she realized must have come from her father.

Who else but a Russian lowlife would have such a fortune to gift to her mom?

She'd only accepted the money because she needed

to make a future for Anne Sofie. She would do anything for her daughter.

She knows that Andrei thinks the money is tainted. And he still believes that the death of his brother Daniel had something to do with the Russian or one of his lackeys.

Frida doesn't agree with Andrei on this point. Ebba, the police chief, had been certain it was just a horrible accident.

Now that she feels better about her inheritance, the guilt over the money has been replaced by a new one. How could she even think that her mom would get involved with someone like Dudnikov?

Frida puts her head in her hands.

If only she knew more about who her mom's mystery benefactor – and most probably her dad – was.

Frida can only think that all the grief and upheaval she experienced during her pregnancy and after Anne Sofie's birth had made her misjudge her own mother. When Alicia's son, her first love, Stefan, died, and she was bereft with grief, she made one mistake. She slept with their mutual friend Daniel.

She cannot regret having Anne Sofie, but all the fresh grief that accompanied her pregnancy and her first months as a young mum were just too much. How did she even survive it?

First, Daniel, who she now knows was trafficked to Åland to work for no pay on Alicia's stepfather's farm, had a fatal accident at sea. Then, just after Anne Sofie was born, her mom died at the care home. Her mom had suffered with alcoholism for years, and then got dementia. She didn't even recognize Frida when she took Anne Sofie to the care home to meet her grandma.

When she was told to go and see her mom's attorney, she was incredulous at first. Why would her poor mom, who'd worked as a waitress at the Arkipelag Hotel, even have an attorney?

When Mr Karlsson told her that she was a millionaire twice over, she didn't know what to think. Suddenly she remembered the rumors about her mom's Russian lover, which she'd dismissed before her mom's death. Who else but a criminal would have such sums to make her mother a millionaire?

The attorney more or less admitted that Dudnikov was the benefactor, and therefore, Frida was convinced, also her dad.

Perhaps Frida should contact the lawyer and show him the DNA results?

She knows that would do nothing, however. The man is as impregnable as a brick wall. Over the months that she's had dealings with him, Frida has tried every trick in the book to get the truth out of him.

But to no avail.

He keeps citing 'client privilege' with her mom's benefactor, even when Frida points out that she, too, is his client.

Luckily, Frida no longer uses Karlsson's services. She has found a younger lawyer in Mariehamn.

Frida hears a cry and gets up to check on Anne Sofie. She tiptoes into the little girl's bedroom and sees that her daughter is fast asleep. She was probably just having a bad dream. She has pushed the sheet that was covering her to one side and is lying on her back with just her diaper on.

She is so beautiful, with her long lashes resting on her rosy cheeks, that Frida is filled with heart-aching love. Whatever happens with Andrei, and whoever Frida's real father is, she will always have Anne Sofie. They've managed on their own before and will again.

As she tiptoes out of the room and brings the door to, leaving a small gap so that she can hear if the girl cries out again, Frida remembers that she has been far from alone over the past two years. She's had Alicia. And now Liam. Not to mention Hilda.

She can't believe that both Alicia (in her condition!) and Liam were involved in apprehending Dudnikov. She can't imagine what happened. Knowing Alicia, she would not have cared about putting herself in danger if she thought she could get the Russian behind bars once and for all.

Ebba had said they were both well after their ordeal. Still, Frida wants to hear for herself. But it's gone midnight, so she sends a message instead.

Are you and Liam OK? Ebba just phoned with news re D. So glad the villain is behind bars.

Frida sees from the small dots that the message has been read and that Alicia is writing a reply.

A bit shaken but fine. Lots of love xx

CHAPTER TWENTY-SIX

Mia Eriksson is fuming. She's sitting alone on the veranda of the family's summer place just outside Mariehamn, which has a stunning view of the sea. It's the afternoon of the hottest day of the year yet, and the sun is still high in the sky.

She's leafing through the latest British *Vogue*, but she can't concentrate. She's wearing a sheer Melissa Odabash kaftan over a bikini, both in her signature white, and crystal-embellished Manolo Blahnik Birkenstocks. Watching the buckles sparkle gives her some pleasure. She got the first pair ever sold in Sweden, delivered to her favorite boutique in Östermalm. She'd had to send several emails, and had personally visited the shop, where she'd bought another pair of shoes she didn't even want just to get to the top of the snooty woman's waitlist.

But the eye-wateringly expensive sandals ('How much did you pay for a pair of clunky German clogs?' her mother had exclaimed when she'd made the mistake of telling her about her triumph) are a poor consolation prize for the humiliation she suffered in Mariehamn.

Why is it that every time she gets closer to Patrick, that woman appears on the scene?

Mia is certain Patrick would have kissed her again, more passionately, if Alicia hadn't appeared in front of them, pregnant and blooming. Mia knows that she could have got Patrick to go further.

He's never been able to resist Mia's advances.

But that woman, looking sexy despite her condition. How can someone so old be so attractive when expecting? Well, Mia didn't think she looked that good, but judging by the rapt expression on Patrick's face, she certainly did something for him.

And now the gossip blog has posted pictures of the two cozying up to each other in a local cafe. How droll!

Why is she still chasing him? After everything, you'd think she'd have learned her lesson and kept well away from Patrick!

Mia doesn't hear her father, until he's nearly standing next to her.

'Beautiful view,' he says.

Mia turns around fully so that she can see her father's face. His voice sounds strange, as if someone is strangling him. He's not looking at her, but over toward the horizon and the islands in the distance, beyond the sparkling surface of the sea.

Mia lowers her large Chanel sunglasses and takes a closer look at him. Something doesn't look right. He is slightly stooped, and his linen suit is hanging off him as if it's at least two sizes too large.

'Are you OK, *Pappa*?'

Kurt Eriksson turns his head abruptly toward her daughter as if he's just realized she is there.

'Where's your mother?' He says straightening up.

Back to normal, then, Mia thinks, returning to her magazine.

'No idea,' she replies.

'And the girls, you must at least know where your own daughters are?'

'Why, dear *Pappa*, are you offering to babysit?'

They are both silent for a moment. Mia longs for her father to leave her alone. She needs to plan what to do next with that woman – and Patrick.

'Look, I need to tell you something.'

Mia's father sits down next to her in one of the white Adirondack chairs Mia's mom bought for the villa last year. She'd seen them in LA and had insisted they'd look good on the sea-facing decking of the villa.

Mia had wholeheartedly approved. Previously, the outdoor furniture had been some awful weather-beaten rattan that had been in vogue years ago. Now the veranda looked the part and could be photographed for any home decor magazine without her being in the least embarrassed about their small island place.

Of course, Daddy would never allow photographers into their home. More was the pity. It would do good for their property business if people saw how wealthy they were.

But Kurt Eriksson was modest, and wanted to keep their real wealth a secret, something Mia just couldn't understand.

'Are you listening?'

There's more than a hint of impatience in her father's voice now.

'Alright, keep your hair on!'

Her father turns his upper body toward his daughter and leans in closer to Mia. He nods at her face.

'Take those off.'

With a sigh, Mia removes her sunglasses.

Her father regards her with watery eyes but doesn't say anything.

'What is it?'

Suddenly, Mia's heart starts beating a little faster. Her father's bronzed, lined face, which is so familiar to her, looks drawn somehow. What does he want to tell her? Bad news?

'Don't tell me you've lost money?' Mia asks when her father doesn't say anything, but just continues to regard her with those sad eyes.

Her comment makes Kurt Eriksson snort.

'Is that all you care about? The money!'

Her father goes to get up but struggles to move. The chairs are low, more suited to young bodies, Mia realizes.

'Let me ...'

But her dad waves his hand at her.

'I don't need your help! These bloody things are ridiculous.'

That's when Mia breaks. She puts a hand up to her mouth to hide her smile, which is threatening to develop into a snigger as she watches her dad move sideways and then, holding onto one of the arms with both hands, finally get himself up.

He comes to stand in front of Mia.

'I said take those things off!'

Mia has replaced her sunglasses so that he wouldn't see how funny she found his difficulty in getting out of a garden chair.

'OK, OK. I don't know what's got into you today, but you are being really rude …'

'Be quiet and listen.' Her father's serious expression makes Mia shiver.

'I have cancer.'

Mia doesn't think she's heard right.

'What?'

But now she can't stop her father from speaking.

'Cancer of the colon. I haven't told your mom yet. The operation is next week, but they are not certain. Not sure that …'

'Oh my God.'

Mia gets up and goes to hug her dad. But his body is thin and weak. He takes hold of her arms and pushes her gently away.

'They are not certain it will work.'

Once again, Mia puts her hand over her lips, but this time it's to stop a shriek escaping from her mouth.

'Dad,' she manages to say.

Her throat feels constricted, as if a hand is grabbing it, the thumb pushing against her windpipe.

'I wanted you to know.'

'Right,' Mia replies. The word comes out in a whisper.

She nods but can't say anything else. It's as if all air has been pushed out of her lungs.

She cannot understand. How has she not noticed that her own father is seriously ill? It's now obvious that he has lost a lot of weight. And his face is gray and lined. It's as if he's shrunk, as if someone had cut the cords holding his body upright.

Mia feels the panic rising in her again just as it did when she was in the restaurant with Patrick. She takes a few breaths in and out.

Don't lose it now!

Her father turns away and gazes out to sea.

'The wind is up.'

Mia needs her mom. She'll know what to do.

'So why haven't you told Mom?'

Her father's eyes are following a small sailing vessel making its way across the water.

'Good wind for sailing. I wish I still had my boat.'

'Dad?'

Mia stands next to her father and takes his hand in hers.

'Yes?'

'Shall we go inside and see if Mom's in her study?'

That same evening after Mia has told Sara and Frederica to go to their rooms, she sits in what used to be her and Patrick's suite in the summer villa. It overlooks the sea and the small beach behind the rocks that her father had made for the girls. A lorry full of sand was poured into the small cove, but Mia cannot now remember if they ever played there.

This morning, she thought that her life was on the rocks, but little did she know how bad it could get. When she'd found her mom, who was busy working on her latest novel in the study, she'd managed to get her father to tell her about his illness.

He'd found out soon after Easter that he had a problem, but he hadn't gone to see the specialist until last week. When her mom, always the practical one, had asked him exactly what they'd said, her father had lowered his head and in a low voice told them that he has a 50/50 chance of survival.

'There's something else I need to tell you,' her dad says after they've been quiet for a long time. He's not looking at them but at his hands, which are resting on his lap.

Her mom is sitting on her high-backed, ergonomically designed office chair opposite her husband and Mia. Her body is rigid, as if any moment a movement would shatter the quietness of the room. She is staring at her husband, but Mia cannot decipher what her expression means. Is she angry at him? Sad? Her mom has always been a bit of a closed book, and distant. Mia thought that's because she pours all her inner life into her prize-winning novels.

She's often wondered who the woman behind the books, described as "full of deep-felt emotion" is. Her mom, the always perfectly turned-out person without as much as a strand of hair out of place, hasn't ever seemed to have any deep feelings inside her body.

Even when Mia was a little girl, it was her dad she'd run to if she had cut her finger or if someone at school had been nasty to her. (They often were, calling her "the poor little rich girl".)

'This heat doesn't help!' Her mom now says, dabbing her brow with the back of her hand. It's as if it was the fault of the weather that her dad has cancer. 'It's about time we installed aircon here, don't you think?'

This is directed at Mia, bypassing her husband, as if the decisions about the house already belonged to the two of them rather than to her dad. Kurt has always been the one with the final say on any larger purchases, even though Mia knows her mom's books bring in almost as much income as her dad's business ventures.

Her dad lifts his head and stares at Mia's mom.

'Well, it'll be more comfortable for you, when you are convalescing after your op.'

Kurt sighs.

'You are not listening to me, Beatrice. I have something important to tell you. To tell you both, he adds, taking Mia's hand in his.

'What is it, *Pappa*?'

Mia is now truly scared. Perhaps this is to do with money as well? Perhaps he's lost it all in some kind of crazy investment in Russia, or something?

As Mia gazes at her dad, who is biting the inside of his mouth in a very uncharacteristically indecisive manner, she admonishes herself. What does money matter if she doesn't have her beloved dad? They may argue a lot and they may be rather rude to each other, but she knows for certain he loves her.

He may be the only person on this earth who truly loves her, warts and all.

Her dad brings his eyes level with Mia's and says, as if he'd been reading her mind,

'Remember, I love you very much.'

Mia can hear her mom's sigh.

'Well, don't keep us in suspense. What other secrets are you keeping from us?'

Kurt gives his wife a brief glance but returns his gaze toward his daughter. In almost a whisper he says, 'I have another child.'

CHAPTER TWENTY-SEVEN

'You have to come over!'

Patrick doesn't understand what is going on. It's gone 10pm and he's in his old apartment, overlooking the West Harbor when he gets the frantic phone call from Mia.

'What is it? Has something happened to one of the girls?'

'Girls?'

'Yes, Mia, our daughters! Are Sara and Frederica, OK?'

Patrick can hear Mia inhaling and exhaling loudly at the other end of the line.

'Of course, they are! They're in their room. Frederica came home from camp this afternoon exhausted. This is not about them, but I can't tell you over the phone, so please, please come over as soon as you can. I need you!'

Patrick hears that Mia has ended the call. He stares at his cell, which now displays the image of his two daughters, both smiling into the camera. He remembers when he took the photo. It was last year when they were visiting him in Stockholm. He'd taken them shopping on the fashionable south side of the city, and they were about to go for a pizza in one of the restaurants near his modest apartment.

He sighs and picks up his keys. Something important must have happened for Mia to swallow her pride and actually plead with him to go to see her.

After leaving the built-up areas of Mariehamn behind, Patrick heads along the road to the tip of the peninsula, water on either side. Suddenly the road narrows, barely fitting the strip of land, before it widens again. The Erikssons' summer house is a large estate, surrounded by the sea, with breathtaking views across the Baltic and the smaller islands and skerries dotted here and there in the distance.

The first time Patrick came here, he was a poor journalist, fresh off the train from northern Sweden. He had never seen such a large villa, and he was nervous that his simple upbringing would show.

The electric gate opens without Patrick having to get up and press the intercom, so he knows someone must have seen him arrive. He parks and still no one shows. The lobby is empty, as is the double height lounge where a curved staircase leads up to the suite he once shared with Mia.

As he makes his way up to the second floor, Patrick's mind is flooded with memories.

In spite of the lingering heat, he shivers as he remembers when their eldest, Sara was ill with a fever that they'd later discovered was meningitis. Patrick had gone with her in the ambulance to the hospital, fearing the worst. They'd been on their own in the villa then, and Mia had had to stay behind with their younger daughter.

Walking along the upstairs landing, he recalls the many midsummer parties held here. During the one two years ago, he'd kissed Alicia in the cove, the small sandy beach that Kurt Eriksson had built for his grand-daughters.

Patrick tries to put Alicia out of his mind when he reaches the door to their suite, which is closed. He stands there for a moment, wondering if he should just walk in. He decides to knock.

Almost immediately, the door opens and Mia flies into his arms.

She's in a flood of tears.

Patrick hugs her for a moment, then pushes her gently away. 'What's the matter, Mia?'

But his ex-wife just continues to sob.

Suddenly he hears a door open somewhere else in the villa. He can pick up what he thinks is Mia's mom speak in a low voice to the housekeeper, but he can't make out the words.

'Let's go inside,' Patrick says. He doesn't want to have an encounter with either of Mia's parents just now. What if they think it's him who has upset Mia?

Patrick half-carries, half pushes Mia inside the suite.

He's shocked when he sees the state of the main

room. The large bed, which is usually beautifully made up with white Egyptian cotton sheets and topped with a mass of different-shaped pillows, is now a complete mess. The bedding is bunched up, clothing litters the floor, and there is a tray of food half-covered with used tissues.

A bottle of some sort of liquor – vodka, Patrick would guess – and a half-empty glass sit on the bedside table, together with more tissues and various bits of makeup.

'What is going on?'

'Oh, Patrick. You have to look after me. I can't do this on my own. I just can't.'

Mia slumps on the bed, picks up the glass and empties it.

Patrick takes it from her and places the glass and the food tray on a large table opposite the floor-to-ceiling windows. The curtains are open, and he can see a figure walking along the shoreline.

It's Mia's mom.

She's wrapped up in a long shawl and is smoking a cigarette. This startles Patrick; he had no idea Beatrice smoked!

Something is very, very wrong here.

Patrick turns his attention back to Mia, who has fallen into the bed. As he gets closer, he sees that Mia is snoring gently.

Patrick lifts Mia's head and places it on a pillow, clearing away the detritus. Taking off her white kaftan-style dress, he covers her with a sheet and quietly leaves the room.

. . .

He finds Beatrice sitting on one of the boulders framing the artificial beach. She is looking out to sea. As he approaches, Patrick sees that there are tears running down her face and that she is wearing no make-up. She looks vulnerable, a description Patrick would never have attributed to his former mother-in-law.

She hears Patrick's steps and turns around.

'Ah, she called you, did she?'

This is a statement, uttered without any emotion.

'Yeah,' Patrick says. He's standing next to her, uncertain what to do.

The sea is calm, as still as it has been for days now, and the sun is halfway down the horizon. It's still warm, although the faintest of sea breezes catches Beatrice's shawl.

'Sit down. You make me nervous, standing there.'

After Patrick and Beatrice have been sitting gazing out to sea for a few minutes, he dares to speak.

'What's going on, Beatrice? Mia is beside herself. And she's been drinking vodka. She fell asleep before I could find out what the matter is.'

Beatrice turns her head, and their eyes meet. He can see a likeness to her daughter, although Mia's features are sharper and her eyes darker than her mother's.

Beatrice wipes her cheeks. 'Kurt has cancer. Probably incurable.'

Patrick is stunned. He thought that the whole of the Eriksson family visited all kinds of medical experts regularly; if anything was wrong, they got world-class treatment pronto.

He places a hand on Beatrice's arm. 'I'm so sorry.'

Beatrice turns back to look at the sea. She lights another cigarette and offers Patrick one, but he shakes his head.

'The fool hasn't accepted treatment, so now he's …' Here the older woman's voice falters.

'I'm sorry.'

Patrick realizes he's repeated himself and swears silently. Why can't he think of anything more intelligent to say?

He's always been in awe of Beatrice's writing and her brain. When he read the novel for which she got the Finlandia prize, he couldn't link the author and the book. The woman he knew as Mia's mom was a cold, unfeeling person. Not the passionate author who could capture the emotions of a family enduring famine and severe cold on the islands in the 16th century.

Patrick had never admitted to Mia that he had read and loved her mom's book. Mia's relationship with her mother was difficult, and the last thing Patrick wanted was to come in the middle of it.

'What's more, he's gone and fathered some kid. Something he only told us tonight.'

Patrick feels certain he's misheard Beatrice.

'What?'

They sit silently for a moment. Beatrice is once again facing the sea. She stubs her cigarette on the rocks and puts it inside the pocket of her loose pants.

'I'm going in. Are you staying? The guest bed is made up.'

Patrick thinks for a moment, but he feels he's been given no choice. He nods, and Beatrice, getting up, adds, 'Kurt is in the apartment in town.'

'I'll look in on the girls before I turn in. I presume they haven't been told yet?' Patrick asks.

'On the contrary. I believe in being honest with children. I told them this evening that their *mofa* was ill and that mom was a little upset about it. They seemed to understand.'

Patrick is staring at his former mother-in-law. There's a fine line between honesty and cruelty.

'Did they cry?'

Beatrice's eyes meet Patrick's. She takes air through her nose and lifts her chin just a little, before replying.

'No. I gave them both a hug and told them to be brave.'

Patrick nods.

That figures.

Poor Sara and Frederica wouldn't dare to show any emotion in front of their grandmother. The two stare at each other for a moment, then Beatrice turns to go up to the house.

'Well, goodnight, Patrick.'

Breakfast is a subdued affair. The girls are not up yet, and Patrick knows, won't be for a few hours yet. He'd been with them last night until they fell asleep. Both had asked a myriad of questions, and he'd tried to answer as well as he could.

When Frederica asked if *mofa* was going to die, Patrick had admitted that, yes, their grandfather was so ill that he may die. At that, tears had filled their eyes, and Patrick had to struggle to be brave with them.

When he'd tiptoed out of their room, he'd been glad that he'd stayed at the villa. His family needed him now.

Around the breakfast table, Mia and Beatrice don't say a word to each other. Patrick tries to make conversation, but the looks he gets from both women soon stop him. When Patrick has finished eating the delicious scrambled eggs and sausages, with freshly baked French rolls, Mia nods at him, indicating with her eyes that she wants to go up to their old suite. Patrick notices that Mia has hardly touched her food.

'Thank you, Beatrice, that was excellent,' Patrick says, and Beatrice raises a brief smile.

Upstairs, Mia sits on the bed, which has been magically made up while they were downstairs.

'I don't know what to do.'

Patrick gazes at his ex-wife. He feels desperately sorry for her, but at the same time, he thinks she has never been more unattractive to him.

It was her confidence, almost bolshiness, that first appealed to him. He remembers when a fellow reporter, a young man from the Swedish upper classes, had introduced her to Patrick. He'd been attracted to her immediately. He realizes now that he'd also been drawn to her power to open doors for him. She came from a wealthy family, but she wasn't Swedish, which was a serious handicap in the circles Mia mixed in. Patrick saw that this dent in her – and Kurt Eriksson's – armor was something he could smooth out. Together they could become a celebrated power couple in Stockholm!

Of course, it hadn't worked out that way. Something in him, whether it was his northern upbringing, or his desire to be a good father, had hindered his career progression. Perhaps Kurt Eriksson didn't have as much sway on the Stockholm newspaper *Journalen* as Patrick had anticipated.

Perhaps Patrick just doesn't have what it takes to be a prize-winning journalist.

Whatever it is, as soon as their daughters were born, Mia lost interest in Patrick. Kurt, too, seemed to be disappointed in him. Each time they'd spend any time on the islands, whether in the Eriksson's lavish place in town, or in the summer villa, Mia's father showed his displeasure with Patrick.

A snide comment about the lack of progress in his career, or his desire to be a stay-home dad, pushed Patrick to spend more and more time on his boat, which Mia had given him early in their marriage.

He had dreamt about taking long sailing holidays in the Finnish archipelago with his new wife, but that had never materialized. He learned too late that Mia hated being on the water.

His ex-wife now lifts her eyes toward Patrick. She's not wearing any make-up, and there are still traces of yesterday's mascara under her eyes. Years ago, when Patrick was still in love with Mia, he would have found her smoky eyes and unkempt appearance sexy, but now he just feels sad for her.

'What should I do?'

This is a question Mia has never asked Patrick.

'I have no idea.'

Mia stares at him.

'Well. That's useful.'

There is a flash of anger in Mia's eyes.

'Don't be nasty.'

Mia comes to stand close to Patrick and he can smell yesterday's booze on her.

'You could try being a tad more sympathetic!'

She jabs a finger at Patrick's chest, which makes him take a step backward.

'Don't blame me. I have nothing to do with this.'

He lifts his hands up, his palms facing Mia.

Mia is still staring at him.

'You are unbelievable. This is your father-in-law we are talking about! Your children's grandfather! What's more, there's another child out there – another person with a right to my dad's estate.'

'Of course,' Patrick says, adding drily, 'this is all about money. And you blame me for being uncaring. You really are something, Mia Eriksson. I don't want anything to do with this.'

Patrick moves toward the door, but Mia takes hold of his arm and pulls him. 'Don't be such a hypocrite. You like the money too. That's why you are here. That's why you stayed here last night. You can sniff out the dollars – or the lack of them – the same as me.'

'I stayed here because our daughters needed me. Have you forgotten that they may too lose their *mofa*?'

Patrick stares down at Mia. He is so disgusted by her that he has to control himself not to push her. Instead, he frees himself from her grip and walks out of the door.

'Come back here immediately! Patrick! You'll regret this!'

He can hear Mia's shrill voice all the way down the stairs.

In the hallway, he is met by Beatrice.

'You've finally had enough, have you?'

The older woman's eyes are pale.

'I'm sorry, Beatrice, I have to go. Say goodbye to the girls for me. I'll call them later.'

Beatrice nods and turns away. She disappears into her study, which is just off the wide hallway.

Before he walks through the door, Patrick glances back through the hall toward the huge living room and the winding staircase. He vows that this is the last time he steps inside this venomous villa. He'll pick the girls up, but he doesn't want to be inside it ever again.

CHAPTER TWENTY-EIGHT

Even though there's only a week before the schools break up, Frida has managed to get a place for Anne Sofie in the local preschool. She's just stepping out of her door, on her way to collect her daughter after the first day, when she bumps into Kurt Eriksson.

'Hello there! Long time, no see.'

The man is extending his hand to Frida.

Kurt Eriksson, the owner of *Ålandsbladet*, the main newspaper on the islands, where Frida had worked as a summer intern before her mom died and she had Anne Sofie, stands expectantly in front of her. She stares at his outstretched hand but can't quite bring herself to take hold of it. What does the man want with her?

Kurt Eriksson's arm hangs awkwardly and Frida doesn't know what to say or do.

This is the richest man on the islands. Some people say he owns Åland, because of his extensive investments in land and property.

'Mr Eriksson,' Frida says at last and takes the proffered hand.

The man grabs hold of it and peers intently into
Frida's face. Placing his other hand on top of hers, he
squeezes it gently. His grasp is surprisingly warm, the
skin of his palms softer than Frida had imagined.

'Kurt, please.'

Frida doesn't know where to look. Kurt Eriksson's
eyes are bloodshot and the wrinkles on his face have
deepened since she last saw him in the newspaper office,
inside the editor's glass cubicle at the back of the room,
where he used to sit during his meetings with old
Nousiainen.

'You've changed your hair,' the man now says, at
last releasing Frida's hand from his grip.

Frida touches the ends of her blonde bob.

'It was, erm, a bit more colorful before. And shorter,'
the older man adds.

Is he coming onto me?

'Yeah, well, it's nice to see you again, Mr... Kurt,
but I must go.'

Frida looks up and down her street. It's quiet, and
she can't think of a reason to get out of talking to Mr
Eriksson.

'You look just like your mother now.'

Frida snaps her head back to face Eriksson.

'What did you say?'

Now the man is quiet. Instead of looking at her, he's
gazing down at his expensive shoes.

Frida glances at her phone and realizes she's late for
Anne Sofie. She takes a step sideways, but Eriksson

takes hold of her arm. 'Look, I need to talk to you. Could I come and see you later?'

When Frida is walking back to the apartment, pushing Anne Sofie in her stroller, her head is full of questions. What does Kurt Eriksson of all people want with her? And how did he know her mom?

Even while talking about Anne Sofie with the nursery staff, who'd said her first day had gone brilliantly, Frida's mind had been on the brief but puzzling meeting with the powerful man. The lives of her mom, a waitress at the Arkipelag Hotel, and the millionaire – maybe even billionaire – Kurt Eriksson could not have been further removed from each other. Perhaps Kurt had seen her in the restaurant, and been served by her, that was highly likely, but why would he mention her to Frida now?

Was Kurt Eriksson another secret her mom had kept from her daughter?

Frida thinks back to how her mom had been before the fall, and even before that, before the drinking had become a serious issue. She'd been beautiful, yes, and Frida remembers that her hair had been mid-length and blonde, like Frida's now. Only the other day, after she'd had some highlights put in by her old stylist in Mariehamn, she'd looked in the mirror and her mom stared back at her.

Then there was the bombshell of the money.

While her mom had been ill, and when she'd been taken into the old people's home, Frida had struggled with money. All her young life, she'd been under the impression that they were poor. A salary from a waitressing job wasn't much, and they had lived simply. Frida had never given a thought to how her mom could afford to send her to the lyceum in Stockholm. She'd assumed there'd been a grant from the state, but she'd never checked.

After Frida has given Anne Sofie something to eat, bathed her, and read her a story, she settles the girl into bed. After dimming her bedside lamp, she tiptoes out of the room. Her baby had been so tired after her first day at pre-school that she hadn't grumbled about bedtime. As Frida stands by the doorway and gazes back into the room, she can see that Anne Sofie's eyes are closed and her chest rising and falling in a steady rhythm. The girl is already asleep.

Frida goes back to the kitchen and sits at her laptop. Since she found out that Dudnikov couldn't be her father after all, she hasn't done anything further. After Alicia told her Dudnikov was through and through Russian, Frida had phoned Ebba to check for herself. The police chief sent her a screenshot showing part of Dudnikov's file. It stated that his parents hailed from Moscow, where he is also registered as a resident. How Ebba got the information, Frida has no idea, but she'll take it. It means Dudnikov is mostly of Russian descent. If only they had his DNA on file, then she could be 100 percent certain.

Alicia thinks she should forget about Dudnikov entirely.

The question is, if the Russian isn't her dad, and her mom's secret benefactor, then who is?

Her only hope is if the research lab can find matches to her own DNA. She's not had any more information from the place that did her test, but they did say it would take a few days.

'It also depends on whether anyone with results linked to yours has agreed to share their data. We take privacy and information ethics very seriously,' the man at the other end of the line had told Frida.

From his tone, she felt as if she'd asked him something she wasn't entitled to know. She guesses that was why she'd told him she didn't know who her dad was.

The guy at the other end had seemed nonplussed about Frida's predicament.

'We get that a lot,' he'd said drily, adding, 'You'll just have to wait for any matches to come through, I'm afraid.'

CHAPTER TWENTY-NINE

Frida decides that she is going to tell Andrei the good news about her paternity and is about to pick up her cell when her doorbell goes.

'Hello, I hope I'm not disturbing bedtime?'

Frida stands at the doorway, unsure of what to do. She'd all but forgotten about her strange meeting with Kurt Eriksson on the street earlier.

Frida really wants to talk to Andrei. She hasn't heard from him since yesterday when he'd seemed very distant. He claimed he was tired, but Frida was nearly in tears after the conversation. She felt that what she'd feared after leaving Romania was now happening. The love affair that had been so passionate and the connection that had been so strong while they were still in Mariehamn was quickly dissolving, like a wave sweeping over a sandcastle on the beach.

'Look, I'm not ...'

Kurt Eriksson's face, which had been serious just now, lights up. His whole body seems to relax.

'That's fine. I'll catch you at a more convenient time.'

And with those words the man is gone, walking briskly out of the outer hallway and the main door.

For a moment, Frida stares after him. What could he possibly want with her? Did he need someone to work at the newspaper? Surely there would be many takers for a junior position at *Ålandsbladet*? And it wouldn't be Kurt Eriksson who'd come and talk to her about something like that. There were many people working for the paper who could contact Frida, by phone or email, if that was what he wanted.

No, it had to be something else. But what?

Just as Frida is about to close the door, Kurt Eriksson reappears in front of her.

'I'm sorry, Frida, but I must tell you something. It can't wait, I'm afraid. Can I come in?'

The look on his face of desperation and – yes, fear – makes the decision for Frida.

'Of course. But please be quiet, I've only just settled Anne Sofie.'

The old man nods. Watching him walk inside her apartment with an uncertain gait, his back stooped, Frida wonders how old he really is. When she worked for his newspaper, Mr Eriksson would only occasionally come in, if there was an important meeting with the editor, or if there was a particularly significant news story about to break.

One such time was when poor Daniel's body was found in the archipelago. No one at the time knew that he was a very close friend of hers, nor that she was expecting his child.

Kurt Eriksson stands awkwardly in the middle of the room, like a man who is not used to waiting for permission to sit down.

His eyes are a paler blue than Frida remembers from those meetings in the *Ålandsbladet* office. Then his bright blue, piercing gaze, framed by his tanned face, had intimidated even Frida, who'd cared little about what the entitled millionaire thought of her. Now he seemed wary of her, rather than the other way around.

What is going on?

'Please sit down.'

Mr Eriksson lowers himself down, wincing a little as his behind hits the sofa.

'You OK?'

The older man lifts his head and now his lips form a smile.

'That's very kind of you. In fact, I am rather unwell.'

'Oh.'

Frida seats herself opposite Mr Eriksson.

Why is he telling me this?

'Can I get you anything? Coffee, beer? Water?'

'A glass of water would be good.'

When Frida returns with the water, she sees that the man is leaning back on the sofa. His eyes are shut and for a moment she thinks he might be asleep, but as soon as she's close enough to hand him the glass, he straightens up and gives her another grateful smile.

'Thank you.'

Frida returns to her seat. She looks at her cell and

sees it's gone eight o'clock. The heat from the day is finally abating, and a sea breeze drifts across the room from the windows, which she's left open in order to get some cool air into the apartment.

'That's better,' Mr Eriksson says.

Frida isn't certain if he is referring to the glass of water or the cool air wafting through the room. She decides not to ask. Small talk will not make the powerful man in front of Frida tell her why he needs to talk to her. So, she waits.

Mr Eriksson coughs and places the empty glass on the table between them.

Frida fights the urge to ask him why he's there.

'Are you aware that I knew your mother?'

Frida cannot hide her frustration.

'Mr Eriksson, she worked for decades as a waitress in Arkipelag, a hotel complex you own. Most people knew her,' she snaps.

The old man lifts his hand up and looks at her carefully, before saying, 'We were intimate.'

'What?'

Frida gets up. She stares at the man on the sofa, who's face is pale. His eyes are pleading.

'Please, sit down,' he says, and continues, 'I'm not well. In fact, I'm dying. I wanted to let you know before... before it's too late. And I would very much like to meet your little one, Anne Sofie, isn't it?'

Frida is glued to the spot. She's still looking at Kurt Eriksson, not comprehending what he is talking about. At the same time, she knows exactly why he is here.

And who he is.

CHAPTER THIRTY

'Calm Down, Frida! Start from the beginning.'

Alicia is in her office, going through a set of figures that Liam sent her, when she gets a call from Frida. She sounds almost hysterical and seems to be saying that she knows who her father is.

Alicia feels guilty. She and Liam had discussed Dudnikov's claim that he knew the identity of Frida's father in the hours after the scary night. In truth, neither Alicia nor Liam believed him, so they'd decided to postpone telling Frida. They'd been at the hospital checking on the baby (a scan showed that all was fine) and Liam's injuries, which were minimal, thank goodness. Since then, he's healed quickly and now has only faint bruising on his body, though he's got to wear a brace around his ribs for a few days.

Alicia had felt so elated over Dudnikov's apprehension, that, truthfully, she'd forgotten all about Frida's real dad. Besides, she'd not been certain she should pass on the Russian's gossip.

'Surely that's good news?' Alicia adds when she hears Frida's rapid breathing.

'No, it isn't. You don't understand. It's, it's …'

'Who?'

'Kurt Eriksson!'

Alicia doesn't know what to say and Frida starts talking fast, recounting how the multi-millionaire had come to her apartment and told her how he had known her mom and that he was her father.

'But he's ill. Very ill. Cancer.'

Alicia can hear Frida's sobs now.

'It's so unfair. After all this time, he tells me now!'

Still Alicia cannot speak. But it makes sense. Who else could have given all that money to Sirpa Anttila? The list is very short once Dudnikov had been removed. Of course, it could have been someone from outside the islands, but how likely was it that a visitor would have remembered and taken care of Frida's mom for all those years. Those sorts of things only happen in fairy tales, or soppy romances.

Now that Alicia thinks about it, it had to be someone who was buying Sirpa's silence. She'd mistakenly thought that it had to be the Russian villain.

Alicia glances at the numbers on her screen. She can hear Liam making food for them in the small kitchen. It's gone 9pm, and finally the heat is abating a little.

'Do you want me to come over?'

'Oh, I don't know. I just don't know what to think.'

Alicia can hear the desperation in the young woman's voice.

'Look, I'll get Liam to drive me. You don't mind if he comes along too, do you?'

Alicia can hear Frida sniffle and her voice is full of gratitude when she replies, 'Of course not. Thank you, Alicia.'

Frida's mind is a jumble of questions.

She knows now that her father is one Kurt Eriksson, who according to his own words had met and fallen in love – he used those words – with her mom about a year before she fell pregnant with her.

They met when Sirpa came to work for Arkipelag. Kurt was dining in a private room with some of his business associates at the restaurant and Sirpa was their waitress.

'It was a group of loudmouthed show-offs from Sweden. They kept making jokes about the islands and about how we spoke 'Moomin Troll Swedish' here. I was fed up with them, but I couldn't say anything. I needed their money. Two of them were bankers and one was a property magnate, who then owned the best parts of the city. I was planning to build a sports complex in Mariehamn, you know the one?' He paused for a moment and looked up at Frida with those watery eyes of his.

She'd nodded.

'Anyway, I was worried because I wasn't sure they would back it. It was more a project to benefit the islanders than a tourist attraction, so I couldn't do anything but laugh along with them.

'When your mom came to serve us coffee and cognac, she caught my eye. The property magnate was then going on about how Åland was really just a poor man's Las Vegas. "Without the gambling," he added to laughter from the others.

I knew that she understood from my expression and inability to laugh with the other men that I didn't agree with them.

'When she began pouring coffee for the Swedish property magnate, he put his hand out to squeeze your mom's bottom, saying, "The women are pretty though, and easy to please, I hear? How much for a night in the sack with you, love?"

'Your mom straightened herself up and poured the coffee right into the man's lap. It took all my self-control not to howl with laughter.

'Of course, the man wanted your mom to be sacked, but I said I'd dock her pay and eventually he accepted that. I asked the restaurant manager to replace your mom and send her home, but I didn't forget her. A few weeks later we bumped into each other in a cafe and the rest, well the rest is …well, you.'

Frida couldn't listen to him anymore. She sent Kurt, as he insisted she should call him, away. She told him she needed to think.

CHAPTER THIRTY-ONE

W hen Frida opens the door, she flies into Alicia's arms.

Alicia hugs the young woman hard before peeling her off and saying, 'You must be in shock. Let's make you a cup of coffee.'

They settle into the living room, Alicia next to Frida, and Liam opposite. They sip their coffee (Alicia has hot water with a slice of lemon) and eat the cinnamon buns that Hilda insisted on sending over after hearing Frida's news.

'Look, I had to tell my mom, but she swore she would not breathe a word of it to anyone,' Alicia says, taking a large bite of her bun.

She's got to a stage in her pregnancy when she is always hungry, yet cannot eat very much before feeling full again, so she's constantly snacking.

Frida glances at Alicia and nods at her bump, 'You've got a lot bigger in the last few days. Are you sure your dates are right?'

'Thanks!' Alicia laughs, which makes Frida's face fall.

'Sorry, I didn't mean …you look gorgeous.'

Frida seems a lot calmer now, so Alicia allows herself a smile as she passes one hand over her tummy.

'That's OK. I know what you mean. I'm definitely a lot larger than I was with Stefan.'

Alicia steals a glance at Liam, whose face is a vision of happiness. Seeing his expression makes her think back to her meeting with Patrick and those stupid online reports. She wishes she'd taken a moment to tell him the full story, but with everything that has happened with Dudnikov and Frida, she hasn't had the time.

Besides, it all seems highly irrelevant now.

'I'm sorry to drag you into Mariehamn tonight,' Frida now says. Her head is bent and she's looking down at her hands. 'But I can't get my head around what Mr Eriksson, Kurt, told me. I mean, it can't be true, can it?'

'Would you mind telling us everything from the very beginning?'

Liam's calm voice and sensible question seem to do the trick and Frida starts to recount what Kurt Eriksson told her.

When she finishes, there is a moment when no one speaks.

Frida is wringing her hands and Alicia can see that there are tears in her eyes.

She covers Frida's hands with her own and looks at her. 'It does sound feasible. Of course, the lawyer, Karlsson, can verify it all.'

Frida nods, but then lifts her eyes toward Alicia and

says angrily, 'He's another man who could have told the truth from the beginning. Instead, he deliberately led me to believe that I was the result of some kind of tryst with that awful Dudnikov! All these years, I thought ...'

Alicia squeezes Frida's hands tighter.

'I know but he was bound by client confidentiality. His hands were tied. It wasn't his choice.'

'Alicia is right,' Liam says. 'On the face of it, if you take away the timing, this is good news, isn't it?'

Frida looks over to him.

'How do you make that out?'

'Well, as I understand it, and apologies if we've broken your confidence, but Alicia told me about Andrei's objections.'

'That's OK'.

Liam nods and smiles at Frida, 'Isn't it easier with Andrei if your father isn't the Russian after all?'

Frida sighs and nods.

'Have you spoken with him since you found all this out?'

Frida shakes her head. Again, her eyes become watery.

'I'm afraid that it's not that. What if he just doesn't want to leave Romania? What if ...' Frida gives Liam a sideways glance as if she is embarrassed about what she's about to say.

Liam smiles.

'Don't worry, Frida, I really do understand a little of what you two are going through,' he says and gazes gently at her.

Alicia's heart fills with so much love toward her

husband that she thinks it's going to burst. His eyes meet Alicia's. She knows he, too, is thinking how hard the last two years have been for them. Grieving the loss of their beloved son, living in two different countries, not being able to share their feelings.

And now, they've come through it all. Alicia wants to put her arms around him and rest her head on his chest and tell him what a wonderful and kind man he is.

Frida searches their faces. 'What if he doesn't want to be with me after all?'

Instead of hugging her husband, Alicia takes Frida into her arms.

'Oh, Frida. It's scary, but you do have to tell him. You want to be with him, right? And you want to know if he can't leave his farm, don't you?'

Liam gives a cough.

'Speaking as someone who has moved to another country to be with the love of his life,' he gives Alicia the sweetest of smiles and Alicia feels herself blush, 'I just want to say that you have to give him time. Tell him what you've learned about your real father as soon as possible, but then allow him to get used to the idea.'

'Oh, Liam,' Alicia says, and turning to Frida adds, 'He's right you know.'

'I know he is.'

'Why don't we go, so that you can talk to Andrei?'

Liam's words are so sensible. His fatherly attitude makes Alicia' heart spill over with love for him.

There was a time when Liam and Frida didn't get on at all. It was when Frida thought, wrongly, that their late son Stefan was her unborn baby's father. For Alicia, her misjudgment, or possibly lie, had been the result of deep-felt grief that she was unable to express. She forgave Frida almost as soon as she told them the truth – that it was Stefan and Frida's friend Daniel who was Anne Sofie's true father, the result of them drawing close after the devastating shock of Stefan's death.

Alicia believes that Frida wanted her son to be the father so badly that she convinced herself that he was. But Liam had always been skeptical, and when the truth came out, he couldn't accept that it wasn't maliciously intended.

Those bridges are thankfully now well and truly mended.

CHAPTER THIRTY-TWO

Andrei is leaning across a wooden gate, surveying his land. In the far end of the field, the cows are grazing happily in the early afternoon sun. A slight breeze ruffles the leaves of the large oak tree, which has stood in the middle of the grassland for hundreds of years. Or so his father used to claim.

Andrei inhales deeply and thinks about the many times he has stood here, overlooking the land of his fore-fathers. He wonders what it is that keeps him rooted to this smallholding. Is it because of the hard work of all those farmers before him, who gave their lives to the land to put food into the mouths of their families.

It has never been easy. There's been religious perse-cution, famine, war, revolution. His father never tired of telling him about the years of Communism, when the country suffered widespread poverty.

'Looking healthy, aren't they?'

Andrei hasn't heard his little brother, Mihai, walk up to him.

He nods and returns his younger sibling's smile.

For a moment, they both stand there, Mihai smoking a cigarette, a habit Andrei no longer nags him about. He's already 18, over the age of consent.

'Pining after Frida?'

Mihai nudges Andrei with his elbow while exhaling smoke.

'A disgusting habit,' Andrei grumbles and wafts a hand over his face to get rid of the smell and vapor.

'Don't change the subject. I thought the plan was to leave me in charge here and for you to start a new life on those dreamy islands in the North?'

Andrei turns to look at his brother, who's dropped the cigarette on the ground and is grinding the stub with his foot.

He looks so young to Andrei, with his dark brown hair curling at the nape of his neck. He recalls vividly when their mom died, how he comforted his younger brothers. Daniel didn't shed a tear, but Mihai, just a year his junior, was inconsolable. Later, he wished he could have cried, but it wasn't in his make-up. Just as it wasn't in his nature to discuss his relationship with Frida.

'That's still the plan,' he says, turning his gaze toward the field. 'They're looking healthy, and the milk yield is up,' he adds.

'Don't change the subject.'

Andrei takes a step back and turns his whole body so that he is facing Mihai.

With one arm leaning on the gate, he says, 'You think you can look after all this on your own?'

Mihai purses his lips but doesn't look at Andrei.

'That's just the vote of confidence I need.'

With these words, his kid brother lifts his eyes toward Andrei. Mihai's eyes are darker now, full of emotion.

He is angry at me again.

Andrei takes hold of Mihai's arm. 'That's not what I meant. It's difficult for me to let go. You know that.'

Mihai shrugs his older brother's hand away.

'And you don't trust me. I don't know why. We now have a new farmhand, someone who knows the business well enough and can help me. And there's Maria. And all this fancy equipment your rich girlfriend bought us. And we can FaceTime now that we have fast broadband. Again, courtesy of Frida and all her money. What more do you need? I can do this!'

Andrei tries to take hold of Mihai's arms, but he steps away, continuing to stare at him with an angry expression. His eyes are the spitting image of their mother's and suddenly Andrei has a lump in his throat.

'Look, I haven't really spoken to Frida properly in days.'

'What?'

Now Mihai's expression changes. His eyes are no longer full of anger, but wide and questioning.

'Have you two broken up?'

'No, no. It's just ...well, I don't know.'

Mihai looks hard at his brother. 'You're a fool if you

are going to let her go. She's the best thing that has ever happened to you.'

Andrei wants to call Frida so badly, but he doesn't know what to say. He knows she'll ask him when he is coming over to the islands and that's the one question he doesn't know how to answer. He wants to be with her more than anything.

More than the pull of his family's land?

Each night as he tries to get to sleep in the double bed they collected from IKEA in Brasov, he misses Frida's lithe shape next to him. How he loves the scent of her hair, and the way she sighs with contentment when they make love. Needing to be quiet so as not to let his brother or sister hear them through the thin walls of the old farmhouse, Frida's quiet gasps were the only indication to him that she was close to climaxing. He could then let go, so that they'd share the pleasure of their bodies coming together.

Andrei stares at the light fitting above his head. It's a bamboo affair with a crisscross design that reflects the faint light coming from outside. Frida chose it, one of the few items she changed in this, his parent's bedroom.

They had replaced the lumpy mattress filled with horsehair in the old wooden sleigh bed, with a modern, thick one. But the bare wooden floors remained, along with the rug that relatives from Bucharest had given his parents when they married. He had begun sleeping in this room after his mother died, and before making the journey to Finland to find the truth about his brother Daniel's death.

What he found was love.

If he is honest with himself, he knows that he'd leave the farm if it wasn't for the other thing that he found out in Mariehamn while falling in love with Frida. The fact that he hasn't been able to confront his brother's killer haunts him every second of every day. He doesn't believe the police chief's explanation that Daniel had an accident at sea.

How could he have done?

His younger brother was always careful, and although he didn't have much experience of fishing or rowing, or the sea in general, he was a strong lad. Andrei just cannot accept that he would have drowned just like that.

And then there is the man that he knows – just knows – is responsible for Daniel's death. That Russian devil, Alexander Dudnikov. The same man whose dirty money he has accepted from Frida, his illegitimate child.

Andrei took the money because he was desperate. Without it, the farm would have gone under. They badly needed a new generator with solar panels to reduce the cost of running the new milking machines. They had needed more cattle, plus a new farmhand to help them with the increased herd. Now the farm is making a profit, and he does know that Mihai, with his careful supervision, can run it day to day.

Andrei turns over in bed and presses his eyes shut, trying to stop his thoughts darting between the farm, the Russian, poor Daniel, and Frida, but he cannot settle.

If only he was able to explain to Mihai, why he cannot bring himself to leave the farm and move to the Åland Islands to be with Frida. If only he could discuss the dilemma with him. His brain is a jumble of thoughts.

He tries to imagine leaving Romania. He tries to picture a future with Frida on the beautiful islands, where, she has told him, winters can be bitterly cold, and the snow can stay for months. Andrei had laughed; he knew all about cold winters. When they compared temperatures, Frida was surprised at how low it could go in Sibiu.

But what would he do in Åland? Frida told him he could do anything he wanted. But what would that be? He didn't want to tell Frida he had no ambition to be anything but a farmer. All he has ever known is looking after the cows and the land. He began milking the heifers when he was tall enough to hold the bucket between his legs, and strong enough to withstand the occasional kick the animals gave anyone who had the audacity to touch their udders.

With breaks for school and university, he's worked seven days a week since then, with no holidays. Being away from the farm last summer had been strange. It was both a wonderful break, a painful search for answers about his brother, and an astonishing revelation about himself.

He had no idea that he could feel what he felt about another person. He'd had girlfriends, including a girl in the village before he went to university. By the time he got back, she had found someone else and was married with a kid.

Then there was a beautiful young farmer, whose father had wanted them to marry, but in the end, they both decided their relationship wasn't strong enough. It was Laura who realized he didn't care enough for her. Looking into the dark pools of her eyes, he couldn't disagree. After Laura, Andrei had decided he wasn't suited to being a husband, or even a boyfriend.

And then there was Frida.

Something happened to him when he first saw her, standing on the threshold of her apartment in Mariehamn. To begin with, he'd thought it was his extreme tiredness after days of traveling and sleeping badly on various buses. Or the unfamiliar surroundings – the light nights and being surrounded by water. Or he'd thought that his grief for his younger brother, and the guilt he felt for allowing him to go to the islands in the first place, had made him feel a strong and strange attachment to the young woman who wanted to help him uncover the truth about Daniel.

Soon, however, he realized that he had found true love. It had been the blinding love he felt for Frida that had kept him from going crazy with longing for the farm and his homeland last summer.

So how can she expect him to leave it all behind?

Doesn't she love him with the same passion? Doesn't she want him to be happy?

She expects him to come over to the islands and live off her money. The tainted money from a criminal who has most likely earned it on the back of other people's misery. The same man whom Andrei still suspects killed his brother.

How can Frida think he can possibly accept all this? Forget about the farm, his loss, the Russian villain, and start a new life with her?

Andrei opens his eyes and gazes up at the strange shadows Frida's lamp makes on the back wall of the room.

Tomorrow he will take the lampshade down and replace it with the old simple one.

CHAPTER THIRTY-THREE

fter Alicia and Liam have left her alone and she is able to think a little more clearly, Frida grabs her cell and taps out a message.

Can we talk tomorrow?

She waits for the gray dots that indicate Andrei is writing a reply, but none appear. It's gone half past ten and Andrei is probably already in bed.

She knows mornings start early on the farm, which means that he may already be asleep. She tries not to read anything into the lack of response. It's happened before – Andrei often forgets to take his phone to bed with him and leaves it on the kitchen table downstairs.

Frida thinks back to the life on the farm with Andrei. She wasn't exactly unhappy there. Living together felt so right. Cuddling in bed together at nighttime was wonderful and the love making… Frida hugs herself and tries to keep the tears at bay. She misses Andrei's touch so much. Those dark eyes that gazed at her with such passion! She's never felt this way about anyone.

Not even Stefan.

She realized when living with Andrei that Stefan was just a teenage fantasy. This is something else. She'd never tell Alicia and Liam, of course, but she doubts whether she and Stefan would have made a couple as real grown-ups.

Andrei is a man, not the boy that Stefan was.

Frida glances at her cell again, but there is no response to her message. She tries not to let that worry her.

Tomorrow morning, she will call Andrei and tell him who her real father is. She will try not to ask him about his plans. Liam is right, he will need time to process what Frida has learned in the last few days.

A sudden thought prompts Frida to get up quickly and go to the full-length mirror on the inside of one of the wardrobe doors in her bedroom. She studies her face, bringing it close to the mirror. She then searches for Mia Eriksson on her cell and puts one of the many images that come up next to her face.

No, there are no similarities.

Wait, perhaps she has the same nose? Frida lifts her chin up, just as Mia has in the photo, and there it is: they have the exact same chin! And her lips have the same neat curve and a very similar Cupid's bow. Mia's is enhanced with bright red lipstick and, Frida wouldn't be surprised, a little filler, but there it is: they have the same mouth too.

Frida continues to stare at her own face.

Does Mia know that they are half-sisters?

This thought makes her giggle, and she starts to

laugh uncontrollably. She has to share this thought with someone, and she sends a quick message to Alicia.

The reply comes immediately.

I know. How strange.

Alicia's reaction makes Frida grow serious. She knows how much her friend has suffered from Mia's antics over the years, but now the Erikssons, including Mia, are her family. Will it make her relationship with Alicia more complicated?

Frida doesn't think Mia even knows she exists, whether as her father's other daughter, or as a person in general. She saw Kurt's first daughter (what a thought that is!) occasionally when she was working for him at *Ålandsbladet*, but they never said as much as hello to each other. What Frida is certain about, however, is that Mia will not be pleased with the news.

CHAPTER THIRTY-FOUR

As the ferry makes its slow progress toward Mariehamn, Andrei gazes out of the window. It's a beautiful scene. The sun's rays glitter on the surface of the cobalt sea, which is only intercepted by an occasional skerry. It's gone 6pm, but it could be the middle of the day. The sun hardly sets at this time of the year, Andrei reminds himself. No black nights like the ones they get on the farm.

Andrei cannot but compare this journey to the first one he made to the islands. He had no money and made the trip on several buses, and finally a ferry. He slept badly for the duration of the trip, which lasted for days.

Now he could fly, with only one stop, from Sibiu, the nearest large town to him in Romania, to Stockholm. Then it was just a matter of catching the ferry to Mariehamn.

He is also a completely different person now. Then the pain of losing his brother was new and raw. And he was angry. He needed answers from the people he felt had let his brother down.

The first person on the islands he sought out was Frida.

Her appearance on the doorstep made him forget, momentarily, about his brother. The blue eyes that looked almost as sad as he knew his did. Holding little Anne Sofie, she looked like the Madonna that hung in his parents' bedroom.

When they talked that first evening, it was as if they'd known each other in another lifetime.

Andrei now realizes that he fell for Frida the moment he saw her. That he dreamt of having her in his life from the start.

Why now, when that impossible dream could be true, has he decided that it can't happen?

The journey back to the islands has weakened Andrei's determination. When he left early in the morning, having told his brother Mihai his final decision, he'd been certain about his future. But now, as the small skerries and islands dotted in the sea become more numerous, and there is more land than water, which means they are nearing his destination, he's beginning to doubt himself.

Can he really live without Frida?

When Frida opens the door, she nearly drops the cup of coffee she is holding.

'What are you doing here?'

But Andrei doesn't reply. Instead, he steps inside,

and ditches his backpack on the floor. Frida's cat wraps herself around Andrei's legs, purring loudly. Andrei leans down to pick up the creature.

'You've missed me, have you?'

He's talking to the cat, but instead of looking at Minki, his eyes are burning into Frida's.

She puts her hand out to stroke Minki, but this is too much for the jumpy animal and she leaps out of Andrei's grasp. Immediately, he steps forward and takes Frida into his arms.

Too late, Frida realizes what she was holding in her other hand.

'Ouch,' Andrei exclaims and soon they are both laughing.

Frida has spilled her drink all down Andrei's back.

'Just as well the tea was only warm! Take it off and I'll put it into soak.'

But when Andrei begins to unbutton his shirt, and Frida gets sight of the strong muscles of his bare chest, she presses herself against him again.

'I've missed you,' Andrei whispers in her ear.

'Me too,' Frida says. She pulls herself away and looks into his eyes. She wants to ask him why he is here. Has he come to stay for good?

But before she has time to utter a syllable, Andrei has covered her lips with his and Frida forgets everything. All her nerve endings are in this moment, in this kiss, his touch that she has so longed for.

Her whole body tingles as Andrei begins to stroke her neck, then runs his fingers down her back, only stopping at her bum. He gives it a gentle squeeze and pulls Frida toward him, her back against the wall.

Frida's body is on fire. She unbuttons her top while Andrei unzips her skirt, at the same time stepping out of his jeans.

Frida can feel how hard he is, and she places her hand there. She hears Andrei gasp at her touch.

They can't seem to stop kissing.

Andrei rips at her knickers, and when he finds her innermost place with his fingers, Frida thinks she might faint.

But Andrei has hold of her, and she relaxes, almost reaching a peak.

Andrei has stopped kissing her and is now whispering in her ear.

'Anne Sofie? She sleeping?'

Frida hasn't got the strength to talk, but she nods, and at that moment, Andrei lifts her up, holding her buttocks with both hands, and enters her.

Afterward, they are sitting on the sofa. They are eating a takeaway pizza and drinking beer straight from the bottle. Frida steals a glance at Andrei, who has Minki curled up on his lap. She's just finished a large slice of mushroom and cheese calzone.

'I tried to contact you all day today!'

Andrei swallows a large piece of pizza and takes a swig of his beer.

'I wanted to surprise you.'

Frida leans in to give him a kiss on the cheek and

feels the graze of his dark stubble. She has a flash of memory of his face buried into her neck moments earlier. Feeling the heat rise to her face, she begins to smile.

'What's so funny?' Andrei asks, with a mouthful of pizza.

'Nothing.'

Andrei grins and squeezes Frida's knee, before going back to eating.

Frida doesn't know if this is the right moment to start the serious conversation she knows they have to have, but she cannot keep her thoughts to herself any longer.

'I have a surprise for you.'

Andrei lifts his dark eyes toward Frida and raises his eyebrows, his face a question mark.

'But perhaps we should talk tomorrow? You've had long journey, and …'

Before Frida has time to finish, Andrei has taken her hands in his.

'Tell me now.'

After Frida has told him about the DNA test, and about Kurt Eriksson's visit, Andrei is quiet for a long time. He isn't looking at Frida, but at the last slice of pizza in the brown cardboard box in front of him.

'Say something,' Frida demands.

Andrei turns slowly toward her, his eyes serious and his mouth set in a straight line. 'What do you want me to say? This is a great surprise, but it doesn't change anything.'

Frida's heart begins to beat faster, and her stomach turns over. She feels sick.

'What do you mean?'

Suddenly Frida understands.

'You've come to tell me you're going to stay in Sibiu.'

Andrei turns away from her and, resting his elbows on his thighs, gazes at his hands hanging between his legs.

Frida gets up and goes into kitchen with the pizza cartons. She needs to put a physical distance between her and Andrei now.

Her fears were correct.

Andrei's reluctance to move away had nothing to do with Frida's parentage. He just doesn't love her enough to leave Romania and his family farm behind. Tears prick her eyes, but she takes deep breaths and places the leftover food in the refrigerator. She puts the empty cartons on top of her recycling bin and looks out of the window.

The night has finally fallen, although it never gets fully dark at this time of the year. At nearly midnight, there's a kind of dusk. The lights on the mast of the old barque, the *Pommern*, twinkle in the West Harbor.

Having spent nearly six months at Andrei's farm, Frida now knows that she couldn't leave Mariehamn. She couldn't imagine denying Anne Sofie a childhood in Åland, something she now realizes is a rare privilege in a world full of poverty and suffering.

In Romania, life isn't as easy as it is on the islands. Of course, they have money, which makes all the difference, but what of her daughter's heritage? She needs to be where her mom and grandmother lived. She needs to speak Swedish, rather than Romanian. Frida knows she's being selfish and unfair, because, after all, half of Anne Sofie is Romanian, and Frida is denying her daughter the opportunity to get to know her father's country.

But she will try to visit. She owns half of the farm anyway, so even if Andrei doesn't want her there, she has a right to go.

Suddenly a wave of anger washes over Frida.

Andrei had promised that he would move back to the islands with Frida, once he had ensured that his brother was able to look after things on the farm.

Now he's changed his mind, after Frida has invested God knows how much in the farm.

Frida sits down at the kitchen table and puts her head in her hands.

Of course, the money doesn't matter to her. The farm is also her daughter's heritage, so she was glad to help out. It's the family homestead and it was important for Frida to ensure its future.

No, that's not it.

Frida's breath catches in her throat, and she feels as if her lungs are contracting. There's a hollow feeling in her tummy. She tries to take slow breaths. How is she going to manage without Andrei in her life?

Frida hasn't heard Andrei step into the kitchen. It isn't until he kneels in front of her, taking her hand away from her face that she even notices him.

'Frida …'

Frida pulls her arm away from his grip and gets up.

'It's late. You must be tired. I'm going to make you a bed in the spare bedroom.'

Andrei also gets up and looks at her with those dark eyes. 'Please, we need to talk about this.

'I don't think there is anything more to say.'

Frida doesn't want to look at Andrei. She walks past him and stops at the doorway. 'On second thoughts, you can make your own bed. You know where everything is. Good night.'

Trying to stop the flow of tears that she can feel welling inside of her, and keeping herself upright, she walks through the hall and into her bedroom. She closes the door as quietly as she can with her shaking hands and leans against it. Putting a hand over her mouth, she tries to muffle the cry that escapes from her mouth as soon as she is alone.

What am I going to do?

CHAPTER THIRTY-FIVE

Before he's managed to make up his bed in Frida's spare room, the little cat, Minki, has already settled herself at the foot of it.

At least she loves me.

Andrei knows he's being ridiculous. It's he who has let Frida down, not the other way around.

He knows she loves him.

He's dog tired, but when he lays down on the bed, he feels wide awake. It's still hot, with the air hardly moving in the small bedroom. Andrei gazes out of the window, which has thin curtains on either side. Opposite is an old wooden house, painted in pastel colors, with white framed windows. It's so picturesque, just like everywhere on these islands, where wealthy people live in their large, beautiful homes.

Is he crazy to turn down a better life in Northern Europe with the woman he loves?

Of course he is.

But his country means so much to him too. He will

never forget how his father taught him to look after the farm, and how he struggled over the years to keep a roof over their heads. Andrei took on the task willingly, even if it wasn't easy. How he wishes he'd never let Daniel go. If Daniel hadn't come here, he would never have come here either.

He would never have met Frida.

No, no, he doesn't wish that.

Before he traveled back to Åland this time, he thought his mind was clear. He'd made his decision and he would not be swayed from it. He saw that Mihai was disappointed when he told him he wasn't going to be running the farm on his own after all. But that could not be helped.

He has to admit it was a surprise to hear that Frida's father was a local businessman and not the villainous Russian.

As he watched Frida talk of her discoveries, and of the confession of her real father, now gravely ill, he began to understand that the source of the money that has saved his family farm was just an excuse he'd used to make up his mind.

It wasn't fair on Frida, he knows that, but the truth is that he cannot imagine his life here.

All of this wealth and wellbeing makes him feel as if he's the poor relative. Everyone is kind to him but underneath it all, he knows they feel sorry for him.

Or despise him.

He saw the looks he and Frida drew when he stayed here last summer while trying to find out about his brother. He'd fallen hard for Frida, and to everyone's surprise, they'd soon become an item.

Andrei is certain there were whispers about how he must be with Frida for the sake of her money. He saw the disapproval in Alicia's mum's eyes when Frida first took him to the farm in Sjoland and introduced him as her friend.

Even Ebba, the police chief, had raised her eyebrows when she had realized that Frida was romantically involved with Daniel's brother.

The policewoman also thought that Andrei was using Frida.

He's a proud man and he cannot abide the thought of living off a woman.

No, no.

He has taken enough money from Frida already.

The next morning, when Anne Sofie wakes up at the crack of dawn as always, Frida gives the little girl her breakfast and gets her ready for nursery. Feeling exhausted after a sleepless night, and guilty that she is glad her daughter will be out of the way when she has to say goodbye to Andrei.

She has decided that she is not going to cry anymore. If Andrei doesn't love her enough to stay in Åland, so be it. She cannot make him stay.

She will be happy watching her daughter grow up on the islands. She was alright before she met Andrei, and she will be fine again.

While she helps the little girl to eat her porridge,

Frida keeps an ear out for any movement in the spare bedroom. She has to walk past the door as she carries Anne Sofie to her bedroom to get her dressed, and back again on their way out, but there is just silence.

Is Andrei waiting for her to leave, so that he can sneak out of her apartment like a common thief while she's away?

Frida speaks softly to Anne Sofie as she puts on her new pink sandals, but anger surges inside.

'You like these shoes, don't you?'

'New shoes, new shoes,' Anne Sofie pipes up and claps her tiny hands.

'You want to walk or sit in the stroller?'

Her daughter tries to jump up and down with only one sandal on, shouting, 'Anne Sofie walk.'

'OK,' Frida says, 'but you must stand still so mommy can put your other shoe on.'

When they are finally ready to go, it's already gone half past eight, and they are late for the nursery. Frida tries to convince her daughter to go in the stroller after all, but when she sees Anne Sofie's face crumble at the suggestion, she gives in.

Just as she's struggling to get the door open, while pushing the stroller with one hand and holding Anne Sofie's with the other, a familiar shape appears in the hallway.

Andrei is wearing a pair of boxer shorts and nothing else. Frida tries not to look at his lean, muscular torso, or the coarse hair on his legs, or what lies in between.

'Hello,' he says.

His dark hair is tussled, and his eyes look sleepy.

'Hi.'

Frida tries to take her eyes away from the man's body. She thinks back to all the mornings they woke up together in Romania. They'd often take Anne Sofie into bed with them, and it had felt like they were a proper family.

When the little girl gets sight of Andrei, she turns around and runs into his arms.

'Addy, Addy,' she says.

Frida's resolve not to cry anymore nearly crumbles as she hears her daughter repeat the nickname she's invented for Andrei.

'Anne Sofie, please, we are late for nursery.'

Andrei gives Anne Sofie a squeeze and then, placing her down on the floor as if she is a China doll, tells her, 'Go on, I'll see you later.'

He doesn't look at Frida.

Frida takes her daughter's hand and closes the door behind her.

CHAPTER THIRTY-SIX

Once she has deposited the little girl at the nursery, Frida walks back to her apartment more slowly than usual. Her feet just don't want to carry her home today.

She decides to stop off at the small grocery store at the corner of Norragatan and Ålandsvägen. It takes her out of her way, but she needs time to think. As she walks along the aisles, she bumps into someone.

'Sorry!' the man says and suddenly, Frida sees it's her new neighbor, Ollie.

Frida looks up into the man's blue eyes and sees that she wasn't lying to Alicia when she told her that he was handsome. Ollie is wearing a faded light blue T-shirt and jeans, and his mid-brown hair nearly touches his shoulders. He brushes strands off his face and smiles at Frida.

'Can't decide what to have for breakfast?'

Ollie looks pointedly at Frida's empty basket.

She laughs. 'Yeah, sorry, I was miles away.'

They stand there for a moment looking at each other.

Frida is still embarrassed about the incident with Minki. She's apologized several times when they've passed in the hallway to the apartments, but he's told her to forget about it. To this day, Frida can't imagine what got into Minki.

'I'd better get my brain in gear and buy something,' Frida now says.

She's trying not to blush. The man's gaze is so direct that she feels he can see what she's thinking. That he can tell that she is sad, lonely, and about to be dumped by the boyfriend she thought she was going to spend the rest of her life with.

That first time they met, when Ollie came over to borrow some coffee, and before the incident with the cat, she could tell he was interested in her. She had a feeling he might want to ask her out. Luckily, he didn't, because Frida would have had to say no.

Frida had been relieved. She didn't want to explain her complicated relationship with Andrei to a stranger. Besides, having a relationship with someone in the same small block – however handsome – was a bad idea.

'Unless you'd like to have breakfast with me at the bakery around the corner? You must know that their butter buns are famous? You could tell me all the gossip in our little apartment block over fika. I hear the man in No. 4 never talks to anyone and that the couple in No. 2 have loud parties.'

Frida laughs.

'Isabella is quite the gossip, isn't she? I bet she told you all sorts about me!'

Ollie's face grows serious, and he tilts his head to the side.

'No, she said you were lovely. And I can see she was right.'

Now Frida knows she's blushing like a teenager. Is this man flirting with her?

For goodness' sake, she's a mom and in a serious relationship. Or is she? Didn't Andrei try to tell her last night that it's over?

When Frida doesn't reply, Ollie says, 'Apart from your cat, of course.'

'Oh, please, I really don't know what got into her.'

Ollie takes hold of Frida's arm and squeezes it gently.

'Please stop apologizing. But how about it? Are you up for some coffee and a butter bun this morning?'

Frida considers taking her handsome neighbor up on the offer but then thinks how unfair that would be to the man. She is in love with Andrei, whether he wants her or not, and Ollie is obviously looking for something more than just a neighborly relationship.

Frida glances at the man, and then at her watch.

'I'm sorry, I have to get back …another time, perhaps?'

'OK, I'll take a rain check. Hope you find inspiration,' Ollie says gazing once again at her empty basket.

Frida watches him move away toward the chilled section of the store. She quickly picks up some bread, tomatoes, and lettuce, plus some grapes. Anne Sofie has become very fond of them lately.

As she gets to the self-service check out, she sees

Ollie is at the next one. She nods to him and pays for her groceries. They leave the store at the same time.

'You going straight home?' Ollie asks.

Frida nods and regrets not leaving the shop empty-handed.

She doesn't know what to say to her new neighbor, but as they begin the walk up the hill to the small apartment block, which is really one old house divided up, she finds that Ollie is good company.

He tells her that he is a graphic designer and that he was born in Sweden, but his parents are from the islands.

'I used to come here for two months each summer and vowed to live here when I grew up. It took a few years, but now I'm freelance, and can decide where I live, it was a no-brainer to move to Mariehamn.'

Frida tells him about her mom, and how she had bought the apartment after she died.

'I'm sorry for your loss,' Ollie says.

There's real emotion in his eyes when he says it and this makes Frida wonder if he, too, has lost a parent. But before she has time to ask, they are at the door to their small apartment block. As she's about to open the door, Ollie takes a step toward her and gazes into her eyes.

'I'm very happy I chose this place to live. I love my neighbors already.'

Andrei is sitting at the kitchen table, looking out at the street below when he sees Frida walking with a tall, blond guy toward the house.

What the hell?

They walk very close to one another, their bodies almost touching. Frida is laughing at something the guy says, and then they come to a stop outside the door to the apartment block. The man takes a step toward Frida, and at that point, Andrei gets up and runs through the main lobby to the outside door.

He's just in time, because he's certain the guy was just about to try to kiss Frida. He hasn't even left the country yet and she's already making out with someone else!

His suspicions are confirmed when he sees Frida's cheeks redden at the sight of Andrei.

'Hi, this is Andrei,' she says, taking a step away from both Andrei and the guy. Not meeting Andrei's eyes, she adds, 'And this is my new neighbor, Ollie.'

'Right. Good to meet you,' Ollie says.

The guy doesn't seem in any way embarrassed that Andrei very nearly caught him in the act. Has this been going on for long? Was Frida already moving on while he was back in Romania agonizing over the future of their relationship?

'Hello,' Andrei manages to say. He takes the hand the guy offers and squeezes it hard.

'OK, I'd better get breakfast on the go,' Ollie says and moves inside the building. 'Bye, new neighbor, I'm sure we'll bump into each other again soon.'

He smiles brightly at Frida. He's acting as if Andrei wasn't there.

. . .

Frida is fuming. After Ollie has disappeared inside the building, she walks past Andrei, not daring to look at him, and opens the door to her apartment. She drops her bag of shopping onto the kitchen table and turns toward Andrei, who's followed her into the room.

'What the hell was that?'

'I ask you same question,' he says.

Frida can't believe her ears. Blood is rushing so hard between them that she is surprised she can hear at all. Even her vision is blurred. How can this man make her so angry?

'What right do you have to tell me what to do or who to talk to? Ollie is a new neighbor who, as unlikely as it seems, wanted to ask me out for breakfast. I said no, but we walked home from the store since we both live in the same building.'

Frida crosses her arms over her chest and glares at Andrei.

But instead of seeing his dark eyes become even blacker as he challenges her, she sees him lower them and sit down at the table in front of an empty cup of coffee. He puts his head into his hands and lets out a loud groan.

Frida stares at his bent head, not knowing what to do. She cannot but notice the bulging biceps as he flexes his arms. He's wearing the same shirt he had on last night, rolled up at the sleeves. Suddenly he starts to shake, and Frida sits down opposite him, placing her hands on his wrists. She tries to pull at them, to see his face, but he is stronger than her.

'Shh, it's OK,' she says and begins to stroke his arms instead.

For a while, they sit while Andrei sobs so hard that his whole body shakes. When he calms down a little, Frida gets up and fetches a box of tissues.

'Here,' she says and puts them on the table in front of him.

Only then does Andrei remove his arms and lift his eyes to look at Frida.

'I'm sorry,' he says.

Frida has never seen a man cry. She grew up without a father, thanks to Kurt Eriksson's selfishness, and she never had a male role model in her life. None of her past boyfriends were criers. Even Stefan, Alicia's sensitive son and her first love, never shed a tear each time they had to part, while Frida cried her eyes out. The tears she'd shed for him after he died made her almost numb to any emotion. It wasn't until Anne Sofie was born that she began to have normal feelings again.

Now that Andrei is so upset, the powerlessness she's felt ever since she returned to the islands has left her. She feels strangely strong. Perhaps it's motherhood that has made her more capable of holding onto her own tears and controlling her emotions.

'It's OK,' Frida now says, because she doesn't know what his tears, or his apology, mean.

Is Andrei sorry because he cried? Or because their relationship is ending? Or because he realizes that if he leaves, Frida might – one day – move on to someone else. Is he sorry for himself or for acting stupidly over Ollie.

She wants to ask but is afraid there will be another flood of tears.

Andrei takes Frida's hands in his, and with a shaking voice says, 'I love you.'

And just like that Frida loses control of her emotions.

'I love you too,' she says and feels the tears pool in her eyes.

'Don't cry,' Andrei says and gets up to take her into his arms.

'But I can't bear it if you leave,' Frida sobs against his chest.

All her resolve to let Andrei go without pleading for him to stay has left her. She wipes her eyes and pulls herself away from him to look into his eyes.

'I'm not leaving.'

Andrei bends down to kiss her lips.

CHAPTER THIRTY-SEVEN

P atrick is packing when he gets another message from Mia asking to meet her urgently. He looks at the words on his cell and shakes his head. He's told her after the argument in the villa, and after another one over the phone when Mia shouted at him about his 'lack of interest in the girls' futures', that he was leaving for the north.

That piece of news led to another shouting match, and in the end, Patrick put the phone down.

He doesn't need the hassle.

Mia's outbursts remind him of their marriage, much of which was spent fighting. Rather, he was forced to listen to Mia's nagging or raving.

Besides, if Patrick can't have Alicia, he isn't going to take Mia as a second-best prize. It wouldn't be fair on him or Mia.

Patrick spent the rest of the previous day, right after the tongue-lashing from Mia, with his daughters. They'd had a fantastic time on the beach, and he told them about the job he'd been promised in Luleå.

'I'll miss you, Pappa,' Frederica, the youngest, had said, and her words nearly broke his resolve.

But then Sara said, 'Don't be stupid. We'll probably see more of him than we do now. Besides, Luleå is cool!'

Both girls had hugged Patrick and they'd planned for the girls to visit him by train.

Patrick is so proud of Sara. She's an avid follower of Greta Thunberg, the young environmental activist. She's been vegan for over a year now, wears only second-hand clothes and refuses to fly.

This naturally annoys Mia.

Patrick hopes that Sara's social conscience is not just a teenage rebellion against her mother. Looking at her now, he's certain it isn't.

Frederica, too, has grown into a confident, kind young girl. Patrick knows he will miss them, but he also knows that he has to get away from the Erikssons.

And the islands.

He can't stay to watch Alicia have a child and see her marriage to Liam flourish. He knows he should be selfless, and that loving somebody means also setting them free. He can do that, but he can't be there to witness it.

Perhaps sometime in the future, but not now.

When his phone pings again, Patrick gives a sigh. When will the woman give up?

But when he sees that the message is from Alicia, he immediately opens it up.

I have some great news about Dudnikov. Can you come over?

Alicia is standing at the door to the farmhouse in Sjoland. She's wearing a yellow cotton dress, showing off her pregnant form. She looks radiant, and Patrick cannot but smile as he walks from his car toward her.

When he's reached the doorway, he hesitates for a moment, but Alicia takes a step closer and gives him a hug. He holds her tightly, as far as her tummy allows. He closes his eyes briefly and enjoys the scent of her. When he opens his eyes again, he can see Hilda in the kitchen. She has a wide smile on her face, but then turns away and disappears from view.

Alicia lets go of him and they gaze at each other for a moment.

'Thank you for coming over.'

'It's always lovely to see you.'

Alicia's eyebrows shoot up.

'Please, Patrick.'

Hilda comes into the hallway. 'Come on, the coffee is getting cold.'

As he steps inside the kitchen, Patrick sees that Liam is sitting at the other side of the table, which is laden with a plate piled high with Hilda's famous cinnamon buns, as well as a lemon cake and a tray of open sandwiches.

'Liam,' Patrick says and the other man nods. He too, though, is smiling widely.

'Are you going to tell me what you are celebrating?' Patrick adds as Hilda gestures for him to sit down opposite Liam.

Alicia settles herself next to her husband.

'I think Alicia should tell the story,' Hilda says, lifting the plate of sandwiches and offering them to Patrick.

CHAPTER THIRTY-EIGHT

'You did what? But you're, you're …'

Patrick cannot believe what he is hearing.

'I tried to tell her that she was in no condition to start chasing a dangerous criminal around the islands in the middle of the night,' Liam gives Patrick a conspiratorial look, 'but you know what she's like.'

'The end result is that Dudnikov is behind bars. At last!' Alicia says, ignoring both men.

She lifts her mug of tea and adds, 'So I think that merits a toast!'

The others raise their cups too, and clink them together.

'I think we need champagne, really, but we'll wait until you've had the baby,' Hilda says. Patrick sees that her eyes are moist.

'When I think about the danger you were in …'

Hilda wipes her eyes with her napkin, and Alicia reaches over and puts her hand over her mom's.

'Don't worry, Hilda, she's not going to pull another stunt like that again,' Liam says.

Patrick is surprised to see that Alicia just smiles and gives Liam a loving look. He knows that he'd have been shot down by Alicia if he had ever said something like that.

But she was never pregnant with Patrick's child.

'When did this happen? I haven't heard it in the news or seen anything about it online.'

Patrick can't believe that none of his journalist friends have contacted him with the news. They all know his interest in the Russian.

'Oh, it's being kept under wraps for now, until he is moved to the mainland,' Liam says. 'That's why we wanted to tell you in person. You cannot trust the internet or the phones anymore. He is being transported to the mainland as we speak.'

Patrick gazes at Liam and nods. The journalist in him wants to leave right now and report this to the world.

'We'd appreciate it if you didn't breathe a word about this to anyone,' Alicia says, her eyes fixed on his.

She knows me too well.

'Of course not.'

'She means it, Patrick. We're counting on your discretion,' Hilda says.

The suddenly stern expression on the older woman's face reminds Patrick of the shameful events of last year, when he wrote an article about how the farm in Sjoland had been employing trafficked labor from Romania and other former Communist countries. He hadn't even consulted Alicia before publishing it in the main Swedish newspaper, *Journalen*.

'I do mean it, Patrick,' Alicia adds. 'If the story comes out too soon, it could jeopardize the whole operation of getting that man in front of a court to answer for his vile criminal actions. We have no idea who his associates here are. We can't even be certain that he hasn't got contacts in the Russian consulate in Mariehamn. He was pretty bold moving around here, so Ebba is being ultra-careful.'

Patrick nods.

He can't believe that these good people, whom he has treated so badly in the past, would let him into their confidence.

He thinks back to the day he thought he spotted the Russian, wondering if it really was him after all. He looks around the table, from Liam to Alicia and to Hilda, and decides he's not going to tell them about the sighting.

It's no longer relevant.

Besides, he knows Alicia would be disappointed in him because he hadn't told her, or the police chief, about spotting the criminal on the islands.

Alicia inhales deeply. 'I myself saw Dudnikov a couple of days before he was caught, but I convinced myself it couldn't possibly be him.'

'I did too!' Patrick blurts out before he knows what he's doing.

Instead of showing disappointment, he sees Alicia is smiling. She shrugs her shoulders.

'By the East Harbor?'

Patrick nods.

'But I thought it couldn't possibly be him. He was onboard this huge yacht …'

'*Babushka*?' Alicia says, interrupting Patrick.

'Yes! I was walking along the jetties, dreaming about having a sailing boat again, and there he was.'

As his eyes meet Alicia's, he gets an image of the two of them making love in the forward cabin on his old yacht. He knows Alicia, too, is thinking about it. A faint blush covers her cheeks, and she looks away, before getting up.

'Well, we should both have trusted our instincts,' she says and leaves the table to refill her mug of tea. Hilda too goes to the kitchen counter to get more coffee to pour into their cups.

The two women sit back down and for a moment everyone is quiet, deep in their own thoughts.

Patrick is the first one to speak.

'I appreciate you telling me all this and I promise not to write about it until it's out, but,' here he gazes at Alicia, ignoring the alarm he sees in Hilda's eyes, 'could you ask Ebba to let me know as soon as I can. I would love a scoop.'

Patrick holds Alicia's gaze for a moment, and then lowers his eyes.

'Going after the Russian did send me to hospital,' he adds quietly.

There's another moment of silence and Patrick thinks he's blown it.

'I have to ask, I'm a journalist and it's my duty to report important events,' he pleads, lifting his eyes again.

He glances at the others around the table, who are exchanging looks.

'I think that's a reasonable request,' Liam says after a while. He's speaking slowly, his eyes on Alicia, who sighs deeply.

'I'll talk to Ebba, but I can't promise anything.'

Patrick smiles at Alicia.

'I better get going,' he says.

Alicia gets up and walks him out to his car.

'Thank you for agreeing to talk to Ebba.'

They're standing by Patrick's car. He's got his keys in his hands and he's holding Alicia's eyes.

She gives him a lopsided grin.

'I can't promise anything. You're not exactly her favorite reporter right now.'

Patrick nods.

Her expression changes when she speaks again, 'By the way, I meant to ask you, how is Kurt? Frida told us about his illness and about the rest of it. I can hardly believe he is her father!'

Patrick looks down at his feet.

'He's not so good. Mia is all over the place, but you know how she is. Mainly angry at me.'

Alicia's eyebrows shoot up.

'Didn't look like that when I saw you in Mariehamn together.'

'No, but I guess she wants more from me than I'm able to give right now.'

Patrick gazes at Alicia. Her expression is neutral,

she's not sad, angry, or happy. She shrugs her shoulders and says, 'I'm sure the two of you will work it out.'

'Well …' Patrick starts but Alicia stops him by giving him a quick hug.

'Bye, Patrick.'

She turns to go back to the house. A sudden breeze catches her yellow dress revealing the roundness of her pregnant form.

'I'm moving back up north,' Patrick blurts out.

He bites his lip. He wasn't going to tell Alicia about his plans. He's not sure why, but he wanted her to find out from someone else, perhaps Frida via the family.

In his dreams – or fantasy, more like it – he wanted her to feel a pang of regret at the news that she would never bump into him while out and about in Mariehamn. Or be able to call on him whenever she wanted to, for a chat, or whatever.

Not that she ever did that anymore.

But seeing her now, glowing in her pregnancy, and together with her husband, to whom she has been married for more than a decade, maybe even two, has shown him that she belongs here in Sjoland and not with him.

Alicia is not the same person that Patrick fell in love with. And perhaps he isn't that same person who fell in love with Alicia.

Alicia turns around slowly: 'It's none of my business but doesn't your family need you right now?'

CHAPTER THIRTY-NINE

'I don't want to talk to you.'

Once again, Kurt Eriksson is standing outside the door to Frida's apartment.

She's not replied to any of his messages. She's just not had the headspace to deal with Kurt bloody Eriksson.

Her time has been taken up by Andrei and his sudden reappearance. His insistence that he would not move to the islands, followed swiftly by a complete turnaround, has been an emotional rollercoaster. Frida is deliriously happy, but at the back of her mind there's a tiny doubt about Andrei's resolve.

What if he doesn't get employment on the islands? She's told him over and again that he doesn't need to work, but he insists that he wants to make his own money and not rely on her inheritance.

But every time she sees him sitting at the kitchen table, head bent down at his phone, she knows he will stay. When he lifts his head and smiles, his dark eyes meeting hers, she is convinced that they will never be apart again. When he takes her into his arms and makes love to her, quietly in the evenings, when Anne Sofie is asleep next door, and with more abandon during the day, when they are alone, she cannot imagine life without him.

The dramatic way Dudnikov was apprehended has also occupied her thoughts, as has the fact that he isn't her father after all. Frida simply doesn't have the capacity to think about a new candidate for the post of her wealthy, absent father.

Kurt Eriksson's tan face crumbles at Frida's unfriendly demeanor.

Is he about to cry?

Frida takes pity on the man.

Sighing, she moves away from the door and lets Kurt into the apartment.

Frida is on her own. She's just dropped Anne Sofie off at pre-school and Andrei has gone into town to find out about language courses. Frida had offered to go with him in case he needed an interpreter, but he had insisted on doing things for himself.

'You can't babysit me forever,' he'd said kissing Frida on the mouth.

Frida indicates with her hand for Kurt Eriksson to come into the living room.

'Take a seat. Do you want a coffee?'

She follows him and watches as the old man slumps down on the sofa facing her. Since she last saw him, he's lost weight. He looks diminished, somehow.

'Thank you,' he says.

His face, although tan, is gray-looking and his eyes are sunken and bloodshot.

'Are you OK?'

Instead of going into the kitchen to get the coffee, Frida sits opposite the man. The man who says he is her father.

A weak smile forms on Kurt Eriksson's face. He places his hands in his lap. Frida sees the deep veins and liver spots that cover the backs of them. She wonders how old he is. How old he was when he started the love affair with her mom.

Love affair. Was true love ever part of the affair?

To stop the anger rising inside her, she gets up to make the coffee.

Frida brings a cafetière, two cups with saucers (the best ones that her mom left) and some of Hilda's cinnamon buns that Alicia and Liam brought over the other day.

'How lovely, thank you so much.'

Kurt picks up a coffee cup, but Frida can see his hands are shaking.

'Would you like a cinnamon bun? They're made by Hilda Ulsson, you know Alicia's mom?'

Again, a smile briefly brightens Eriksson's face. His pale eyes meet Frida's. 'Sorry, I can't …my appetite has gone now. It's very nice of you, though. I hear they are the best on the islands.'

Frida nods and Kurt sets the cup of coffee down on the table between them.

'But I didn't come here to talk about Hilda's baking, as wonderful as it is.'

'No.'

There is a brief silence between them. Frida cannot face eating anything either, so she just sips her coffee.

'I worshipped your mother.'

Kurt Eriksson's eyes are on her, challenging her to face him. Frida meets his gaze. Is the man opposite her, the most powerful man on the islands, really her father?

'So you claim.'

Kurt Eriksson lowers his eyes and looks down at his hands. 'It was difficult.'

Frida snorts. 'I bet!'

Kurt owns more property and businesses on these islands than anyone else, including the largest super-market and the main newspaper. He has the grandest house in town with uninterrupted sea views, and an estate covering a whole vast peninsula only a few minutes' drive from Mariehamn. His daughter swans around town in her designer gear, and his wife is a cele-brated author, wealthy in her own right.

How could it be too difficult for such a man to divorce and marry another woman if he truly loved her?

'Would you ever have told me the truth if you hadn't fallen ill?'

Kurt Eriksson lifts his head. He is visibly affected by Frida's words as if she'd slapped him. For a brief moment, Frida regrets her harsh tone.

When she remembers the sorry state her mother was in during the last few years of her life, she knows she has the right to ask the man in front of her these sorts of questions.

If he had left his wife and been a proper partner – even a husband – to her mom, and a father to her, how different would their lives have been?

'As I said, it's been difficult, but I provided well for Sirpa – and you.'

Frida can't believe her ears.

'Money isn't everything!'

She almost spits out the words, and again Kurt looks hurt. He leans backward and holds onto his stomach. He takes a few deep breaths in and out.

'Are you OK?'

Suddenly, Frida is filled with pity. Surprised by her own feelings, she gets up and sits next to the man.

His eyes are closed, and he is gasping for air.

Frida places a hand on his shoulder.

'Can I do anything?'

Kurt shakes his head, but it's obvious he's in pain and cannot speak because of it. Frida doesn't know what to do.

'Should I call an ambulance?'

When he doesn't answer, Frida sits and waits. She regards the man sitting next to her. Even though he is slumped on the sofa, as if his very bones are too heavy for his spine to support, there's something familiar about the line of his shoulders and the length of his fingers.

Slowly, it dawns on Frida that she can see aspects of her little daughter. Kurt has the same curve to his shoulders, and the same, almost stubby arms jutting out of his torso. The chin, too, is one that she recognizes in her daughter. And herself. It's square with a very determined air to it. She also has Kurt's high forehead.

'If you are up to it, you can meet Anne Sofie later today.'

CHAPTER FORTY

A licia cannot believe the change in Frida. Her face, lately etched with worry, is relaxed and there is a glow about her that Alicia hasn't seen before. They're sitting in the Svarta Katten cafe, sipping their drinks.

Alicia has ordered an Ålandspannkaka, but after eating just a couple of mouthfuls, her tummy begins to press against her ribcage.

'I love to see you so happy.'

A faint blush rises to the young woman's face.

Frida looks down at her hands, and suddenly Alicia spots something. Something glittery on Frida's ring finger.

'Goodness, congratulations! Why didn't you tell me?'

Frida's smile reaches from one side of her face to the other. Alicia cannot remember seeing her this happy. Of course, she was overjoyed when Anne Sofie was born, but the effort of having just given birth had also been evident.

Frida lifts her hand and turns it around to show Alicia the ring. It's truly magnificent. A cluster of diamonds beautifully arranged in a gold setting. Alicia has never seen anything like it. It's brilliant and unique.

'It just happened. That's why I wanted to see you. I didn't want to tell you about the news over the phone.'

'Come here, I want a hug and it's too cumbersome to lift myself to give you one!'

Frida gets up and wraps her arms around Alicia's shoulders.

'When are you due again?' Frida asks when she's settled back down opposite Alicia.

'Oh, I've still got too long to go, but I don't want to talk about me. Tell me everything. How he proposed, everything. And show me that ring again! It's beautiful!'

While Alicia is examining what is truly a magnificent piece of jewelry, Frida begins to speak. She is breathless, and when Alicia lifts her eyes from the ring to the young woman's face, she can see how excited she is.

Affection for Frida fills Alicia's heart. When they first met at the *Ålandsbladet* offices over two years ago, she had no idea what a capable and strong woman Frida would turn out to be. She was then just an angry teenager, who Alicia had no idea was grieving for the same person as her – her son. When she found out that Frida had been Stefan's girlfriend and was pregnant, she assumed, or hoped, that the child was Stefan's. Her own desire to have a baby, something of Stefan, in this world, was so overwhelming that she had encouraged Frida to go along with that dream.

That's all gone and forgotten now. Even if Anne Sofie isn't her real grandchild, the little girl and Frida feel like family. And that's what's important.

Perhaps in the future, Frida will have another child, and all their children can become honorary cousins.

Alicia places a hand on her belly. The baby is moving inside her. She's certain it's a boy again, even though she's refused to be told the sex of the baby.

'This is Andrei's great-grandmother's ring. He had it couriered from Romania. It's somehow survived all the troubles that the country has suffered. His great-grandfather was originally from Russia, and Andrei's mom kept it hidden and refused to have it sold even when they hardly had enough money for food. Isn't it wonderful?'

Smiling, Alicia nods.

'And did he go on bended knee?'

Again, Frida blushes.

'He did. Last night. I couldn't believe it. You know when Kurt came to see me, Andrei had just gone into town to find out about something. He refused to allow me to go with him. I'd invited Kurt back to meet Anne Sofie and Andrei was behaving a bit strangely. I thought it was to do with suddenly discovering that Kurt was my father, but when he left and we had put Anne Sofie to bed, he hugged me and told me he wanted to talk to me. I was so scared. I thought …'

A single tear runs down Frida's cheek.

'Oh, darling girl! It's been a roller-coaster of emotions for you, hasn't it?'

Frida wipes the tear away and nods.

'Instead of telling me he'd changed his mind about staying, as I'd feared, he went down on one knee and brought out a small box from the pocket of his jeans. I was so shocked!'

'There is something else I want to talk to you about,' Frida adds.

Alicia looks at her young friend. Her expression is open, and a wide smile covers her face.

'You know I appreciate everything you – and Hilda – have done for me over the years?'

Alicia's face grows serious, and she places her hand on top of Frida's.

'What's the matter?'

'Nothing. It's just …'

Alicia removes her hand and leans back in her chair.

'Oh, no. You're not moving to Romania with Andrei, are you?'

Frida gives out a short laugh. It comes out more like a snort.

'Oh, no! We've agreed that we will live here. I feel very selfish, but I just can't leave the islands.'

Alicia lets out a long breath. She places her hand on her belly and smiles again.

'Phew. You say we've done so much for you, but it's mutual. I don't know how I would have managed these past two years without you and Anne Sofie.'

Alicia glances down at her tummy again.

'And soon she'll have a little friend to play with. I want to say cousin, but …'

Frida leans across the table so that she's closer to Alicia's face.

'I consider you as my true family here on the islands.'

Alicia opens her mouth and then closes it again. She nods a few times and then bites her lower lip. Perhaps Frida is worried about her newfound blood ties to the Eriksson family?

She takes Frida's hands into hers and looks into her eyes.

'You know I don't care for Mia. She's got her own problems, I'm sure, but she's been quite nasty to me ever since I settled here. And well, even before. At school she was a bully.'

Frida looks down at their linked hands and lifts her eyes to meet Alicia's She doesn't know what to say.

'But you can't do anything about genetics. Mia is your half-sister and I'll just have to live with the fact. Have you spoken to her yet?'

Frida shakes her head. Kurt Eriksson, or her dad, as he now wants her to call him, has sent messages to her nearly every day since she let him meet Anne Sofie.

'Kurt wants us all to meet.'

Frida can't look at Alicia. Instead, she gazes at her belly, which is almost touching the table. Alicia is wearing a pale-yellow dress with short frilly sleeves that flutter in the air from a nearby fan.

Alicia removes her hands from under Frida's and lifts her chin up so that she can look into her eyes.

'Look, Patrick and I are over. Have been for ages now. I don't care for Mia, but perhaps it's her problems that have made her nasty. You never know what people are going through. You must keep an open mind and give her a chance. For Anne Sofie's sake.'

Frida nods. She can't speak. Alicia's kindness is too overwhelming.

'I also know that her two daughters, Sara and Frederica, are very nice. I'm sure they'll adore you. And they will fall in love with little Anne Sofie!'

As Frida walks home to her apartment, where she knows Andrei is waiting, she wonders again how it will all work out. The islands, and the city of Mariehamn, are so small that even if she goes against Kurt's wishes (she still can't bring herself to call him 'Dad') and refuses to meet his family, she will bump into members of the Eriksson clan eventually.

Then there's Anne Sofie.

She wants her daughter to feel as if she belongs here. And that she is part of the Eriksson family, just as she is one of the Tamas in Romania. Frida knows that she'll always be part of the Ulssons in Sjoland, even if there is no blood relation.

Another of her worries is Andrei. Will Mia and her mom look down on her Romanian boyfriend?

Frida touches her ring with her thumb. The unfamiliar sensation on her finger makes her remember that Andrei is much more than a boyfriend now.

He is her fiancé!

As she opens the door to the apartment block, she decides that if they don't like her or Andrei, so be it. It wasn't Frida's choice to be part of that family.

It's all Kurt Eriksson's doing.

CHAPTER FORTY-ONE

The villa nestles behind a set of wide gates, which open automatically as the car sent to get them approaches.

Frida puts her hand on Anne Sofie's knee. She's sitting in a child seat between her and Andrei. Over the little girl's head, she gives what she hopes is an encouraging smile to her fiancé.

He is looking as handsome as ever in his linen trousers and shirt. He'd asked about a jacket, but Frida told him not to bother. The temperature was once again approaching 30°C, with little or no wind, and Frida doesn't want him to be uncomfortable all afternoon.

She glances down at her own dress, a lime green wrap-around Stine Goya number that she ordered online a few days ago. It's loud, but that's Frida. Even though her hair is now her natural hue, she still loves color.

She's embarrassed about how long it took to get herself and Anne Sofie ready.

While she discarded one outfit after another Andrei

sat on the sofa in the lounge and read – or pretended to read, Frida isn't certain – that day's copy of the *Ålandsbladet*.

'You know that's owned by him – or them, don't you?' Frida shouted to him through the door. She was in her underwear and instead of answering, Andrei lowered the paper and gave her a wicked smile.

'I think you go just like that.'

Frida had grinned and wiggled her chest at him before pushing the door to with her foot.

'Yeah, that would get the day off to a wonderful start.'

'What you doing, mamma?' Anne Sofie piped up.

Anne Sofie was sitting on her (their!) bedroom floor, surrounded by her favorite toys. Her soft unicorn, tons of Moomin books, and wooden bricks that she used to build a tower only to let it topple halfway through construction.

'Mommy is being silly, darling.'

In the end, Frida had settled on the dress she'd planned to wear all along. Anne Sofie also had a frock in the same neon color, but hers had white dots. She knew it was silly, but she wanted to match her clothing to that of her daughter. It was irrational, but for some reason Frida felt she needed to show the mighty Eriksson family that Anne Sofie was hers and hers alone.

Mia glances down the row Erikssons, all of whom are standing in the front garden as if waiting for a royal visit.

Pappa had insisted that they should all be there,

including his two granddaughters, and – more surprisingly – Patrick. It hadn't been as difficult to get him to postpone his move up to northern Sweden as it had been to get her two teenage daughters to join the family lunch.

'Mamma, what are we going to do all day? It's going to be sooo boooriiing.'

Sara had drawn out the syllables of the last two words as long as she could, infuriating Mia even further. As if this 'family lunch' wasn't stressing her enough.

They'd been in her and Patrick's bedroom, Mia putting on her makeup and the two girls, still in their ripped jean shorts and loose-fitting T-shirts, standing behind her.

Mia had stopped applying mascara and stared in what she hoped was an authoritative way at her daughters' reflection in the mirror.

'You will both be there. That's my orders, and what's more that is also what your grandpa, *mofa*, has …'

Suddenly Mia's voice had broken down. She lowered her eyes, gazing at her dressing table and the mess of pots and jars and other makeup. Thank goodness their old housekeeper would come in later and sort it all out. Frankly, Mia just didn't have the energy to put everything back. Not when she had so much else to deal with.

She pushed back the tears that threatened to fill her eyes and looked back at the girls. 'You know *mofa* isn't very well. He'd like you to meet Frida and her daughter and boyfriend, so …'

Almost in unison, Sara, the older leader of the small pack, and her little sister, Frederica, lifted and lowered their slender shoulders. At the same time, they each took in a breath and theatrically pushed it out again through pursed lips.

Mia resumed brushing mascara onto her lashes.

She looked at her reflection and was satisfied. That's when she noticed that her daughters were still standing behind her.

'Get ready, they'll be here in about fifteen minutes!'

But neither of them moved.

It was Frederica who spoke. In almost a whisper she asked, 'Is *mofa* going to die?'

Mia had managed to convince the tearful Frederica and even Sara, who'd been gazing at her with mistrust in her eyes, that their grandfather wasn't going to die anytime soon.

She was furious when she heard that Patrick had told them the exact opposite. She would have to speak to him later.

But now, standing in line like a goddamn welcoming committee to royalty, she looks past Patrick and the girls, at her father and isn't certain how long she can keep up the pretense with her daughters.

Kurt is thin and he's holding onto a stick like an old man. It's something the hospital in Sweden has given him. He is now going there three times a week, on a small plane that he chartered each summer.

Not that Mia was often given the opportunity to use it. Even when Patrick was living in Sweden, she wasn't allowed to take the girls on the plane to see him.

'That's not a business trip!' Her father would bellow if she as much as asked.

Mia shifts on her high heels and sighs. At least he's now agreed to some treatment. She knew as soon as her mom got involved that her father would cave in.

No one goes against Beatrice's wishes.

Her mom, standing next to her dad, has her hand around his waist, as if she is holding him upright. She's wearing a pair of wide palazzo pants and a silky top, with flat sandals.

Mia has opted for a simple white cotton Prada dress, which hugs her curves perfectly, and a pair of white Jimmy Choo sandals. Her gold jewelry is all Versace. She's going to show that little upstart what real style is all about.

When the car drives in through the gate, Mia gasps. Her father has sent their best Bentley to collect the trio? She glances at her mom, but she doesn't show any emotion.

Mia has overheard the many arguments her parents have had about Frida Anttila. In their hushed voices, which they always imagine Mia can't hear, they have gone back and forth about why Kurt hadn't said anything until now. About how much money he gave her mother over the years. (A couple of million, it seems.)

Mia isn't certain, but she believes this lunch is a reward for all those trips to the hospital and his agreement to have treatment. That must mean that her mom has forgiven him the affair, keeping Frida a secret, and all the money he gave them.

That's a lot to overlook.

Mia doesn't think she'd be able to be so magnanimous.

Although she forgave Patrick his sordid little affair with Alicia, that was a short relationship compared with her dad and the waitress.

A waitress! How crass.

CHAPTER FORTY-TWO

Frida has to carry Anne Sofie out of the car. She has suddenly become very shy. She's probably picked up the tensions of the occasion, which Frida completely understands. She wishes she had her mom with her too. The thought of all the suffering her mom had to go through suddenly gives Frida strength and she steps forward.

The first person to meet them is Beatrice, Kurt's wife, the famous author.

'We've been so looking forward to meeting you,' she says, taking Frida's hand in both of hers and moving it up and down a few times.

'Thank you, Mrs Eriksson.'

'Please call me Beatrice.'

Leaning on a stick, Kurt takes a slow step forward to introduce her to Mia.

'This is my first daughter, Mia,' he says, smiling at Frida.

Frida can see that his words have a terrible effect on Mia. Her smile, which had been a smirk at best, drops. She gives Frida a quick, limp handshake.

'And Patrick you already know,' Kurt continues, taking another step along the line of Eriksson family members, which looks more like a welcoming committee.

'And who's this?' Patrick says, smiling at Anne Sofie.

He makes a fuss of the little girl, and for the first time, Frida sees how Alicia might have fallen for this man.

His daughters, the two slender teenagers, who at first looked as if they'd rather be anywhere else, now also start to play with Anne Sofie. When Frida puts her down and she starts to totter around, the atmosphere suddenly changes.

'She's adorable,' the younger of the two girls exclaims, melting Frida's heart.

Anne Sofie gives the girl a brilliant smile and reaches out her arms.

'May I?' The girl asks and Frida nods.

'She may be heavier than you think, Frederica,' Patrick says. He glances quickly at Frida to make sure it really is alright for his daughter to pick up Anne Sofie. Frida nods.

Beatrice, who looks elegant in loose-fitting pants and top, stretches out her hand and smiles at Frida. 'Let's go over to the back terrace and get some drinks. Please.'

The two teenagers are taking Anne Sofie around the

house. She has decided to walk again, and totters between the two girls, holding their hands.

Frida can't quite believe her eyes. Anne Sofie is a friendly little child, but she's never taken to strangers as quickly as she has to Sara and Frederica. Does she sense there is a blood connection?

If only it was so easy for all of us to accept a new family.

Before following Mrs Eriksson, Frida glances back at Andrei, who is now talking to Patrick. They're deep in conversation, but then Kurt Eriksson nudges Patrick with his stick.

'Come on you two, surely you're thirsty in this heat?'

There is a glint in Kurt's eyes that Frida hasn't seen before. He looks more like a kindly uncle than the scary former boss, or the sad, sick man who visited her. Perhaps the treatment he is taking is working after all?

He makes his way past the two men and toward Frida.

'Give me your arm, young lady,' he says

They move forward slowly, Frida adjusting to the old man's restricted pace. As they walk along, Frida glances back at the only person who hasn't moved from the front patio.

Mia is standing as still as a statue. Her white dress is adorned with chunky gold jewelry. She's also wearing high-heeled sandals that show off her bright red toenails. She looks as if she's on a fashion shoot rather than on the Åland islands, with its relaxed vibe and summer visitors looking for the simple life. Unwittingly, Frida shakes her head at Mia, who is looking down at her hands. Suddenly, Mia lifts her head and sees Frida's eyes on her.

She brings her hands together and gives Frida a silent clap.

CHAPTER FORTY-THREE

The long table on the terrace overlooking the sea is covered with a white tablecloth, which flutters in the gentle breeze. It could be a scene from an interiors magazine.

Or more like a TV drama.

As they sit down at the 'informal lunch', as Mia put it when she asked him to postpone his return to the north, Patrick can't pretend that he isn't enjoying the spectacle of the Eriksson clan's discomfort.

As he looks around the table, only his girls and – amazingly – Kurt seem to be at ease. He feels sorry for poor Frida, who sits next to Kurt. She's listening to him with her head slightly cocked and holding her daughter in her lap. At the same time, she's taking in the table setting and trying to keep the little girl's legs from kicking it.

The scene reminds him of the first time he was invited to dinner with the Erikssons. It was at their town house in Mariehamn. He was worried about which pieces of cutlery to use, or whether he would break anything.

Today, Beatrice has gone all out as usual. Polished silver cutlery sits next to antique white and blue China plates. The tablecloth is white linen, the napkins ancient lace that he knows belonged to Beatrice's grandmother. There are three different glasses, all cut crystal.

They are served wine and water.

'Beer?' Andrei asks when the server asks whether he'd like red or white.

There's a hush and everyone's eyes turn to the Romanian.

The young waitress lifts her eyes toward Beatrice, who gives a nod.

'What kind would you like?' she asks, to which Andrei just replies, 'Normal?'

'He likes Stallhagen, if you have it?'

Frida's cheeks are slightly flushed, and she directs her words toward Kurt, not Beatrice.

'Of course, please, could you find it for our guest?'

Beatrice gives a quiet cough and nods to the server.

'I'll have a beer too,' Patrick says, and smiles at Andrei.

They didn't have the best of starts when, last summer, Andrei was looking for answers to how his brother Daniel had died on the islands. Patrick had got hold of Daniel's diary, and when Andrei found out, he was angry with Patrick, even though Patrick had already handed it over to the police.

Andrei seems a lot calmer now, thank goodness, and he returns Patrick's gesture when he lifts his glass in solidarity. Perhaps being engaged to Frida and becoming a stepdad to his brother's daughter has helped him with his grief.

Even though Patrick isn't going to be living on the islands, he will return to see his girls often. It'll be good to have a male ally in the family.

Although Frida looks uncomfortable in this setting, there is a marked change in the young woman Patrick knew at *Ålandsbladet*. Gone are the spiky multicolored hair and the heavy boots. Gone, too, is the anger. It's been replaced by a calmer, much more confident woman.

Perhaps motherhood did that for her?

Patrick glances at Mia, who's sitting next to him, glaring at her dad and Frida.

Becoming a mom had the opposite effect on his ex-wife. Having a newborn who totally depended on her seemed to make Mia irritable and impatient. Of course, Patrick remembers how hard it was with two young children, especially when they nearly lost Sara to meningitis.

Those were tough times.

As if reading his mind, Mia looks at him. He places his hand on her knee under the table, and immediately Mia's expression softens.

Patrick leans toward her. 'It'll be OK,' he whispers.

Mia's shoulders relax and for a brief moment, she leans against Patrick, before straightening up again. She picks up Patrick's hand and places it between hers. Looking into his eyes, she says softly, 'I need you.'

Patrick thinks he has misheard.

He gazes at Mia's eyes. For the first time in years, even before the children were born, he sees true tenderness toward him. Even last year, when she was dead set on getting him back – or rather, ending his relationship with Alicia – she hadn't seemed genuinely in love with him.

Can this Mia be the woman he fell in love with and married?

He's too stunned to reply.

'Let's talk after this farce is over?'

Mia releases his hand and plasters a forced smile on her face as Kurt gets slowly to his feet.

'You don't have to stand, Kurt, we can hear you well enough,' Beatrice protests.

She's sitting on Kurt's right side, opposite Frida.

But Kurt Eriksson doesn't do things by half. Holding onto his stick for support, he begins to speak.

'I know these past few days have been difficult for you, my dear family.'

He nods toward Mia, the girls, and finally, his wife.

Patrick can see that both Mia and Beatrice are fighting tears. Two women who never show emotion suddenly appear the most vulnerable at the table.

'But thanks to my dear wife,' here Kurt extends his hand and touches Beatrice's neatly manicured fingers.

When he nearly topples over, everyone instinctively rises from their seat. 'For goodness' sake, Kurt,' Beatrice exclaims, 'you must sit down.'

With difficulty but refusing help, he lowers himself into his chair. He then lifts his glass, and starts speaking again, this time directing his words to Frida and Anne Sofie, who is munching on a biscuit that Frida has brought.

'I would like you all to celebrate the new members of the Eriksson family. I know I should have welcomed you before, and I am profusely sorry for my cowardliness. Because that's what it was. I hope that we have time to make up for my past mistakes. I also hope that you may find it in your hearts to forgive me. If not today, then perhaps sometime in the future.'

Beatrice is now visibly weeping.

This is in such contrast to her normal behavior that everyone around the table is silent, including Kurt.

'Excuse me,' Beatrice says and leaves.

Immediately, Mia, also gets up, scraping her chair against the stone slabs of the terrace.

Patrick hesitates. Should he go after them? Or would they be embarrassed?

While he contemplates what to do, Frida gets up and, handing Anne Sofie to Andrei, follows the two women.

CHAPTER FORTY-FOUR

Beatrice Eriksson and her daughter are sitting in the lounge, on one of two large white couches. Mia is comforting her mom, who is dabbing her eyes with a tissue.

The room is vast, made even more impressive by the double ceiling height and the two wide staircases snaking up to a landing on the second floor.

When the two women see Frida, they stop talking.

She approaches slowly, as if walking toward two angry, wild animals.

'I'm so sorry. We shouldn't have come.'

Mia gets up from the sofa and faces Frida.

'How astute of you. A bit too late now, though, isn't it?'

'Mia!' Beatrice says, rising from her seat.

'Well, it's true. It's far too early. We've only known for a matter of days, and now …'

Mia crosses her arms over her immaculately cut white dress.

'I just wanted to apologize before leaving.'

Frida turns to go, but Beatrice places a hand softly on her arm, removing it almost as soon as it lands there. Frida's surprised by the cool touch of her fingers. The heatwave still hasn't abated after nearly two weeks, and even this close to the shore, the air feels oppressive. Yet, Mrs Eriksson is as cool as a cucumber, even when visibly upset.

How does she do it?

Beatrice sits back down and smiles at Frida, indicating for her to join her on the sofa.

'Please excuse my daughter. She's still in shock over everything.'

For a moment, Frida hesitates. She glances toward Mia, who's standing stock still. Only her eyes move, from her mom to Frida and back again.

Beatrice keeps her eyes fixed on Frida, who has little choice but to obey her.

'You too, Mia. Please sit down.'

Mia gives an exaggerated sigh, more suited to her teenage daughters than a grown woman, but follows suit. Instead of sitting next to her mom and Frida, however, she chooses the sofa opposite. She perches on the edge, arranging her legs in a prim manner.

Perhaps she thinks she is entitled to create dramatic scenes, Frida thinks.

She's behaving like a child, even though she must be at least ten years older than I am.

Frida just wants to leave this chaotic, but powerful family. She bitterly regrets that she agreed to come. She's seen how uncomfortable poor Andrei is, even if

Patrick is trying to make amends with him. The only person who has been at ease is her little daughter. Never before has she been so well-behaved, or so interested in her surroundings.

'I hear congratulations are in order?'

Beatrice nods her head toward Frida's hands, and more specifically at the large stone on her left ring finger.

Mia groans, showing her disapproval at the direction the conversation is taking.

'Thank you,' Frida says and casts her eyes down to her ring. It's so beautiful and feels so heavy on her finger that she is constantly surprised by its presence.

'And what a beautiful ring.'

Frida lifts her eyes toward Beatrice, who is smiling at her with what seems like true emotion.

Is this real? Is she really interested in my life?

As far as she understood from what Kurt told her, his wife and daughter were both shocked and 'disappointed' by the news that he had fathered another daughter. That was totally understandable, of course, and the reason why Frida had been so surprised that a lunch had been organized, only days after the secret had come out.

'Have you set a date yet?'

Beatrice's eyes are still kind. She seems genuinely interested in the answer.

Frida shakes her head.

'It was rather a surprise. Andrei needs to go back to Sibui to sort out his affairs, so I'm not sure... well, we haven't discussed dates yet.'

'Kurt would be delighted to give you away.'

Frida doesn't have time to reply before Mia flies out of her seat.

'What are you doing?'

Beatrice ignores her daughter, apart from indicating with her hand that she should sit back down again. Mia obeys but continues to give her mom an angry stare.

But Beatrice isn't deterred. Her face is serious, and she adds, 'You know he hasn't got much time. A wedding here would make him very happy. Give him something to look forward to. Naturally, we would cover the costs, but I am more than happy for you to make all the decisions. Your beautiful daughter would be the perfect little flower girl and I know her half-cousins, Mia's daughters, would love to help her with her duties. They seem to be getting on very well already.'

Frida doesn't know what to say.

Is this what Mrs Eriksson had been planning all along? Is this why they had been invited over so soon?

When Frida doesn't reply, Beatrice continues, 'There's no need to decide now, but as you know, time is of the essence with these kinds of things. It's June now, so we could perhaps make it September? It would be such a wonderful thing for Kurt to look forward to, don't you think? It would give you (and me, if you let me help you) enough time to organize the dress, the catering and, of course, decide on who is going to be your maid of honor, Andrei's best man and so forth.'

While Mrs Eriksson has been speaking, Mia has stood up again and is staring at her mom. With her hand on her hips, she says, 'I need to talk to you. Now!'

Beatrice sighs.

She touches Frida on her arm again and gets up.

'Please consider it. You would make Kurt so happy.'

CHAPTER FORTY-FIVE

'Alicia, please do not carry anything!'

Alicia smiles at Liam whose face is peeking out behind two cardboard boxes. She is bending over in Hilda's – now their – kitchen, trying to start the unpacking.

'I'm just looking for our coffee cups.'

Liam places the boxes down and sighs heavily. 'That's a good idea, I need a break.'

Once they are seated at the kitchen table, Liam with his cup of black coffee and Alicia with a mint tea, she asks, 'How's Mom settling in over there?'

Liam shrugs his shoulders.

'You know her better than me. I think she's OK.'

Alicia sighs. She looks around the large, modern kitchen with its marble tops, double depth island with an additional sink and barstools. The house swap was always going to be difficult for Hilda. She's lived here for nearly forty years and remodeled it several times. Alicia knows she was happy here with Uffe.

But it was her idea for Alicia and Liam to move out of the cottage, which for years had served as Uffe's farm office. After he died and Alicia took over the running of the estate, Hilda insisted she would turn half of the building, which had been used for storage, into Alicia's living quarters.

Hilda was good at interior design. She had an eye for it which – frankly – Alicia lacked, so she was glad to let her mom make all the decisions.

The results were stunning. With floor-to-ceiling folding windows overlooking the sea, a kitchen between the two ends of the cottage, and an alcove for Alicia's bed, she'd been more than happy to move in from the sauna cottage where she'd been living temporarily after returning to the islands from London.

Now that Alicia and Liam are once again a married couple, her mom suggested they swap places. She'd made the decision even before they'd found out that Alicia was expecting. At first, Alicia had rejected the idea, but her mom and Liam, united as always, convinced her that it made sense.

But as they've been packing and moving their personal stuff back and forth, Alicia has noticed her mom's mood getting lower and lower.

'Is Mom really OK?' Alicia now asks Liam again.

'Hmm,' Liam doesn't look up from a large IKEA bag he is gazing into.

Alicia sets the cups down and walks over to him.

'Liam, is Mom OK?'

His eyes finally meet Alicia's.

'Yes, of course, why wouldn't she be?'

'You haven't noticed anything?'

Alicia sighs and sits down on one of the chairs around Hilda's kitchen table, which they've all agreed should stay. So many pieces of furniture have to stay put, since there's hardly any room in the cottage opposite. Which is what worries Alicia.

How will her mom get used to the much smaller space?

'You mustn't worry.'

Liam comes over to Alicia. With practiced hands, he takes hold of Alicia's wrist and starts to take her pulse.

Alicia sighs but lets him do his thing. She wonders briefly if he misses being a surgeon, or even just a family doctor, which is what he did for a while before continuing his training in London.

'You seem fine,' Liam says, smiling and giving Alicia a peck on her cheek. Moving back to the pile of boxes and large carrier bags in the middle of the room, he adds, 'It's bound to be strange to move out of a home you've been living in for several decades. She's probably feeling a bit emotional about the loss of Uffe too. Just give her space, and she'll be fine.'

How little he knows my mother, Alicia thinks, but frankly she is too exhausted to worry about Hilda now.

The islands are still in the grip of a heatwave, and in the middle of the afternoon, the temperature is unbearable. Especially when you are moving heavy boxes back and forth in the sun.

'Why don't we take a break? It's just too hot for this today,' she says, looking pleadingly at Liam.

Just them Alicia's phone starts to bleep.

'Hello, Frida, how are you?'

Alicia listens as Frida tells her about the lunch with Kurt and his family. Alicia's forgotten all about it, amidst the move.

'I'm glad it went well. How was Mia?'

Alicia gives Liam a quick glance. Although they've talked everything through, Liam still doesn't particularly like hearing what the Erikssons, and by extension Patrick, are getting up to.

But Liam continues to sort out items in the pile on the floor, putting the contents of two cardboard boxes into one. Although she's good at interior design, Hilda is hopeless at packing.

Alicia is glad he's not heard Mia's name and is unconcerned about what the Erikssons are getting up to.

'What?'

Alicia cannot believe her ears.

'What did you say?'

Now Liam has noticed that something is the matter and gazes at Alicia. She puts her hand up in a gesture to let him know everything is well, while continuing to listen intently to Frida's voice at the other end.

Alicia has to bite her lip.

Although she is Anne Sofie's unofficial grandma, she's always tried not to interfere in Frida's life. She'll give advice if Frida asks for it, and she looks out for her, but this – Kurt's revelation that he is Frida's absent father, and her late mom's lover, and her benefactor, leaving Frida a fortune after her death – was something else. And now this!

Alicia thinks for a moment.

No, she can't tell Frida that she thinks it's a bad idea. Although Frida is young, she has had a lot to cope with in her life already. She's a mom, and she is forging a new life with Andrei. Where and when they get married is their own choice.

'If you think that is the right thing to do. It's very generous of you to share your big day with them.'

Alicia hopes that her words do not betray how she really feels.

'I am certain. We've talked about nothing else all night,' Frida says.

They end the conversation by agreeing to meet up for coffee the next day.

'What was that all about?' Liam asks her.

'You won't believe it, but Beatrice Eriksson has offered to host and pay for Frida and Andrei's wedding. At the summer place in September!'

CHAPTER FORTY-SIX

Hilda surveys the mess in front of her. She should get it all sorted before the day is over, but suddenly she has no energy. She sits down on the unmade bed that Alicia and Liam are leaving behind for her. It's made-to-measure, ordered by Hilda, so there's no reason to move it to the main house. Liam has bought a fancy new bed for the two of them from Sweden, which Hilda is happy about. Even though she would never have admitted it, somehow it doesn't seem right for her daughter to sleep in the same bed that Hilda shared with her dear husband.

Hilda sighs.

She knows she's being too emotional about this move.

It was her idea, because it makes absolute sense.

It would be crazy for her to continue to occupy the large house, while a young (well, younger than her at any rate) couple with a baby on the way, live in the cramped two-room cottage.

Hilda looks around the space. What amounts to one large room, with a sitting area and the bed in an alcove, is well designed, even if she says it herself. The tall floor-to-ceiling windows, which open to a small area of decking, beyond which lie the reefs and the sea, give the place an airy feel.

The tall ceiling is painted white, with natural wood beams. The idea to break into the loft area to give the living room a vaulted ceiling had been hers, and she is pleased with the effect.

A vintage chandelier, which Hilda found at a second-hand market in Stockholm, hangs in the middle of the space, with one tall standard lamp in the corner. There is a sense of the old mixed with new, which has made the room look quite special and even spectacular.

On the downside, the kitchen is small, but she has plans to knock through into the office next door, creating a large chef's kitchen with an island and an eating area.

'It'll be a nice new project for you,' Alicia said when she heard of her plans.

Her daughter knows her far too well. Perhaps, she now thinks, she should get one of the reporters from *Ålandsbladet*, or even a fancy interior design magazine published in Sweden, to write an article about the renovation when she's done.

She needs to get going with the remodeling before Alicia's new baby is born, because she intends to be a hands-on grandma this time. She was too far away to be of any help whatsoever with Stefan. In fact, when she and Uffe visited Alicia and Liam in London for the first time after his birth, she'd felt more of a nuisance than anything else.

The new baby will be a chance for Hilda to show her credentials as a doting granny, and she cannot wait to be there for Alicia this time around.

'Let's take a break for a minute, shall we?'

Alicia sees her mom sitting on the unmade bed. Her face brightens into a smile, but she can't entirely dispel the sad expression she had when Alicia walked in.

'Mom, it'll be OK. We're just across the yard and you can pop over at any time.'

Hilda takes Alicia's hands into hers and nods. 'I'm fine.'

Alicia puts her head on her shoulder, while Hilda touches her belly.

'We won't have time to be maudlin when this little darling is born.'

'No.'

Suddenly Alicia remembers the phone call with Frida.

'Guess what, Mom. I just had some very strange news.'

'I always thought she was such a cold fish, that woman,' Hilda says after Alicia has told her what Frida had said.

'Frida says she wants Kurt to have something to look forward to.'

Alicia is struggling to understand why Beatrice

would go to such trouble to arrange a wedding for her husband's secret lover's child.

Frida told her that, at first, the lunch had been very awkward, mainly because Mia had been so unfriendly. Beatrice, she said, had been polite but cold, which was exactly what Alicia had experienced whenever she'd met the woman. It wasn't until Kurt himself had spoken with Frida at the end of the lunch, saying how much he would appreciate celebrating her wedding at his summer place, that Frida had made up her mind to do it.

'We should have it here instead,' Hilda now says.

'Gosh, that hadn't even occurred to me,' Alicia says staring at her mom.

'Although…'

'I'm due in late September, the same month they're thinking of having the ceremony,' Alicia says, voicing her mom's thought. 'And I think it's up to Frida, don't you?'

Hilda nods.

'As long as we get an invitation!'

Alicia laughs and puts her arms around her mom, giving her a hug.

'Of course, we will!'

'This is the last trip over today,' Liam says when Alicia is back in the large house, having left her mom unpacking at the cottage.

'I'll come with you,' Alicia says and begins to heave her body off the chair.

'You'll do no such thing. Stay here and rest, or better

still, go upstairs and lie down on our new bed. I've made it up so it's ready to go.'

Alicia smiles and is overwhelmed by so much love for Liam that she can feel tears pricking her eyelids.

'It's OK, I just want a quick word with Hilda and then I'll go and rest.'

Liam gives her a sideways glance, but his smile turns to a frown when he notices the expression on her face.

'What's the matter, lovely? Are you in pain?'

Alicia attempts a smile, but tears force themselves out. She wipes her cheek with the back of her hand and puts her arms around Liam's neck. She rests her head on his shoulder and tries to control her emotions.

'I think my hormones are going wild. I'm just so happy. The news about Frida and Andrei, wherever they get married, has taken me over the edge, I think.'

Alicia can feel Liam's chest rise up and down as he inhales deeply. He takes hold of Alicia's shoulders and looks into her eyes.

'I'm very glad to hear it because I have never been this happy either. And I am not hormonal, nor does it have anything to do with anyone else. I love you more than ever.'

Liam gazes over the large kitchen.

'I think we are going to be very happy here.'

CHAPTER FORTY-SEVEN

T he day of the wedding is one of those warm, yet cool late September days when there is more than a hint of autumn in the air. Frida is up early, and she can see the sun just about to rise above the sea from the window of the attic room. It's a stunning scene, but Frida can't enjoy it.

She's so nervous.

Her tummy feels hollow, as if she is starving. As if she hadn't had anything to eat for days. Yet, she can't even think of food. The memory of the delicious meal of smoked fish, salad and new potatoes that Hilda had prepared yesterday now makes her feel queasy.

She spent her last night as a single woman with Alicia, Liam and Hilda in Sjoland, while Andrei stayed in the flat in town with his sister and brother, who traveled to the islands a couple of days previously.

In a couple of hours, she will need to get dressed into her silky cream wedding outfit, which she bought with Beatrice Eriksson and Alicia in Stockholm.

She had tried on dozens of gowns, but in the end had chosen a jumpsuit with a tight bodice and a cape made of see-through silk tulle that reaches down to the floor like a veil, making it appear more like a traditional wedding gown.

It's beautiful.

Frida fell in love with the outfit as soon as she saw it, although she could detect from Beatrice's expression that she had hoped for something more traditional.

'That's so you!' Alicia had exclaimed, making it impossible for Beatrice to protest.

Frida is still amazed that everything has gone so smoothly. Planning a wedding can be stressful at the best of times, let alone with a woman who's just found out that the bride-to-be is her husband's secret love child.

Alicia has been a wonder as usual, putting aside her own problems with Mia. Luckily, her half-sister (the thought that she's related to Mia Eriksson is still foreign to Frida) has been keeping out of the way, preferring to spend the last two months in Stockholm.

Frida tries to calm her breathing. She thinks of Alicia and Liam and the joy that exudes from them.

Now that Alicia also has a new baby to care for, Frida will have to be less reliant on her. Little Theo is just two weeks old and, according to Alicia, no trouble at all. Frida only heard a little cry out of him in the early hours of this morning, when Alicia must have given him his nighttime feed.

Still, Alicia and Liam will be busy with their new business too, which seems to be going from strength to strength. And Frida will be a married woman with a whole family of her own.

The image of Andrei's face makes Frida smile, and the thought that they will soon be officially husband and wife makes her heart swell with warmth and happiness.

Alicia wakes early. She can hear Theo fussing in his cot next to their bed. She picks him up, leaving Liam fast asleep next to her, and walks across the landing and into the nursery to change him. The baby's eyes open and stare at her.

The bright blue color of his eyes and the beauty of his little features still take Alicia's breath way.

'Good morning my little darling,' Alicia whispers, and she blows bubbles onto his tummy.

Gurgling with happiness, Theo punches the air with his arms and kicks his legs, making it harder for Alicia to change his diaper.

'Calm down, little fellow,' Alicia smiles.

When she's finally got him ready, she picks him up, settles herself onto the rocking chair, and guides the baby onto her breast.

When her son nurses, Alicia closes her eyes, but she opens them again when she hears a noise from the attic room above. She glances at her watch and sees it's just gone 6am.

It's Frida's wedding today. She must be nervous if she's up this early.

Alicia decides to go and see her after Theo's feed.

She sighs and realizes that she too is a little apprehensive about what the day will bring. All the arrangements have gone smoothly, as far as Alicia can tell.

Luckily, Mia hasn't been around, and the few times Frida has asked Alicia to help with anything involving Beatrice, things have gone smoothly.

Alicia isn't looking forward to seeing Mia, or Patrick, who she's heard through the grapevine (Frida to be more precise) isn't moving to northern Sweden after all. He and Mia are going to try to give their marriage another go.

When Alicia heard this, she wasn't at all surprised. She knows how much Patrick loves his daughters, and she knows that if Mia wants Patrick back, she will do everything in her power to make it happen. Perhaps her little nudge was all he needed to make the right decision. She hopes Patrick really wants to be with her.

Patrick's happiness is no longer Alicia's concern.

Apparently, they've moved back to Stockholm, which is a relief. But she knows they will be there today.

Then there's her dad, Leo.

Hilda has been in touch with him again and she has asked him to accompany her to the wedding. Alicia isn't certain this is a good idea, but Hilda had argued that weddings should not be attended alone. And when her mom has decided on something wild horses can't change her mind.

'I could of course ask Nils?' Hilda had said with a glint in her eye.

She knows Alicia isn't at all certain about the Swedish man she met on the ferry last year.

'You know I don't want you to be upset.'

'We are just friends now, I promise,' Hilda had replied and hugged her daughter.

Leo is due to arrive on the morning ferry from Helsinki, which docks in the West Harbor at 8am. Hilda had also pointed out that this will be a great opportunity for him to meet his new grandson, something that Alicia couldn't argue against.

'It'll be alright, you'll see,' Alicia now coos as she places Theo onto her other breast. She's saying it more to herself than to the baby.

It makes her feel better to hear the words out loud.

CHAPTER FORTY-EIGHT

The sun is just above the horizon and the view is breathtaking as they fly above the archipelago. Patrick watches the dark green and gray skerries dotted in the inky blue sea below as the helicopter prepares to land.

He sees the Eriksson villa complex just in front of them, and the West Harbor where two large cruise liners are docked, in the distance. He takes hold of Mia's hand and smiles. His wife returns the gesture with a grin. Although they're able to talk through the headphones, they've said little to each other during the short flight from Stockholm.

They decided to arrive for the wedding on the morning of the ceremony rather than the night before.

Mia's new obsession with a private helicopter service between Stockholm and Mariehamn has made short trips in and out of the islands possible. In the past, when Kurt was still in charge of the business, he vetoed money spent on things that would seem extravagant to the islanders.

Mia has no such qualms.

Patrick doesn't get involved in the running of the Eriksson empire; he leaves it all to his wife. Instead, he's writing a novel. To his surprise, he's not missing chasing after news stories, and he revels in the freedom of having his own schedule. There are no fixed deadlines, and no editor is breathing down his neck to produce a certain kind of piece at a certain time.

Yet he has managed to write regularly and hopes to have a manuscript ready before Christmas.

Mia wants him to approach publishers now, but Patrick is holding off. He needs to be certain that what he has produced is up to scratch first. He wants to be a success and that means he needs to polish his words and make them as good as possible. He hasn't divulged what the book is about to anyone yet.

Patrick is shaken out of his thoughts when the helicopter lands and Mia gives him a shove with her elbow.

'We're here,' she says, before taking off the headphones and stepping off the aircraft.

For the second time in her life Hilda is a guest at the Erikssons' grand summer residence. This time she is a guest of honor, rather than somebody who was invited just because her daughter happened to catch the eye of their Swedish son-in-law.

Hilda glances down the first row of seats in the vast grounds of the estate. It's filled with her family, including Liam and Leo, and Alicia, who's holding the newest member, her grandson Theo.

The baby is wearing a beautiful white and blue sailor's romper suit, which Hilda bought for him in a new shop that had just opened in Mariehamn. He's fast asleep, showing off the beautiful dark eyelashes resting on his pink cheeks.

Low music is playing out of invisible speakers somewhere. Hilda smiles at the baby and then at Alicia.

Her daughter looks tired, but there is a new softness to her features, which Hilda knows means she is finally happy again. Gone is the grief that had etched her face for so long. She's certain there are times when Alicia still feels overwhelming sadness at the loss of her first son, but she hopes these occasions are rarer now.

Hilda herself is still grieving Uffe. She doesn't think she will ever get over his death but living without him is getting easier day by day.

A new grandson, as well as happy events like this, Frida's wedding, help.

Hilda faces the front again, admiring the arrangement where white and pink foliage is draped over an arch. A table covered in a white cloth, with flower arrangements in each corner, sits in the middle. A pastor stands by the table, holding a Bible, and talking to the groom, Andrei.

He glances behind him and catches Hilda's eyes. She nods to him and smiles reassuringly. The boy looks nervous, as he should be. If you're not anxious on your wedding day, something's off in Hilda's opinion.

Hilda had expected the setting of the wedding to be

spectacular, but the scene when she walked down the aisle still took her breath away.

The white chairs, with white satin seats and chiffon bows, are set in two wide rows facing the flower arch at the front. Behind the arch where the ceremony will take place, the view opens up to the blue-gray sea, which glitters in the sunshine.

It's as if the mighty Eriksson family could even summon the sunshine on demand.

'They are lucky with the weather,' Hilda whispers to Leo, smart in his dark suit and white shirt.

He turns his head toward Hilda and smiles.

Suddenly the memory of their wedding, a lifetime ago, comes clearly into Hilda's mind. It was a small affair in the Kallio church in Helsinki. She was so happy and young – oh, so young. She was also four months' pregnant, though nobody would have guessed she was with child. Her bump didn't start showing until she was in her third trimester. In the 1980s, it would have been a scandal, which neither her parents nor Leo's wanted.

The first chords of the wedding march bring Hilda back to the present. She glances down the aisle and sees the three girls, with little Anne Sofie in the middle, waiting at the top of the aisle. They look a picture in their flower headdresses and pink outfits.

But her eyes widen in surprise when she sees that behind the bridesmaids, Kurt Eriksson is standing by Frida's side.

So, the old man is giving Frida away!

Hilda doesn't have time to make any comment about this fact, or even glance down the row of seats to Alicia, before everyone stands and the girls, Frida and Eriksson move slowly down the aisle.

The old man is holding a stick and it looks as if Frida is supporting Kurt rather than the other way around.

What a turn of events!

As the pair move closer to Hilda, she notices how beautiful Frida looks in her, admittedly unusual, wedding dress. Or is it a trouser suit? Hilda can't prevent a smile forming on her lips when she thinks what Beatrice would have thought about the outfit.

Alicia has been totally secretive about the gown, even when Hilda had tried to get her to describe it.

But when Kurt Eriksson gets closer to her row of seats, Hilda's expression changes. The old man is smiling widely, but he looks awfully gray, and so very thin. His smart suit is hanging off him and he's visibly out of breath.

His eyes sweep briefly over Hilda and the rest of the Ulsson clan. Hilda struggles against the tears welling inside her eyelids.

Luckily, old women often cry at weddings, but Hilda's tears are not for Frida's joyous day. At this moment, she wants to weep for all that the Eriksson family are about to lose. She knows what it's like to be left alone after decades of marriage. She knows how a daughter feels about the loss of her father.

For the first time during her life spent on the islands, she feels sorry for the Eriksson family.

CHAPTER FORTY-NINE

Mia can't believe that this is happening.

Each time her mom phoned to give her a running commentary of the wedding preparations, she'd tuned out, merely making appropriate noises down the line.

When Beatrice asked her along to buy Frida's wedding dress in Stockholm, she'd managed to get out of it by claiming she had important business meetings that day. When she'd put the phone down after that conversation, she'd been thankful that she'd been listening to her mom for once.

When the wedding march starts and everyone gets up to greet the bride, she's astonished how stylish the imposter looks. She'd been expecting an old-fashioned blancmange, but the dress – or is it a jumpsuit? – is actually stylish and very modern. She has no idea how her mom let that go.

Mia's gaze moves to her dad, and she can't help but

gasp. She saw him only two weeks ago, but the change in him is shocking. His face is even more lined and pale than before. He's almost bent double as he moves with obvious difficulty, leaning on a stick on one side and Frida on the other.

Rage rises in Mia.

He shouldn't have to do this!

'You OK?' Patrick whispers and covers one of her hands with his palm, which he only now notices are bunched up tightly at her sides.

She relaxes and lets Patrick take her hand. Her gaze still on the wedding party, she nods without looking at him. Instead, her eyes move toward her two girls, walking slowly in front of the bride and clad in pale pink dresses that come just below their knees.

She'd heard from Sara how 'lame' the outfits were, but Mia must admit that the girls, both holding little Anne Sofie's hands as she walks between them, look gorgeous. All three wear crowns of pale pink and white flowers that match the bride's bouquet.

Mia smiles at Sara, who, surprisingly, beams back at her.

During the weeks running up to the wedding, all she heard from Sara were complaints about her role in the proceedings, but now she seems to be enjoying herself. Patrick had been trying to convince both girls that it would be a fun day, but Sara had just rolled her eyes at her dad.

Mia had almost hoped that Sara would refuse to take part, but she didn't want Patrick to find out that she wasn't fully behind this charade.

'It's what your dad wants,' he kept reminding her.

Mia has lost count of how many times she had to drive her nails into the palms of her hands to stop herself from shouting at him. She needed to keep Patrick on her side. Getting him away from Alicia, the Home Wrecker, now smiling smugly on the other side of the aisle, holding her new brat in her arms, was a real coup.

She needs to play happy families for a while longer.

'You did a wonderful job, thank you,' Kurt says to Beatrice as they walk slowly up the wide staircase to their bedroom.

The wedding is still carrying on downstairs in the lounge, where Beatrice has set up a dance floor. Music that Kurt recognizes from the stuff his granddaughters listen to flows up.

'Anything for you,' Beatrice says softly, adding, 'Do you want to stop for a bit?'

Kurt hates being so weak, but he nods and leans on the banister.

'We should look at those home lifts again. The engineer said they could install one in a week or so.'

Kurt turns his head to catch his wife's eyes.

He sees her features are etched with worry. Despite the clever makeup, there are visible bags under her eyes.

She must know he may not last as long as a week.

'You should sleep in the room next to ours tonight. I know I keep you awake.'

Beatrice rubs his back and shakes her head.

'Now, let's get going again?'

After what seems like a momentous effort, they finally reach the bedroom in the east wing of the house. With Beatrice's help, Kurt lowers himself onto the bed with a deep sigh. He had one glass of Champagne to toast his daughter's marriage, and it's made him incredibly tired.

He closes his eyes. All he wants to do is to lie down and sleep, but he knows Beatrice wants him to change into his pajamas, so he kicks off his shoes. He doesn't open his eyes when he feels his wife peel his socks off. He reaches for his flies and undoes his trousers, then tries to shake off his jacket, but Beatrice gets there first and pulls it off gently. Kurt manages to loosen his tie, but soon his wife takes over that too.

There was a time when they did all of this in the throes of passion.

Naked, Kurt opens his eyes but tries not to look at his withered body. Instead, he searches for his wife's face.

Beatrice is leaning over the bed, undoing the buttons on his night shirt, which their housekeeper has left on top of the comforter. She is stylish in a bright pink dress that hugs her slim body, with a short jacket in the same color. She's wearing the pearls he bought for her years ago. She's so beautiful, Kurt's heart aches. She should not be looking after an old, dying man. She should be dancing and enjoying herself downstairs.

'I love you.'

She settles her eyes on him and smiles. He spots the single tear running down her face before she has time to wipe it away with her hand.

She runs the fingers, still damp from her tear, down his face.

'I love you too.'

CHAPTER FIFTY

The view out of their Havsvidden villa, hunched on the top of the cliffs at the very northern tip of the islands is spectacular.

Frida had kept the location of their honeymoon a secret from Andrei. He'd feared that Kurt Eriksson had organized a stay in some fancy resort in the Caribbean, but Frida, when she got wind of his unease, had placed her hands on either side of his face and smiled.

'I promise that Kurt or Beatrice Eriksson have nothing to do with our honeymoon. Apart from Beatrice and Mia's girls helping Alicia with the baby-sitting, that is.'

They had arrived last night after darkness had fallen, so Andrei hadn't seen the view until now. It's just gone seven in the morning and the sun isn't quite up yet, but there is a streak of orange on the horizon, between two dark islands in the distance. It's going to be a sunny day.

Andrei still finds it difficult to have a lie-in after years of getting up at sunrise to milk his cows, so he leaves Frida asleep, creeping quietly out of bed and into the large open lounge. He makes himself a coffee and sits down to gaze out at the indescribably magnificent view.

He thinks about the new job that Alicia and Liam have offered him. Their business is growing fast and they need someone to oversee the production of the potatoes. As a cattle farmer, he's never grown potatoes, but he knows how to look after the land. Alicia told him she trusted him and he would learn the ropes quickly enough. Andrei cannot believe his good fortune.

The wind has got up and the teal-colored sea is littered with white tops. Although he can't hear them through the triple-glazed windows, he can see the waves crashing into the rocks all around their villa.

This place, which Frida had only yesterday revealed she'd bought as a holiday home for them, has finally made Andrei understand why Frida loves these islands so much.

The heat of the summer gone, and with it the tourists, the islands have returned to a sleepy state. The streets of Mariehamn are quiet and here, in the middle of nowhere, he truly feels at one with nature.

There is the same sense of his own insignificance, or perhaps his own small role in the universe, that he gets when inspecting his fields in Romania.

How did Frida know he needed such a place to escape to?

. . .

The Erikssons' villa seems almost unoccupied when Hilda and Alicia drive through the gate, which had opened as soon as they pulled up.

Hilda has insisted on coming with Alicia to collect little Anne Sofie and fulfill their part of the babysitting arrangement.

Alicia suspects that she just wants to show Beatrice and Kurt Eriksson her new car. It's another open-top Mercedes, but this time it's bright blue with cream-colored leather upholstery. Alicia had asked Hilda if she wasn't worried about getting this dirty, seeing that Anne Sofie likes to have a snack in the car.

'Oh, that's OK,' Hilda had replied. 'This leather is incredible, you can wipe away anything, even chocolate.'

'OK, Mom,' Alicia had replied.

When they park, Alicia is struck by the quietness of the place. Gone are the flowers, the strings of lights, and the marquee at the back. Instead, Alicia has a clear view of the sea beyond the main house. Mariehamn, only twenty minutes' drive away, seems further off.

Hilda gets out of the car, followed by Alicia.

'Perhaps we have the wrong day? No one seems to be home.'

Hilda dangles the car keys in her hand.

'They let us in through the gate, didn't they? Someone must be here,' Alicia says just as the door opens and Beatrice, dressed in loose pants and a large sweater, appears. She's not wearing any make-up at all, and her eyes are red and puffy.

Alicia gives Hilda a sideways glance. Has her mom noticed that Mrs Eriksson has been crying?

'Please come in,' Beatrice says. 'Anne Sofie is with the girls and Mia in the TV room.'

She indicates with her arm for Alicia and Hilda to come through the door.

Once inside, Beatrice closes the heavy wooden door and promptly leans against it as if standing without support is too much for her.

Hilda steps toward her and places her hand on Beatrice's arm.

'Is everything OK?'

Alicia is rooted to the spot. She glances around but cannot see the children anywhere. An awful thought enters her mind. Why would Mia be here otherwise?

This is when something strange that Alicia has never seen happens.

Beatrice covers her face with her hands and collapses in a heap on the floor.

'There, there, dear,' Hilda says, kneeling beside Beatrice.

'Mamma!' A voice behind Alicia makes her turn around. Mia runs toward her mom and takes her into her arms. She begins to rock her back and forth repeating, 'Just let it go, Mom, just let it go.'

Sara and Frederica, with Anne Sofie standing between them, holding their hands, appear in the large hall.

Quickly, Alicia turns toward the children and kneels down to Anne Sofie's level. 'Were you watching a film or cartoons?'

Gently, she takes Anne Sofie's hand and leads all the girls back into the TV room.

'Is Grandmother OK?'

Frederica's eyes are large, and Alicia can see the concern in her young face. Sara and Anne Sofie also turn toward Alicia, waiting for her reply.

'She's upset. I'm not sure why, but I will find out and come back to let you know. You stay here, OK?'

All three nod and Alicia hurries out of the room and back to the hall.

The space is now empty, but she can hear voices from a room to the left.

Mia and Beatrice are sitting facing each other on a leather sofa, and Hilda is seated opposite them on a matching chair.

'I'm so sorry for your loss,' Hilda says.

Kurt has passed.

Alicia catches Mia's eye.

'They're are asking what's going on,' she says moving her head toward the TV room.

Mia nods and turns to speak softly to her mom.

'I'll explain to the girls and sort Anne Sofie out. You stay here.'

Hilda moves to take Mia's place next to Beatrice, who's sitting with her head down, holding a piece of tissue over her eyes.

Mia moves toward the hall again, and Alicia follows her. Hearing the footsteps behind her Mia stops and turns around, facing Alicia.

'When…?' Alicia asks.

Mia sighs. Alicia sees she too is without makeup.

Alicia hasn't seen her barefaced since they were at school.

'He just didn't wake up this morning. The nurse said it was painless in the end.'

'I'm so sorry,' Alicia says.

Surprising herself, she places her arms around Mia and gives her a hug. At first, the other woman's body is rigid, but then she relaxes and puts her arms loosely around Alicia.

'You should have called, we could have come earlier,' Alicia says when she lets go of Mia.

'We knew it was coming and it had all been arranged. The undertakers came quickly …'

Mia's voice breaks and she places a hand over her mouth, breathing heavily in and out.

'You don't have to explain. I'll get Anne Sofie's things if you just tell me where they are.'

'I've got them,' a voice behind Alicia says.

She turns around and is face to face with Patrick.

For a moment, Alicia feels panic rise in her chest, but as quickly as the sensation arrives, it disappears. She smiles at him and takes the pink Moomin backpack and the larger carryall from him.

'Thank you. I'll go and get her. Could you let Hilda know we're going? And can you also give my condolences to your mom? I don't want to disturb her anymore.'

Alicia addresses these words to Mia, who's recovered now, although she is still pale with grief. She nods and attempts a smile.

Patrick has moved next to his ex-wife and is holding her by the waist.

'Let me know when the funeral is. I'd like to come and pay my respects,' Alicia adds.

Mia nods.

'I will.'

'Goodbye Patrick. And Mia,' Alicia says and turns toward the TV room.

CHAPTER FIFTY-ONE

I n the car, as she stops herself telling Hilda not to drive too fast, Alicia wonders about Patrick and Mia. Will they remarry? And will it last? She'll give it six months, but really it has nothing to do with her.

She is glad that Mia has someone to support her over the coming months, and years. Losing a dad is hard, Alicia knows this far too well. Although her birth father is still alive, Uffe was her real dad.

She sends a quick message to Liam to tell him about Kurt Eriksson and gets a reply saying he's sorry.

Alicia turns toward Anne Sofie, who is sitting in the back. She smiles at the little girl who returns the smile with a shake of her hand. Her fingers are holding onto a chocolate biscuit and her hand and mouth are covered in the stuff. Just as well the seats are wipeable, Alicia thinks and grins.

'Good girl,' she says to her.

Alicia turns back around to face the front. She hopes

that Anne Sofie doesn't understand what has happened to Kurt. That she's just lost the grandfather she's only known for a matter of months.

A thought occurs to her.

'What are we going to do about Frida? Should we let her know or wait until she's back from the honeymoon?'

Hilda turns toward Alicia and nearly drives into the ditch but corrects herself just in time.

'Mom!'

'It's OK, no harm done.'

'So, what do you think?'

Hilda is quiet for a moment. They are on the road leading to the farm in Sjoland, having just passed the swing bridge over the canal. They drive in silence, both women deep in thought until Hilda pulls up to the farm.

Liam opens the door and starts walking toward the car. He takes Alicia into his arms and hugs her tightly. He understands how someone else's bereavement can trigger Alicia's own sad memories.

'I'm OK,' Alicia says releasing herself from his embrace. 'Where's Theo?'

'Fast asleep. I have the baby monitor just here.'

Liam pulls the device from his jacket pocket and turns toward Hilda, putting one arm around her.

'How about you, mother-in-law?'

Hilda smiles. 'I'm a tough old bird, you know that. We've been talking about this little one's mom, though. Should we let her know?'

Liam comes toward Alicia and Anne Sofie, who's undoing the lock on her car seat.

'Hello, darling.'

'Am!' Anne Sofie says lifting her hands up for Liam to lift her up.

'I love my nickname,' Liam grins at the girl, and he carries her toward the house.

After Liam and Alicia have settled Anne Sofie and the baby down to sleep at the end of the day, they step into the lounge and see Hilda sitting in what used to be Uffe's seat in the corner of the room. She's fast sleep, with her mouth slightly open.

'She'll be mortified if she knew we found her like this,' Alicia whispers to Liam, and they tiptoe out of the room and into the kitchen. They begin to prepare dinner, making a little more noise opening the cupboard doors and setting down a pan of boiling water for pasta than they'd normally do.

After a while, Hilda appears at the kitchen door.

'Little ones asleep already?'

Liam nods.

'We're making pasta Bolognese. Do you want to stay?'

Hilda moves toward the hallway and picks up her coat and handbag. 'No, no. You two enjoy your time together.'

Alicia moves into the hall and takes hold of Hilda's coat.

'Nonsense. We need to talk about what we are going to do about Frida.'

'I've just opened a rather nice Sangiovese. You want a glass?'

Liam's comment finally convinces her mom to join them for dinner. This is a ritual they go through a couple of times a week.

When Hilda suggested they should swap houses, Alicia had been concerned that either she'd constantly be in her old house, or that she'd shut herself away in the cottage opposite.

Neither of these scenarios became the norm. Rather, Hilda would wait to be asked to join Alicia and Liam for meals, and would often refuse initially, allowing them to change their minds. At the same time, she made herself available for babysitting or any other kind of help they needed, night or day.

'Let's drink to Kurt Eriksson. May he rest in peace.'

All three lift their glasses to Hilda's mournful toast and take a sip of wine. Alice lets the liquid touch her lips just for a moment. The midwife told her she could drink the occasional glass of wine while breast-feeding, but she really doesn't want it.

Liam clears his throat and, casting his eyes first toward Alicia, and then Hilda, says, 'I may not under-stand exactly how Frida might be feeling, but I vote that we don't tell her until they're back from Havsvidden. Today is Friday, there are only two days left of their honeymoon. Why spoil it? The funeral won't be for a week or so, so she has plenty of time to prepare herself mentally, don't you think?'

'But it will be in the local news online,' Alicia says.

'Ah, I hadn't thought of that,' Liam replies.

'OK, I'll give her a ring.'

'I think that's for the best,' Hilda says immediately.

Alicia suddenly feels the loss of her stepfather acutely. She swallows, trying to stop the tears, and lifts her eyes up to Hilda.

'I know darling, it's hard, but Frida hardly knew Kurt. It's not the same as Uffe.'

'Oh, Mom.'

Just then, the baby monitor on the top of the kitchen cabinet starts to crackle and they all turn toward it.

'I'll go, he needs a feed anyway,' Alicia says and gets up before she hears any protest from Liam. Cuddling Theo is just what she needs now. The little miracle baby is what is holding her together.

And Liam, of course.

I'm lucky, so stop being sad.

As she sits and nurses the baby in the semi-darkness of the attic bedroom, a complete sense of peace descends upon her, as it often does when she's feeding Theo.

After she has put the baby back down, she dials Frida's number.

CHAPTER FIFTY-TWO

The day of Kurt's funeral is rainy. Dark clouds have hung over the skies all morning and when the time comes for Alicia to give Theo his final feed and hand him over to Brit, her good friend who is going to babysit while she and Liam attend the ceremony, the heavens open.

'How apt,' Hilda says as she steps inside the large kitchen.

Although she has made herself up perfectly as always, Alicia can see that her eyes are liquid with tears ready to escape.

'It brings it all back, doesn't it, Mom?'

It's only just over eighteen months ago that they lost Uffe.

Alicia goes over to hug her mom, but Hilda gives her daughter a cursory peck on the cheek.

'We need to get going. Where's Liam?'

'Here', Alicia's husband says, walking down the stairs. He looks handsome in his dark suit and black tie.

Alicia smiles at Brit and kisses the baby's cheek.

'Be good for Auntie Brit, now, won't you?'

'We'll be just fine. He's such a good little boy, isn't he?'

The baby turns his head to look at Brit. His eyelids are heavy.

'Just put him down when we're gone. He can nap until we're back. If he gets hungry, the milk is in the fridge. And ....'

Interrupting her friend, Brit places a hand on Alicia's arm.

'I know. Go, we'll be just fine!'

St George's Church in the center of Mariehamn is full to bursting when Alicia, Hilda and Liam arrive. There's still half an hour before the service is due to begin, but already people are lining up to find a space in the red-brick building. Once inside, a female curate wearing a long black robe recognizes Hilda and ushers the three of them toward the altar and the second pew from the front.

As they walk along the long aisle, Alicia gazes at the coffin set on the catafalque. A large bunch of lilies is set on top and two candles are burning on either side.

Alicia sees Frida at the front, sitting between Andrei and Patrick. On Patrick's left is Mia and next to her their two teenage daughters. Right at the end, on the aisle seat, is Beatrice. She's wearing a wide-brimmed black hat. When they arrive, she lifts her head and Alicia and Hilda nod toward her.

When they are seated, facing the coffin, beneath the

beautiful stained-glass window, Alicia pauses. The last time she was at a funeral, she was burying her stepdad.

Liam places his hand over Alicia's.

'Are you OK?'

She squeezes his fingers and nods, and then, leaning forward, taps Frida on the shoulder. The two women hug. She nods to the rest of the people in the front row and sits back down.

The music plays softly as more people pile inside the cool church.

To try to change the track of her thoughts away from Uffe, Alicia thinks how strange it is that Frida is sitting at the front, an integral part of the Eriksson family. She glances at Mia and Patrick, who are talking in soft tones and whose profiles she can see. They look settled together, which pleases Alicia. Although she knows she'll never be friends with Mia, or Patrick, she doesn't want them to be unhappy.

She also knows how difficult it is to lose people close to you. It's something she'd never wish for her worst enemies.

After the service, on the ancient stone steps of the church, Alicia and Liam make their excuses. Together with Hilda, they walk down the steps to the street, where she asks her mom if she minds attending the wake at the Arkipelag on her own.

'Don't worry about me,' Hilda says and puts her arm around Alicia.

'We'll look after her,' a familiar voice says.

Frida and Andrei are right behind them. It has stopped raining, and the skies are clearing.

'You young people! I don't need looking after,' Hilda protests, but she gives the newlywed couple a weak smile. Alicia can see her eyes are red. She heard her sniffles and saw her dab at her eyes repeatedly during the ceremony. She must have been thinking of Uffe.

'Oh, Mom, are you really OK?'

'Yes, don't fuss.'

Alicia shakes her head and turns toward Frida and Andrei.

'I've got to go and relieve Brit. Her little one is only nine months' old and quite unsettled still. I'm not sure Jukka is such a hands-on-dad, so he'll be pleased to have Brit home as soon as possible.'

'Of course,' Frida says.

'I'm lucky. Anne Sofie is with her cousins at the villa...' Frida pauses and then adds, rolling her eyes, 'with the housekeeper.'

Her expression makes Alicia smile, but her demeanor changes when she spots Frida's eyes following Mrs Eriksson as she walks between Mia and Patrick toward a black limousine. It's almost as though they are carrying her.

'Beatrice has taken it hard. She's not left her bed since Kurt passed,' Frida says, her eyes pooling with tears.

Alicia places a hand on Frida's back.

'It must be difficult for you too.'

The young woman sighs. Andrei puts an arm around her and smiles at Alicia.

'I look after her.'

Alicia nods and hugs the young couple, before turning to her mom once more.

'I'll see you later.'

She takes Liam's hand, and they walk slowly to their car.

CHAPTER FIFTY-THREE

'I feel a bit bad about leaving my mom alone,' Alicia says as they make their way toward Sjoland.

Liam turns to look at her.

'You could still go to the wake. I can look after Theo. There's some milk you expressed in the freezer, and he's fine taking it from the bottle.'

'You're a good father, but I don't want to be away from him. My boobs are aching already.'

They smile at one another.

As the car slides over the swing bridge and Alicia sees the lights of Mariehamn in the distance, her heart fills with joy at the beautiful landscape. It's true that the days are getting shorter, though. It'll soon be October, and then the first snowfall. What a difference it'll be from the long, hot summer, the most protracted heatwave the islands have ever experienced. But Alicia is looking forward to the winter, and their first Christmas in the farmhouse.

What's more, their new business is doing well. The order book for high-end potato chips is nearly full and they are planning on buying more land to expand production.

'I feel a bit guilty about being so happy. We've just been to a funeral!' Alicia exclaims as their farm comes into view and Liam turns into their yard.

Liam switches off the engine and takes Alicia's face between his hands.

'Please don't be, darling. I'm sure Kurt Eriksson, and even Beatrice, would wish us to be happy. Besides, we've had our share of sorrows. It's about time we enjoyed life, don't you think?'

Alicia gazes into Liam's face, and into his dark eyes. His hair has begun to recede a little, and she can see gray strands on his temples. His eyes, which were so bright when they met all those years ago at Uppsala University student café, are a little paler now, but he's still the handsome man she fell in love with. Alicia leans into Liam and touches his lips with her own. They linger over the kiss, and Alicia begins to feel the warm sensation of desire in her tummy.

That's the other reason she's feeling so guilty. Their sex life is like that of a newly married couple. Since they got back together, Liam and Alicia can't seem to keep their hands off each other.

When, early in the New Year, she'd found out that she was pregnant, she wasn't that surprised. They had made love so many times after deciding to try for another baby. Although, at their age, it was a miracle that it happened so quickly.

Or at all.

Reluctantly, Alicia pulls away from the kiss and says, 'We'd better go inside. I'm sure Brit is keen to get back to her own baby.'

Liam smiles and sighs.

'Can you wait just a little while longer? I want to ask you something. I was going to do it before, but then Kurt died, and … I know this isn't the ideal time either, but if I don't say something now, I'm afraid I never will.'

Alicia gazes at Liam. He's looking down at his hands, which are resting on the steering wheel. Suddenly, she realizes he's nervous. A chill creeps up Alicia's spine and her heart starts to quicken. She cannot imagine what Liam wants to tell her that would be so difficult to say.

'You're scaring me. What is it?'

Liam turns to face Alicia once more. His expression is soft and loving, which makes Alicia's heart beat a little less fast. He takes both of her hands in his and says, 'I wanted to ask you to marry me.'

Alicia stares at Liam.

'But we're already married.'

Liam grins.

'I know. But, with everything that we've been through, I think we should do it again. I want us to renew our vows. Perhaps here on the farm. Not a huge ceremony, just your mom, Leo, Frida and Brit with their families. The summer would be perfect, don't you think?'

'Oh, darling!'

Alicia doesn't know what else to say. She can feel a tear running down her cheek, and wipes it away.

'I wanted to do it properly, you know, go down on one knee, but there's not been a moment …'

Liam can't finish his sentence because Alicia is covering his face with kisses. 'How I love you!'

'Well, that's OK then. I was also thinking that we could take a little honeymoon, if we can leave Theo with your mom by then? It'll be nice to have one without you being pregnant.'

Alicia's smile is now even wider than before. She remembers their first honeymoon, when she was six months' pregnant with Stefan. They had a wonderful time in the Canary Islands, but it's true that the heat didn't exactly agree with her pregnancy.

'You've thought of everything.'

Liam smiles back at her.

'That's my job. To make you and our little family happy.'

A FREE STORY!

The Day We Met is a prequel short story to the *Love on the Island* series.

This short story is only available FREE to members of my Readers' Group.

Go to www.helenahalme.com sign up to my Readers' Group and get your free story now!

ALSO BY HELENA HALME

ABOUT THE AUTHOR

Helena Halme grew up in Finland and moved to the UK via Stockholm and Helsinki at a very tender and impressionable age. She's a former BBC journalist and has also worked as a magazine editor, a bookseller and ran a Finnish/British cultural association in London.

Since gaining an MA in Creative Writing at Bath Spa University, Helena has published 15 fiction titles, including six in *The Nordic Heart* and six in *Love on the Island* series.

Helena lives in North London with her ex-Navy husband. She loves Nordic Noir and sings along to Abba when no one is around.

Find Helena Halme online
www.helenahalme.com
hello@helenahalme.com

Printed in Great Britain
by Amazon

20923405R00192